AN HONOURABLE ESTATE

England, 1315. Famine and unrest are spreading across the country, and when Sir William Bradshaigh joins Adam Banastre's rebellion against their overlord, the Earl of Lancaster, things do not go to plan. Sir William is lucky to escape with his life after a battle at Preston and, as a wanted man, he has no choice but to become an outlaw. Meanwhile, the lands at Haigh are forfeit to the king, who gives them to Sir Peter Lymesey for a year and a day ... while Lady Mabel Bradshaigh must make a hard choice if she is to protect her children and herself.

Books by Elizabeth Ashworth
Published by The House of Ulverscroft:

THE DE LACY INHERITANCE

SPECIAL MESSAGE TO READERS

THE ULVERSCROFT FOUNDATION
(registered UK charity number 264873)

was established in 1972 to provide funds for research, diagnosis and treatment of eye diseases. Examples of major projects funded by the Ulverscroft Foundation are:-

- The Children's Eye Unit at Moorfields Eye Hospital, London
- The Ulverscroft Children's Eye Unit at Great Ormond Street Hospital for Sick Children
- Funding research into eye diseases and treatment at the Department of Ophthalmology, University of Leicester
- The Ulverscroft Vision Research Group, Institute of Child Health
- Twin operating theatres at the Western Ophthalmic Hospital, London
- The Chair of Ophthalmology at the Royal Australian College of Ophthalmologists

You can help further the work of the Foundation by making a donation or leaving a legacy. Every contribution is gratefully received. If you would like to help support the Foundation or require further information, please contact:

THE ULVERSCROFT FOUNDATION
The Green, Bradgate Road, Anstey
Leicester LE7 7FU, England
Tel: (0116) 236 4325

website: www.foundation.ulverscroft.com

Elizabeth Ashworth is an author based in Lancashire. Her work has appeared in many publications, including *My Weekly*, *People's Friend*, *Take a Break*, *The Lady*, *The Times* and *Top Gear*.

An Honourable Estate has its own page on Elizabeth's website:

www.elizabethashworth.com/an-honourable-estate

where you can read more about the historical background to the story.

You can also visit *An Honourable Estate* Facebook page here:

www.facebook.com/AnHonourableEstate

ELIZABETH ASHWORTH

AN HONOURABLE ESTATE

Complete and Unabridged

ULVERSCROFT
Leicester

First published in Great Britain in 2012

First Large Print Edition
published 2014

The moral right of the author has been asserted

A catalogue record for this book is available
from the British Library.

ISBN 978–1–4448–2107–9

Published by
F. A. Thorpe (Publishing)
Anstey, Leicestershire

Set by Words & Graphics Ltd.
Anstey, Leicestershire
Printed and bound in Great Britain by
T. J. International Ltd., Padstow, Cornwall

This book is printed on acid-free paper

This novel is based on the legend of Mab's Cross and is dedicated to the memory of Lady Mabel de Haigh and Sir William Bradshaw, who can be found lying side by side in Wigan Parish Church.

Contents

Prologue

Mabel de Haigh paused on the edge of the market place. Her bare feet were bloodied and torn and the snow-laden wind made her shiver as she limped forward, bareheaded and dressed only in her linen chemise. In her hand she shielded a lighted taper, almost burnt down now. The villagers who lined her path willed her on and gave her strength. Although the penance for adultery was designed to be a humiliation, these people neither mocked nor jeered her as she passed, but the men averted their eyes from her unclothed body and the women whispered words of encouragement and sympathy.

At last she reached the stone cross and knelt before it to pray to God for the salvation of her soul. She was an adulteress. She freely admitted her sin to God, priest and man. But she prayed that God would forgive her as easily as Father Gilbert, her confessor, and the people of Haigh who stood protectively around her.

'That is enough,' said Father Gilbert as she felt a warm cloak being placed around her shoulders and the hood raised to cover her hair which hung loose and unbraided. 'Come away now.'

She held up her hand in a silent plea for a few more moments of prayer. Then she crossed herself, put out the taper and stumbled to her feet as arms grasped hers and supported her. It was over now and she could go home, shriven, to have her feet bathed and bandaged and to recover from her long penitential walk.

1

Famine

Bending over her sewing in the gloom of a single precious candle, Mabel heard the latch of the outer door click open and William came into the great hall of the manor house at Haigh. His fair hair was stuck tight to his head and water ran from it, dripping onto the sackcloth around his shoulders that was supposed to have kept the rain from his clothes. But when he took it off and shook it in unison with the dogs who accompanied him, showering Mabel with the droplets, she saw that the wetness had soaked through to his tunic and that his hose and boots were similarly sodden and smeared with mud. She sent Edith to fetch some fresh clothes from the coffer in their bedchamber and cloths for him to dry himself. Then she called for one of the kitchen boys to bring more logs to try to kindle the damp wood on the central hearth into a better blaze. The closed shutters rattled at the windows in a sudden gust of wind and the incessant rain seeped through and

3

trickled down the white plastered wall. It was August and it had rained every day for as long as Mabel could recall.

'Another two dead sheep,' said William as he rubbed his hair, making the flames of the fire sizzle from the wet drops, 'and . . . ' He paused to look up at her. Even in the gloom she could see the pain in his eyes. 'The blacksmith's child, the little girl . . . '

'She died,' said Mabel sadly, knowing what he was going to tell her from the expression on his face.

'It was not unexpected. You cannot save them all,' he said in an attempt to comfort her, before he returned to rubbing at his hair, almost standing on the tail of one of the steaming hounds that had spread itself next to the fire.

The hall filled with the mingling smells of wood smoke, wet dog, wet wool and dampness. It was a stench that Mabel had come to associate with the summer of 1315. That and the stench of death as the animals died in the fields and the children in the village.

She had hoped that the blacksmith's little daughter could be saved. She had, with her own hands, prepared an infusion of willow bark and taken it to the family along with what food she could spare: a loaf of coarse

4

brown bread, though by the time the grain had been dried in the oven it contained little nourishment, and, to tempt the child to eat, a tiny portion of the fresh cod that had come from the weekly market at Wigan. But when she had looked down at the little girl, no more than bones, lying in her blankets with her huge blue eyes staring out from her gaunt and colourless face and her belly swollen despite her hunger, Mabel had known that there was little hope. The child had had that look of resignation that comes to those on the brink of death and, despite her prayers and supplications and the lighting of a precious beeswax candle in the chapel, Mabel was not surprised that God had seen fit to take her from this world.

'At least her suffering is over,' she said at last, though they were only words and she knew that she would have to put on her cloak and pattens and walk down to the small house by the forge to see the frail body and try to give what solace she could to the parents; to the mother who had tried to coax some spoonfuls of the medicine into her daughter's mouth in the hope that it might work some miracle; and to the father, whose smithy stood silent and deserted now that there were no animals to shoe or scythes to fashion because the horses and oxen had died of starvation and the crops stood ruined in the wet fields.

William ran his fingers through his damp hair and pulled a rough wooden stool nearer to the blaze, lifting the logs with a long iron poker to encourage the flames.

'Something will have to be done, Mab,' he said. 'We cannot go on like this. Soon it will be Michaelmas and what will happen then?' He shrugged his shoulders in a sign of desperation as he stroked the head of Calab, his favourite dog. 'Even if the rain stops there will be no crop this year but Robert Holland will demand his dues as if the barns were filled — and neither he nor the Earl of Lancaster will go hungry.' He threw down the poker in an angry gesture and the dog jerked back his head. 'They have no care if we or our villagers starve.'

'But what can we do?' asked Mabel as she picked up his discarded towel.

'I could take a deer from the forest and roast it in the yard.'

'And risk having your hands cut off if you are caught? Talk sense, William!' she told him. 'Besides you know that we owe feudal allegiance to the earl.'

'That does not mean I have to like him,' said her husband.

William recalled when he had begun to dislike Thomas, Earl of Lancaster. It had been three years earlier in the summer of 1312. He had been with the earl, fulfilling his yearly knight's service, when the message had come about Piers Gaveston. That Lancaster hated Gaveston was well known. He had been the foremost of the earls who had forced the king to send his friend and companion into exile for a third time and when Lancaster had discovered the man was back in England he had flown into a rage, kicking stools, dogs and servants around his lavish hall and vowing revenge on both Gaveston and the king.

William understood that the Earl of Lancaster had good reason for his hatred of Gaveston. The Gascon and the king had allegedly sworn an oath to be blood brothers, a pact that was more often made on the battlefield or in tournaments, to fight together and to divide the spoils. But the king had begun to treat Piers Gaveston as if he were truly his familial brother, giving him precedence over his cousin Lancaster who had been subjected to more ridicule and taunting from Gaveston than even a peasant could have been expected to tolerate; and all this from a man only the son of a knight of the household. Of course it should have been Lancaster who carried the crown of Edward the Confessor at the king's coronation, but Gaveston had mocked the way he walked and laughed that the ceremony would be spoiled by Lancaster's minstrel efforts. So Edward had appointed his favourite to the honour instead. Worse had come when the king was in France with his new bride Isabella, and Gaveston rather than Lancaster was appointed regent and left in charge of the kingdom. Even though Lancaster had been ill and unable to fulfil the role he had still taken offence at the appointment of his sworn enemy and had sent him a message to say that he would bow down to no one, least of all a Frenchman.

Gaveston had taken refuge at Scarborough, but the Earl of Pembroke had persuaded him to give himself up from the besieged castle, promising him safety if he came out and put himself into his protection to be escorted to London where parliament would decide his fate. But Pembroke had been lax. As the party rode south he had not been able to resist the temptation of a conjugal night with his wife at his manor house at Bampton and, after lodging his prisoner at the rectory in Deddington, he had gone home. In his absence the Earl of Warwick had taken Gaveston and marched him barefoot to Warwick Castle where he had imprisoned him. Lancaster and his men had followed.

William recalled the day they had approached Warwick. It had looked magnificent in the evening twilight and, as they urged their weary horses up towards the towering stone ramparts, William saw that torches had been lit to welcome them in. He had been sweating and thirsty all day. He had a sore on one leg where his lined hose had bunched up under the top of his cuisses and he was looking forward to a long drink of ale, a hot supper, perhaps the chance to wash his feet as well as his hands and a decent night's sleep — even though it would be on a pallet in a tent rather than the comfort of his own feather bed at home in Haigh.

The hot day was still sultry with the promise of thunder in the air and, as William handed his horse to one of the boys who had come forward to take charge of the animals, he saw his friend and neighbour Adam Banastre coming towards him. Adam nodded his head towards the tight-lipped Earl of Lancaster who was climbing the wooden steps to the great hall with an expression of grim satisfaction.

'If ever a man was bent on revenge,' he

remarked, 'it is our lord and master.' And as William watched the earl disappear inside, he agreed that Lancaster would not be satisfied until he saw Gaveston dead.

The next morning William was one of the men whom Lancaster had called to attend him. Once the court was assembled in the great hall the Earl of Warwick had ordered the prisoner to be brought up from the dungeon below where he had been held overnight. William watched as the door was flung open and Gaveston, in chains, was thrust forward and pushed to his knees on the floor rushes. It was the first time William had actually seen Piers Gaveston though he had heard plenty about him and as he studied the tall, well-muscled man he had to admit that it was hardly surprising he fared so well in the jousting tournaments. He had already beaten all the knights of the earls of Arundel, Hereford and Warenne, and they all hated him with a vengeance for his disgracing of them and their households.

Dirty and dishevelled but still defiant, Gaveston looked up at Lancaster and sneered.

'So the Churl thinks he has me in his power?' he asked with contempt, using his dismissive nickname for the earl. 'I don't think the king will be happy when he hears of this. I think there is a dungeon within the Tower of London and a block with your name upon it, Thomas of Lancaster,' he jeered with the confidence of a man who truly believed that no one was able or willing to harm him.

William watched the bloodlust creep up Lancaster's neck and across his cheeks as his anger raged barely within his control.

'I think you will find that it is you who must die,' he seethed, as he glanced at the faces of the assembled earls who all nodded solemnly in agreement — both judge and jury.

William had found it difficult to watch as the look on Gaveston's face turned slowly from disdain to disbelief and finally fear. He found himself an unwilling participant as they were ordered to drag the protesting prisoner out to the courtyard where his eyes streamed tears in the sudden unaccustomed sunlight and the guards taunted him for weeping. William looked to Lancaster, awaiting his instruction, still not convinced that he actually meant to kill the man. But the earl's eyes were filled with contempt and gleamed with the pleasure of exacting his revenge.

'Take him up the hill!' he commanded and the men-at-arms who held him jerked at the chains that shackled the prisoner's hands and feet, kicking out at him as he hesitated.

'No!' he pleaded as realisation at last came that his life was indeed forfeit to his enemies. He had no well-bred stallion to ride or lance to wield now. The man who had been a champion had no chance against the armed guards of the Earl of Lancaster.

William was sickened as they dragged Gaveston, struggling and protesting, to the summit of Blacklow Hill where Lancaster told them to pull the prisoner to his knees and sent a man to find a log to serve as a makeshift block. But Gaveston was not prepared to die; he was not a man to be subdued without a fight.

'God damn you Lancaster! You will rot in hell for this!' he shouted as the gloved hands pushed him down. William held back. He wanted no part in this murder. Surely, he thought, Lancaster must relent now that he had seen the man humiliated. Surely now he would have him beg forgiveness on his knees and be content with that. Even he, for all his hatred and resentment, could not mean to kill the man in such a manner. But as William looked to his master for a sign of compassion, Lancaster signalled to two Welsh knights who had followed them up the hill to come forward with their broadswords.

'Kneel, you traitor!' he yelled at Gaveston

from his saddle, as he watched the man struggle and squirm for his freedom. 'Die like a man at least!'

'Have pity!' begged Gaveston as he fell to his knees before Lancaster, his tone changed as he saw that the earl did indeed mean to take his life. 'I beg you have pity on ... ' William watched in horror and disgust as the man's words were stopped by the broadsword thrust through his belly. He watched as the blood ran, along the blade of the sword that still impaled Gaveston's body, drips at first from the sword point, then a flow and then a torrent gushed as the sword was twisted and withdrawn and the scream from the victim rent the still air and carried around the valleys beyond; it was an inhuman, primal scream that would haunt William's sleep for years to come. He watched, unable to look away, although he wished he could, as Gaveston slowly sank to the ground, disbelief written across his features. As he fell, still conscious, the second knight drew his sword and began to hack off his head, the metal of the blade screeching at the bones of the dying man's neck until at last the head rolled free and came to rest a little way down the slope of the hill, still wearing its expression of surprise. William retched and vomited into the grass, shivering uncontrollably despite the oppressive heat of the day. Then the Earl of Lancaster ordered their return to the castle, leaving the body of Piers Gaveston, still seeping dark, cloying blood, lying beside the road where he had been killed.

★ ★ ★

Mabel watched her husband as he sat and brooded, his eyes unseeing as he stared at the flames and his hand still absently caressing the ears of the dog lounging beside him. Even now, though they had been married for twenty-five years, the sight of him stirred a physical excitement within her.

William sighed and the dog looked up into his face as if it sensed his disquiet. 'It may be time to act, Mab,' he said. 'I cannot just watch as people starve. If I do nothing their deaths will be on my conscience.'

She laid a hand on his damp shoulder. 'Do you think that I don't come home and weep every night when I've been about the village, seeing the haunted eyes of mothers whose children have been buried and the terror on the faces of men who risk their lives to take a hare for the pot to feed their families? Don't you think I pray for them every night and yet give thanks we can feed our own little girls? But what can we do?' she asked him with a note of despair in her voice.

William picked up the stick again and began to stir the fire. Mabel watched the steam rise from his clothes into the damp air. 'Adam Banastre says we must rise up; rise against Robert Holland and against the Earl of Lancaster. I believe that he is right.'

Mabel stared at her husband until at last he turned his head to look at her. 'Don't you agree?' he asked.

'I . . . I don't know what to say. Banastre is brother-in-law to Holland. I thought he would have supported him.'

'There is no love lost between them. He believes that now Holland has been promoted to being Lancaster's secretary he has lost all interest in his own estates, except as a resource to fund his own table and his fine clothes.'

'So Banastre speaks openly of rebellion?' asked Mabel with a shiver. 'That's dangerous talk, William. I wish that you would stay out of it.'

She felt her husband's muscles tense under her hand and he shrugged away from her touch as he threw the stick down again, making the dog growl.

'God damn it, Mab!' he said as he leapt up, knocking over the stool and began to pace the hall. 'I will not stand by and watch children starve to death whilst the Earl of Lancaster does nothing! If he cannot show any compassion then let us act in the name of the king. There is a famine for God's sake, and no one in authority seems to have even noticed. Money needs to be spent to keep people alive not taken from them in dues and taxes when they have nothing!'

'William! Hush!' she warned, reaching out a restraining hand as he passed her. 'Someone may hear,' she said, glancing at the shuttered windows and the door, half expecting armed men wearing surcoats emblazoned with the lions of Lancaster to burst in and arrest her husband for his disloyal outburst.

'Mama?' The voice of their elder daughter Bella, at the door of the bedchamber made her turn. She had left the little girls tucked under a thick fur coverlet to sleep a little. They had both been tired after a thunderstorm the previous night had kept them awake and afraid. Now she saw the fear on Bella's face again, not fear of thunder this time, but of the unaccustomed raised voice of her father. But before she could go to comfort the child, William had crossed the hall in long strides and gathered Bella in his arms, lifting her and carrying her back to the fire where he sat her on his knee and nuzzled his face into her blonde hair. Then he looked up at Mabel and asked, 'Would you have me do nothing?'

She sighed. She knew that her husband hated the unfair treatment of anyone and deep down she had to acknowledge that his anger at those who ill-governed the country did not surprise her. But what did surprise her was that he felt it so deeply that he was prepared to act against the law. It made her afraid for him; proud, but afraid.

'I wish there was something to be done less risky than rebellion,' she said.

'And what about the blacksmith and his wife? What of their loss? How many more children must die?' he asked as he kissed the head of the little girl who clung to him. 'What if the next loss is ours?'

William glanced up into the evening sky that was reddening into a spectacularly bloody sunset. It was the Wednesday before the feast of St Wilfrid and Adam Banastre had told him to be at the Angel in Wingates before dark. William rode at a leisurely trot, beset by doubt and guilt and toying with the idea of turning his horse's head to ride back home again. He recalled his last conversation with Mab. She was set against this rebellion. She said that their success was unlikely and their defeat would mean certain death, and he knew that she was right. He could still see her

17

bright, pleading eyes, her delicate little hand with its slender fingers on his sleeve as she had begged him not to come. She was afraid, he knew, and he also knew that his reassurances that they would prevail, and that they would return home victorious and that things would get better had rung hollow, like a cracked bell chiming tunelessly from a church tower. He loved his wife and he respected her opinion. In the years before and during their marriage they had taken most decisions in agreement with one another. Mab now understood the business of running their manor better than he did himself and he knew he could rely on her to deal with the villagers and the servants whenever he was away fulfilling his knight's service. She had an astute mind and was an unerringly good judge of character. She was adept at seeing an overall picture of any situation and could predict the outcome of a decision with unfailing accuracy, which was why, after riding under the arch at the centre of the stone building and into the mud-caked yard he gave the horse into the care of a stable boy and walked to the wooden door with some disquiet. Since the king's defeat at Bannock-burn it was the Earl of Lancaster who held all the power at court, having replaced most of the members of the royal household with

Lancastrian supporters. To rebel against Lancaster was tantamount to treason.

The hall was full and noisy and the louvre in the roof was making a poor job of removing the smoke from the fire on the central flagstones. A crowd of travellers was already seated at the trestle and, as William glanced around for his friend, the innkeeper caught his eye and gestured upwards with a thumb as he carried in two jugs of ale.

'If you're seeking Banastre, he's taken an upper chamber.' William frowned as he went back outside and up the wooden stairs two at a time. Now was not the time to be whoring and it was not what he had thought Adam had in mind. He wanted no part of it and he would tell his friend so and then leave. He had been faithful to Mab since their marriage and he intended it to stay that way.

He pushed open the door a little too vigorously, causing it to crash back and reverberate on its hinges. The faces of three men looked up in surprise. They were sitting around a scrubbed wooden table on which was placed a pitcher of ale and four cups. A candle burned brightly amongst them, although the outer edges of the chamber were shadowed in darkness apart from the corner where charcoal burnt in a brazier. As far as William could see the men were alone; there

19

wasn't a woman in sight.

He had pushed the door closed behind him before anyone spoke. 'Adam,' he nodded, and recognised the other men as Sir Henry Lea of Park Hall and Harry Duxbury.

'Bradshaigh! A cup of ale?' asked his friend as he kicked out a stool from under the table. 'You know Harry Duxbury?'

'Harry,' said William with a brief nod towards both him and Sir Henry. He sat down at the table and drank at length from the weak brew before putting the cup down in front of him and looking from one to the other of his companions. 'So, what's this all about?' he asked, although he knew full well what was on Adam's mind.

'Holland,' said Adam, almost spitting the name. 'It's time he was stopped. Or are you content to see him bleed this county dry?'

William glanced at Harry and Henry Lea and saw that they were both in agreement. He supposed that Adam would not have asked them to come if he'd not been sure of their support.

'You look doubtful,' he remarked.

William took up the cup again, but didn't drink; he turned it in his hands watching the ale swirl in eddies around the vessel. 'Holland is powerful. He has the ear of the Earl of Lancaster,' he said after a moment's silence.

'And is a greedy, scheming bastard who sends his bailiffs to extract every last penny from us. Damn it, Will! You've seen the starvation and the hardship. We cannot let it continue. It's time to act!' He thumped the table so hard the flagon and cups jumped into the air and Henry Lea thrust out a hand to save his drink from spilling. 'What ails you man? Are you afraid?' demanded Adam.

'No!' retorted William, his anger flaring at his friend's challenge. 'But this needs thought. We need to be sure we have men enough who are willing and able to fight. If they come under our protection we will need to feed and even arm them. Men cannot march and fight on empty stomachs, nor go into battle empty handed. And in this we take on not just Holland, but Lancaster himself, who is as good as king. It is not a decision to be taken lightly.'

'I hear the cautious voice of your wife in your faint hearted reply,' said Adam with a slight tone of rebuke.

'The Lady Mabel speaks with sense, often,' argued William.

'Women are good for only one thing — and it is not their grasp of politics!'

William flung his cup aside and the stool rolled from under him as he leaned across the

21

table to clutch Adam by his tunic and pull his face closer.

'You do not demean my wife!' he threatened his friend. 'Or, by God, I'll . . . I'll . . . '

'That's enough!' shouted Harry Duxbury, banging his cup down hard on the table. 'Sit down and discuss this sensibly — or it stops here. How can we fight against injustice when we can only fight amongst ourselves?' William looked at the man's angry face. He didn't know him well, but there was a zeal that burned in his blue eyes that betrayed his thirst for this rebellion. He let go of Adam and retrieved the stool as his friend pulled his clothing straight.

'You are either with us or you are against us, Bradshaigh. Choose your side carefully. But remember that if you are against us you already know too much.' William watched as the blade flashed and saw Adam run a finger along it to test its sharpness. 'The details can come later. What I need to know now is whom I can trust.' He grasped the knife firmly and without flinching made a cut across the palm on his own hand until the blood oozed out, black in the shadowy chamber. 'Will you swear to live or die with me in this rebellion against Holland and Lancaster?' he challenged, as he turned the knife and held out the handle first to William and then to Henry. Henry Lea took it without hesitation though William saw him wince as he drew it across his own palm. Then he offered his hand to Adam who grasped it tight, mingling their blood.

'Do you swear?' he asked.

'I swear,' he replied. Adam raised his eyebrows, waiting. 'I swear to live or die with you in this rebellion against Holland and Lancaster,' he pledged. Then Harry Duxbury took up the knife, cut his palm and swore the oath.

'Will?' asked Adam. 'Do you swear?'

William reached out and picked up the knife. It was heavy, with a horn handle embellished with scenes that he couldn't quite make out in the twilight. He weighed it in his hand and opened his palm whilst his companions watched him. He flexed his fingers a little as the sounds of laughter drifted up through the floorboards from the hall below. He touched the blade to his skin, clamped his teeth and drew it through his flesh, surprised at the lack of immediate pain. He looked up to find Adam grinning at him. He put his palm to the palm of his friend and then to Harry's and Henry Lea's. 'I swear to live or die with you in this rebellion against Holland and Lancaster.'

'Good man!' Adam thumped him roughly on the back. There would be blood on his tunic and he would have to explain it to Mab thought William ruefully as he raised his cup with the others in a toast.

'To the rebellion!' he echoed and drank again, hoping that his decision was the right one.

'What was that?' Adam was at the door in a moment and William followed him in pursuit of the eavesdropper, just in time to see the man reach the bottom of the stairs. He had an accomplice waiting with a horse in the yard and had swung his leg over the saddle before there was any hope of stopping him.

'Who?' asked William.

'Radcliffe,' said Adam with a sour face as the others joined them to watch as the horsemen galloped off into the dark, moonless night, 'and his brother. I hope they break their bloody necks, riding at that speed through the forest!'

'How much do you think he heard?' asked Harry.

'Enough to run and think he can take his news to my brother-in-law, unless we can prevent him. How many men can you gather?' he asked them.

2

Murder

They called for their horses, each agreeing to ride to their own villages and gather as many men as were willing to come. They were to meet at Bury and then scour the countryside for the Radcliffes and silence them before they could get word to Robert Holland.

As he rode back to Haigh, trusting his horse to find the way through the night, William began a mental inventory of those on whose support he could rely. Harry Palmer, his bailiff, Wistan Bennett, Oscar Fletcher and Dunstan Browne — all men he knew he could count on to fight and to keep silent.

They all came from families who had long been loyal to the Norreys and so to Mab and now to him as her husband. He remembered how he'd been concerned when they first arrived at Haigh that the welcome was for his wife alone and that the villagers might not accept him, but when they had seen the yield of their crops increase and the sheep thrive they had acknowledged that he was a good lord. When he had asked for men to ride with him to fight the Scots there had been no reluctance to volunteer and although there had been losses at Bannockburn, including that of young Bryan Palmer, these men had become his friends as well as his tenants. He would trust them with his life, though he hoped he would not have to do so.

William reached Haigh as a sliver of moon crested the horizon. He glanced at the manor house door and saw that it was in darkness; the fires covered, the candles extinguished and everyone in bed. He knew that Calab would be curled up by the hearth, warming himself by the last of the embers and he was tempted to go and call the dog out; he could be useful. But he knew if he did, it would wake Mab and she would not refrain from giving him a lecture on his stupidity. Was he being stupid, he wondered. He hoped not. But he had sworn a blood oath and he would not go back on his word.

The cut across his palm was stinging as he took the reins in one hand and slid down from the saddle to quietly knock on the door of Harry Palmer's house.

'Harry?' he called urgently. 'Put on what armour you have and bring a weapon. I have need of you!'

At every door William called out his men.

They rose from their beds, trying not to wake their wives. There was no reluctance, but rather a growing excitement that at last they were going to do something to help themselves rather than starve away as silent victims of this accursed famine. Within the hour they were marching quietly out of the village.

* * *

They had ridden, and even walked on foot, for miles. They had carried torches and led the horses through the dense forest, never worried for a moment that their flames might start a fire in the wet undergrowth. As dawn had turned the sky above them from black to a dull grey William had called a halt to the search and, having gathered around him the dozen or so villagers who had been eager to give him their assistance, he had expressed his profound thanks and told them to make their way back home. But unable to give up, despite his tiredness, he turned his horse for one last look before going to explain to Mab where he had been all night.

It was his horse that caught the scent and whinnied softly. William peered through the trees and recognised Adam Banastre's bay stallion, its white forelegs now black with

27

mud. William gave a long, low whistle to alert his friend. He saw Adam turn in his saddle at the familiar signal and the slow grin that spread over his face reassured him.

'We have him!' said Adam as William drew level. 'He was hiding out at the house of the priest, Roger de Freckleton. There was a threat of bloodletting before the priest allowed us through, but he saw reason when confronted with a sharp dagger to his throat and soon showed us where Radcliffe was concealed under the eaves.'

'And his brother?' asked William.

Adam's face grew serious. 'He's still at large,' he admitted. 'I have a party of men gone to seek him at his sister's house at Bury, whilst I still search here.'

'It isn't going to be easy to flush him out of this forest,' remarked William, as the growing daylight revealed the thickly wooded land and tangled undergrowth that dripped with rain all around them. I should have brought the dogs, though we have no scent of the man to track him.'

'And why didn't you bring your dogs?'

William hesitated, then told his friend the truth. 'They were in the hall and I did not want to go in and waken my wife. I did not want to have to tell her what we were about.'

'Because you feared she would forbid you?

I never took you for a henpecked husband, Will!'

'No. It was because I didn't want to worry her. There are, perhaps, some things that it is better she does not know.'

Adam snorted. 'Remember that you have pledged an oath,' he reminded him. 'Whoever is not with me is against me, and both the Radcliffes will have learned that lesson before this day is out!'

As he spoke, they heard the soft thudding of hooves on mud approaching and both men drew their swords as they turned their horses to face the oncoming rider.

'Hold!' said Adam as the horse became visible. 'He is my man.'

'Sire!' cried the boy as he rode up, his mount tossing its head and showering froth from its mouth across his surcoat which bore the arms of the Banastre family. 'Sire, we have John Radcliffe . . . but . . . '

'But what?' demanded Adam as the boy hesitated and glanced at Sir William and then back to his master.

'They have killed Henry Bury.'

Adam swore a curse on their stupidity. 'They were told to shed no blood,' he muttered. 'How did this come about?'

The boy shrugged. 'There was a fight,' he said.

'We had better go to see what must be done,' said William grimly, 'before the sheriff's men come seeking to hang us by the neck for murder.'

'Aye, you're right,' agreed Adam. 'This is an outcome we could have done well without.'

They spurred their tired horses forwards and rode as hastily as they could, without taking the main road, towards Bury's manor house to see for themselves what had happened.

The body of Henry Bury still lay where it had fallen on the threshold. It was surrounded by a group of white faced men who stared at it as if their regret could provoke a resurrection. They stepped back as Adam got down from his horse and walked across to them. William followed and saw that the man had been run through with a dagger which seemed, by chance, to have plunged upwards through his ribs and stopped his heart.

Banastre's men looked at him apologetically.

'Who did this?' demanded Adam.

'It was an accident,' explained one, whom William recognised as Stephen Scallard. 'Did you kill him?' asked Adam.

Scallard shook his head quickly. 'No, my lord. It was William Tegg. It's his dagger that's still in the man.' He looked at Adam Banastre as if he expected him to somehow make everything right.

'And where is Tegg now?'

'When he realised what he'd done he took Sir Henry's horse and rode off like the devil were after him.'

'It's Lancaster's sheriff he needs to fear in this life, though he may face the devil in the next, and sooner than he thinks if the King's Justice lays hands on him,' said Adam. 'For God's sake take the dagger out of him and wash it in yon bucket. Then I'll lose it in the forest. The rest of you head for your homes and make sure your wives will swear you never left your beds all night. I'll clear this up.'

The men needed no persuasion and moments later William and Adam were left alone with the body.

'What shall we do?' asked William as he looked down at the contorted face of the murdered man.

'There's not much we can do, 'cept pray for his immortal soul. Help me get him inside Will,' said Adam as he bent to grasp the corpse under its arms, 'and let us hope that by the time he is discovered we are very far away.'

'But what of his wife?'

'The Radcliffe sister? I've no idea. Do you think she's still here?'

William glanced around the silent and deserted hall as they carried the body inside. 'I doubt it,' he said. 'If she had any sense she would have got out when your men arrived. But if she's out there and she saw what happened we have no time to waste here. Adam, let's just leave him and go,' said William wiping the man's blood from his hands onto his tunic as fear rose and impelled him to run.

★ ★ ★

It was approaching dawn when Mabel woke. There was a greyness rather than blackness in the bedchamber and she was able to make out the shapes of her sleeping daughters on their pallet beds in the alcove. Amelia was whimpering in her sleep and Mabel wondered what troubled her, though as she stretched a hand across the cold and vacant side of her mattress it was her own concerns that worried her. William and she had parted with harsh words before he rode to Wingates to meet with Adam Banastre and he had not yet come home.

She sighed and turned over. It was still early and she could sleep for another hour.

But sleep wouldn't come again as she turned restlessly and at last she pushed the covers back and quietly pulled her chemise over her head, pushing her arms into the short, wide sleeves as it dropped over her thin body. It was no wonder she was still not able to give William the son he craved she thought. The food she ate was barely enough to sustain one life never mind two and there had been no babies born in the village at all that summer. No new lives to heal the hurt of the ones that had been lost.

She put on her summer Tunic and her soft indoor shoes that were becoming worn under the soles. She would need new ones soon, but so would the girls and their needs as always would precede hers. She fastened the clasp on her jewelled belt and hooked on the keys and the seal that she always kept about her. The morning was already oppressive and even without expending any effort she felt the sweat soaking through her linen as she walked into the hall.

The kitchen boys and Edith were already up and their mattresses were neatly rolled away. Calab, the wolfhound, opened his eyes for a moment and feebly wagged his tail as she went around opening the shutters. The thunder clouds were already gathering on the horizon and a steady drizzle fell onto the saturated yard outside, adding to the quagmire. Mabel took a few breaths, trying to find some relief from the cloying dampness. Instead it made her cough and then she heard Bella calling for her.

'Where's Papa?' she asked, standing in the doorway.

'He had to go out early,' lied Mabel, not wanting to tell their daughter that her father had not come home. Mabel just prayed that he was safe and that no harm had come to him. Adam Banastre was a fool and she wished that William was not so friendly with him. Although drunken escapades were one thing, rebellion was entirely different.

'May I have a drink?' asked Bella and Mabel shook off her concerns and looked once more at the little girl. At eight years old she looked much younger and was so thin that Mabel could have counted every rib on her scrawny little body. She worried that the children did not have enough to eat. She was terrified that they would become ill.

It had only been the day before that she had sat and watched another child die. A boy this time. The only son of another of her villagers; his father Thomas had wept great shuddering tears as the child lay still and neither Mabel nor Father Gilbert, her chaplain, had been able to console him. And all the while his wife had sat in disbelief and held her son's hand as if she could will the life back into him.

'Of course,' said Mabel in answer to her daughter's request. 'But there is only small ale. We have no milk.'

Sitting down at the table she poured the pale liquid into a cup and watched as Bella drank thirstily. She took some of the oatcakes that the cook had carried in from the kitchen and put two on the child's platter, and only one on her own.

'Why has Papa not taken Calab?' asked Bella as she chewed at the bread. Mabel looked down at the dog, still stretched out by the grey ashes of the hearth. He was thin too; his coat was dull and coarse.

'I don't know,' she replied. 'I'm not sure where he has gone.'

When Edith came to clear away the cups and platters she expressed surprise that Mabel did not know her husband had returned to Haigh late the previous night.

'Sir William knocked on everyone's door,' she told Mabel. 'He wanted men who would ride with him . . . ' The girl paused and watched Mabel's face. 'Did you not know?' she asked curiously.

'I did not know he had returned so late. He must not have wanted to waken me,' she replied, as if her husband's actions had been the most natural thing in the world. But she saw the shadow of doubt cross Edith's face, doubt and a slight fear.

'My father went with him,' she said. 'What is it all about, my lady?' she asked as she pushed a stray wisp of her dark hair back under her cap.

'Oh . . . something to do with the sheep I think,' replied Mabel, knowing it was a poor lie even as it passed her lips. Edith met her eyes momentarily then nodded briefly. Mabel could see that the girl was as puzzled and worried as she was herself. 'I think we need to brew more ale . . . if there is enough grain . . . ' said Mabel, to fill the awkward silence.

'My lady? What will happen at Michaelmas when we have to pay our rent? What will happen to those who don't have enough?'

Mabel looked again at the emaciated girl. At eighteen years old her young face was etched with tiredness, hunger and worry. She should have been laughing and dancing and dreaming of love and a young husband, thought Mabel, not agonizing about demands for grain that her family simply could not supply.

'I don't know,' replied Mabel honestly. 'But I'm sure that Sir William will not punish anyone who really cannot pay,' she reassured her, deciding that she must discover for herself just how much they could realistically expect to take from their tenants that quarter.

Darkness had fallen. Mabel had seen the children to their beds, had checked the door and the fires and was reluctantly going to the bedchamber herself when she heard the gentle tapping.

'Who's there?' she called as she stood with her candle in one hand and the other on the heavy wooden beam that secured the outer door at night. Her heartbeat was racing as a hundred and one possibilities ran through her mind. But Calab came wagging his tail and whining and, she thought, he would surely have barked had he scented a stranger.

'It's me.'

At her husband's hushed voice Mabel put down the candle and pulled up the beam, cursing it as it squealed against the door and she heard Amelia cough in the bedchamber. Opening the door just wide enough for William to slip through she watched as he quickly secured it behind him. He was breathing hard and when she raised the candle she could see his face looked ashen.

'What has happened?' she asked, half worried and half angry that he had not listened to her advice and had gone off with

Adam Banastre. William hesitated, his eyes flickering over hers yet not able to meet her gaze. Mabel knew that it was something he didn't want to tell her. 'Well?' she asked again.

'Some of Adam's men got out of control. They have killed Henry Bury,' he admitted and as he looked down at his hands Mabel saw they were stained with what looked like blood.

'Dear God!' she exclaimed. 'I knew no good would come of this. Were you involved?'

'Of course not!' He looked down at his hands again. 'Adam and I arrived after it happened. We moved the body inside . . . I must wash them,' he said reaching for the candle. Mabel followed him into the kitchen where he poured a basin of water from the large stone pitcher on the floor and plunged his hands into the cold water, rubbing them together as if he could wash away not only the blood but the memory of what had happened. 'The men are volatile,' he began, trying to explain to her. 'It isn't just the hunger. They've all spent so long fighting the Scots that they miss the excitement. They've become inured to death . . . '

'And you William? What about you? Does a man's life mean nothing to you either?'

'Of course it does!' he snapped back,

angrily. 'It is the loss of men's lives that has driven me to this. Of course I regret this murder, but I wasn't about to stand there and wait for the sheriff's men to come and find me with blood on my hands!' He reached past her for a cloth and dried his fingers carefully as she watched him. The candle flickered between them on the kitchen table in a sudden draught.

'What will you do?' she asked.

'Lay low for a while. Keep quiet.' He paused and then looked at her steadily. 'You will say that I was here?'

'You would have me lie for you?'

'Would you prefer to see me hanged?' he demanded, bundling the cloth into a ball and throwing it to the floor with force.

'No,' she replied. 'I will say that you were here all day and all night and I daresay the wives of the men who went with you will say the same.' She paused. 'You say it was Banastre's men?'

'Yes. It was no one from Haigh,' he reassured her.

Mabel shook her head. 'It is a mess. I wish you had not involved yourself with this, William. Promise me that you will keep away from Adam Banastre in the future.' He stayed silent and she followed his gaze to his hand and noticed the raw cut across his palm.

'I cannot promise that, Mab,' he said. 'I swore an oath . . . '

Without answering she picked up the candle and went to the bedchamber, leaving him alone in the dark. A while later she heard him come in but when he lay down beside her she kept still and didn't speak. She was too angry to trust herself to say anything more to him.

The next day Mabel was still angry with William. She thought that he should have stayed at home and tried to help their own tenants, rather than encouraging them to ride around the countryside committing murders and mayhem.

'It will soon be Michaelmas and the rents and taxes must be paid,' she reminded him. 'No talk of rebellion will keep Holland's bailiff from our door. I have made an inventory,' said Mabel, laying out the parchment with her neat writing on the table in front of William. 'There are some families who cannot pay their dues to us. Mistress Webb whose husband was killed fighting for you at Bannockburn has struggled. She barely has enough to sow seed never mind feed herself and her children over the winter months. And the Rolfes lost all their harvest when the land they work was flooded. Mistress Bennett used to make some money selling her cheese at market, but since their cow drowned in the swollen river she has been unable to do that — and the wool spun from the sheep is only half what it was last year.' Mabel paused with her finger still on the parchment where she had been directing William's attention to the hardships of their villagers. 'We cannot demand the dues,' she said. 'People will die if we take from them what little they have left.'

She watched as William studied her list. After a moment he sighed and pushed it from him as if that would take away the stark truth. 'But I doubt we will receive the same consideration from Holland,' he remarked.

'William . . . '

'I know.' He held up a hand as if in defeat. 'I need no more sermons from you Mab. You are right, of course. I have no intention of demanding what the villagers cannot pay, but we will still have to pay our taxes when Holland's man comes.'

'But we have the money?' she asked.

'Yes, we have the money for this quarter. But if things do not improve I don't know what will happen at the next quarterday or the one after. Once the money and what little grain we have is gone, there will be no way to replace it, then we will be as destitute as the poorest vassal.'

Mabel watched the steady rain that was still falling beyond the window. All through the springtime she had looked forward to a better summer than the last. She had waited for the warm dry days to come and lift her spirits, but without any change in the weather the summer had come and gone unnoticed. The days were becoming darker again and the nights colder. God had sent no summer again and she wondered what sins had been committed that they should all have been so punished.

'Have you the key to the coffer?' asked William. 'I will go to count out what we owe ready for tomorrow.' Mabel unhooked the iron key from the belt that circled her waist and watched as he went into the bedchamber where they kept their heavy oak coffer with its valuable contents at the foot of their bed for safety. She listened to the chink of the coinage as he took out what would have to be paid to Holland's bailiff the next day, hoping that there would be enough left to buy leather for new boots and some thick woollen cloth to sew warm cloaks for the girls.

It was still early when the bailiff arrived. He was a surly man, dressed in a hood and mantle that were both darkened by the drizzle, who appeared to resent having to leave his comfortable hearth. He rode a well

42

fed black stallion and was accompanied by around a half a dozen armed henchmen who looked as if they expected trouble.

Both Bella and Amelia looked alarmed as this stranger stomped into the hall. The dogs appeared to cower and even Calab only gave a half-hearted growl at the sight of him.

'Go to help Edith in the kitchen,' said Mabel, ushering her little daughters towards the door. 'I think she intends to preserve some fruit today and I daresay she would welcome your help.'

The man sat down uninvited in William's chair, took off the hood to reveal an almost entirely bald head, and pushed the wet cloak from his shoulders. Then he pulled a roll of parchment from the large pouch fastened onto his leather belt and consulted it closely. In the tense silence Mabel watched her husband as he stood on the far side of the hearth, only his restless hands betraying his annoyance at the intrusion.

'Bradshaw,' said the bailiff at last, his fat finger pausing above the neatly written figures. 'You owe us twenty shillings.'

'Surely not?' burst out William, staring at the man as if he was sure he had misread the amount. 'We paid less than half that last time, and I have performed knight's service for the Earl of Lancaster.'

The bailiff regarded him for a long moment with an enigmatic expression. 'Times are hard,' he said at length. 'The price of wheat has more than doubled since last year and so rents and taxes have had to be increased.'

'But the king has ordered the price of basic foodstuffs to be brought down!' William's fist met the table as his anger burst out, though the man didn't move or even flinch, merely held up a hand to silence him.

'Sir William, the king deceives the common people. The fruitfulness of living things is in the power of God alone and it is His will, not the will of man, that must determine the price. If you are in financial difficulty then I am sure that some arrangement can be agreed. For the payment of a small fee I may be able to negotiate a reduction . . . '

William stared at him in silence and Mabel watched as a slow smile twitched at the man's lips. They all knew what he was offering. For a sweetener or a bribe he would take what was probably the correct amount. Mabel was about to tell the man exactly what she thought of him, but a glance from William bade her hold her tongue. And when she saw him glance towards the door where two of the henchmen were standing guard she under-stood why. Any reluctance to pay would only result in more being taken by force.

The bailiff smiled and gestured to William to sit down. 'I'm sure we can reach a mutually beneficial agreement,' he said. 'I could cut the tax by as much as a quarter, if it were worth my while.'

'And how much would you charge to cut it by half?'

The bailiff laughed out loud. 'Come, Sir William,' he replied. 'Do not take too much advantage of my good nature. I am trying to do you a favour. Do not trouble me with your insults.' His face grew serious again as Mabel watched him lean closer to her husband and whisper a figure in his ear. 'My last offer,' he said.

Mabel watched as William placed the bag of money that he had counted out onto the bailiff's open palm.

'There is ten shillings,' he said. 'I will fetch you the rest.' Reluctantly Mabel unhooked the key from her belt and gave it to her husband, then listened as he counted out the extra coins — the sound punctuated by the bailiff humming a tune and drumming his fingers on the arm of the chair as he waited.

When William returned and handed over the extra coins the odious man had the audacity to smile and thank him effusively as if it was a gift freely given, although Mabel saw him weigh the bag expertly in his hand and glance inside to assure himself that he had not been cheated.

'It has been a pleasure,' he said as he rose to leave, pulling his cloak about him again. 'Though it was a pity your wife offered me no refreshment.' He stared at Mabel and she felt her heart begin to pound in terror as he looked at her with his greedy eyes. 'Perhaps next time,' he remarked with a slight lift of an eyebrow. Then he swept out of the hall door, signalling his men to follow him. He mounted his horse and, within moments, they were riding away into the all-enveloping mist.

'Damn them! Damn them to hell!' shouted William. Mabel saw him look down at the red line that crossed his palm. 'I will not stand by and do nothing!' he warned her and Mabel trembled with fear — fear for him, for herself and for their children.

★ ★ ★

Later that morning William looked up in alarm as he heard hoofbeats approaching. Surely the man was not returning to demand more, he thought, reaching to check his dagger was sheathed at his belt. He would pay no more, he thought, even it meant committing a crime. But there was only one rider this time and by the time the man had dismounted William was at the door to greet his friend.

'Adam!' he cried. 'What brings you here on such a day as this? Come inside. Come inside.'

'I have a letter!' The excitement in his voice was palpable. 'From the king.' He drew out a parchment and smoothed it flat on a corner of the trestle table that was set out for dinnertime. 'He has granted us permission to act in his name against Thomas, Earl of Lancaster!'

'Good God, Adam! Is this genuine?' asked William as he stared at the writing, at the signature and the seal.

'It is!' said Adam triumphantly. 'I paid a messenger handsomely to ride with haste and pledge to the king our allegiance in his troubles with his cousin Lancaster. Whatever we do now, we do it in the name of King Edward.'

William looked up at his friend's excited face and saw that he meant to pursue this uprising. Still stinging from the money he had been forced to part with to Holland's bailiff, and anxious about the additional hardships that the coming winter would bring, he found himself in agreement — despite his qualms about how he would make his peace with Mab.

'We must gather men and arms, and get what food and supplies we can,' said William.

Adam nodded. 'First we will assemble the men and as many horses as we can find. Then we will gather supplies. Once the men are armed and can be fed we will ride against Lancaster and we will see him defeated!'

'Amen to that!' replied William as a watery sun shone a weak shaft of light in through the unshuttered window onto the hard earthen floor of the hall.

'And I would ask a favour,' said Adam quietly, taking William by the arm and drawing him away from the pantry door so that they wouldn't be overheard. 'My man, Will Tegg . . . '

'The one who — '

'Yes.' Adam drew a finger to his lips in warning. 'He has come to me for help, but the sheriff's men still seek him and he will not be safe on my land. I wondered, will you . . . ? Could you conceal him?' William hesitated. He did not want to bring danger to his manor and his family, but he could not very well refuse. He would not see the man caught and hanged for a moment's recklessness.

'Tell him to come after dark,' he said. 'Tell him to wait behind the barn until I come for him and I will find him a safe place to hide.'

'I'm grateful,' said Adam. 'We must look out for our own now.'

'Yes,' said William as he thought once again of his wife and daughters and prayed that he was doing the right thing.

3

Rebellion

On Wednesday, the twenty-second of October, William woke early having slept only fitfully during the night. He twitched back the bed curtains and saw the clean undershirt and braies that Mabel had prepared for him. His padded gambeson and mail tunic and leggings lay across the coffer at the foot of the bed, along with his surcoat with the Bradshaigh arms of the three black martlets. Before long he would have to get up, but until then he had a few more minutes to lie beside his sleeping wife. As he turned for one last look at her in the privacy of their bed he saw that she too was lying awake.

'I'm sorry,' he said, reaching to take a strand of her fair hair between his fingers. 'Please let us part on good terms?' He searched her stark blue eyes for forgiveness, for understanding. He loved her so much and hated the way that he never seemed able to tell her how he felt. Whenever he tried he always ended by making some jest.

50

She sighed and reached to clasp her hand around his. She looked so small and frail and when he had loved her last night he had been afraid that she might break she had become so thin with hunger and worry.

'Will you give me your blessing before I go?' he asked, leaning to kiss her pale face in the early morning light. 'I . . . I love you,' he mumbled.

'William,' she replied with the smile that always made him feel so tender and protective of her. 'I know. I love you too,' she told him, touching her gentle hand to his cheek. 'Go, if you must — but take care of yourself.' He bent to kiss her soft lips, feeling her yield to him as her fingers tangled themselves in his hair. Then she pushed him firmly away from her. 'No,' she said. 'You must get ready. I can hear the men bringing out the horses already and you must not keep them waiting. I will still be here when you return.'

He knew she was right. The sun was up and it would soon be time to march out to meet up with Adam and the other rebels at Charnock Richard.

He put on his underclothes as Mabel quickly dressed herself and went to ensure that a breakfast was set out for the men who were to ride with him. There was little to share, but he was determined that no one would leave hungry and by the time he took his seat at the top table there was a welcoming aroma of fresh bread and ale filling the great hall. And even though he had assured his tenants that they had a free choice, and that his waiving of their Michaelmas dues was not dependant on their agreeing to accompany him, William was relieved and pleased to see that everyone who was able had turned out, having polished up the armour they had worn on the Scottish campaign. After prayers and a blessing from Father Gilbert, William thanked the men for their loyalty and support then bade them eat.

His wife and daughters had broken their fast in the bedchamber but came to say their farewells as the company rose to leave.

'I will be home soon,' he promised Mab as he bent to kiss her a chaste farewell. He hoped that their love was strong enough to withstand anything the future might hold, even though she had not given him the blessing he craved. 'Take care of our daughters,' he said, as he kissed each of the girls in turn. Then he buckled his sword belt at his waist and picked up his helm and gauntlets.

Outside the door the young son of a villager was holding his stallion, brushed and harnessed. Beside him Harry Palmer held the Bradshaigh banner, fluttering in the sharp wind. He put his foot to his stirrup and easily mounted the tall horse. Then, after a last smile at his wife, William led them out of the village and their womenfolk stood at the doors of the houses to see them go.

Adam was waiting for them. As William led his men towards the market cross he saw that his friend had amassed quite a following too and was surprised at the number of horses he had brought, though many more men were on foot and only poorly armed. Harry Duxbury and Henry Lea had also kept their word and at a quick count William thought that there must have been going on for a hundred men and perhaps two dozen horses milling around the square.

'It's good to see you!' Adam greeted him, his face bright with anticipation.

'Surely you didn't doubt me?'

'Not for a moment,' he grinned.

'And your man Tegg rides with us — under my colours and mounted on Henry Bury's horse,' William told him.

'Good man!' laughed Adam. 'Let's hope we will all survive this fight. Have you seen Sir Adam Walton?' he asked.

'No. Why?'

'He is pledged to the cause but has not

arrived. I think we should send a party to remind him of his allegiance,' remarked Adam as he beckoned to one of his armed and mounted men. 'I do not trust those who change their minds.'

'And if he will not come?'

'He will come,' Adam assured him as he gave orders to the man to bring Walton willingly or under duress. 'Now we ride for Standish church,' he told William. 'We have more supporters who await us there.'

William smiled as he watched his friend urge the men forward and signalled to his own villagers to follow on. The sound of the hooves, the creak of the saddles, the determined marching footsteps of the booted army sent a thrill through him and this time there was no overlord to please; this time the fight and the victory would be all their own.

At Standish he recognised Sir Ralph de Bickerstaffe and John Henry, and Gilbert de Bickerstaffe, who took oath to join them and after they had sharpened their blades on the stone walls of the church they set off again, this time following the Banastre banner towards Wigan. The leaves on the trees were turning to orange and yellow as they rode. They would have been a magnificent sight if the sun had been shining, mused William, but instead the mist clung to them and made them hang limply as the light faded in the early afternoon.

As they approached the town Adam fell back to ride beside him.

'All these men will need to be fed,' he said with a worried frown. William glanced around them. He had advised his own men to bring with them as much food as they could, but what they'd had was long since eaten and the men would expect their bellies to be filled before nightfall. 'Where will we find food?' asked Adam.

'I think I know a place,' remarked William with a wry smile as he recognised Holland's manor house in the distance. Although he was confident that Holland himself was not in residence he could imagine his bailiff lording it over the servants, pleased with his illicit haul of supposed taxation. 'I'm sure Sir Robert can spare a little more than trencher bread to feed our army,' he said referring to the lord's habit of handing out the leftovers from his table to beggars at his gate.

A look of satisfaction crept across Adam's face. 'Indeed he can,' he replied. 'Let's get the men settled and then we'll ride up with our request.'

'And shall we bid the priest open up the church?' suggested William. 'We cannot expect men to sleep in the open,' he said, as the lingering mist turned into a persistent rain with the creeping darkness.

Father Robert de Cliderhou, the rector of Wigan, frowned as William politely explained their request after banging persistently on his door with a gloved fist. But after glancing at the armed men who were standing around his threshold he fetched his keys and reluctantly turned the iron lock in the thick studded door to allow them access.

'I would ask you to keep from the chancel,' he said as he watched men begin to follow them through the doorway, 'and to remember that you are on hallowed ground — and to clear up after yourselves.'

'You have my word,' said William as he reached to take the keys from the priest. 'I will return these before we leave,' he said as weary men began to spread their blankets on the floor and pull off their sodden boots to dry their feet. 'Can you spare us any food?'

'I have little enough for my own needs. I give what I can in alms, but there are so many . . . ' The priest glanced at the throng of men who were laughing and joking with one another as the church filled with the press of wet bodies, a few lean dogs and, had William not held up his hand and shaken his head, horses as well. Though he could hardly blame their owners not wanting to leave them tethered outside when so many had disappeared, probably to be sold as illicit joints of meat from the stalls of unscrupulous butchers.

'Have they brought no food of their own? I cannot see how they can all be fed,' said the priest.

'Pray for a miracle,' replied William, thinking that his dilemma was indeed like the feeding of the five thousand and hoping that it could be as easily solved.

After the priest had left with a backward glance of disquiet, William gathered around a dozen or so men he knew he could trust and horsed them although the underfed animals were weary. Armed men on horseback, he reasoned, would be more menacing than armed men of foot. He made sure each one had sword and dagger as well as a bow and some arrows and after exhorting them to be assertive and insistent he led them towards Robert Holland's manor house.

The house stood some distance from the village and was built from stone surrounded by a wall inside which William could see a fair few cattle and sheep were gathered, safe from wolves and thieves. Beside the house was a sturdy barn which William suspected was quite full. The gate was locked and barred, but he was prepared. After knocking and receiving no reply he dismounted from his horse and unpacked the dry tinder, arranging it at the foot of the wooden gate and striking his flints. Before many minutes had passed there was a steady blaze and the bundle of twigs that he had brought were fed to the fire until the gate itself began to burn. The men behind him raised a skin-tingling cheer of delight.

It wasn't long before men came running with pails of water, but the gates no longer posed a problem and, as William remounted to lead his men forward, he directed them to take as much as they could carry of grain, peas, beans and any salted meat they could lay their hands on.

'And I would have what bread you can spare and a few kegs of ale or wine from your buttery to warm our bellies,' said William leaning from his saddle to speak to the agitated bailiff.

'You haven't heard the last of this Bradshaw!'

'Bradshaigh,' William corrected him. 'Sir William Bradshaigh of Haigh and Blackrod.' He grinned down at the bailiff's infuriated face, lit by the flames from the burning gate. 'I'm sure you can spare it,' he told him. 'And bring whatever weapons you can find!' he bellowed after his men.

An hour or so later camp fires had been lit in the churchyard, a thick broth was cooking in heavy iron pots and bread and ale were being distributed to the men. William and Adam had counted the sacks of grain that had been requisitioned from Holland's barn and had decided that they had enough to feed the men for another day at least.

'We could do with more, though and more weapons and armour,' said Adam as they settled down with their backs against the cold stone wall of the church and dipped their bread into the hot broth. 'Those men who wear only jackets stuffed with straw will be cut down at the first onslaught.'

'They will have weapons and armour at the castles at Halton and Clitheroe,' said William. 'And maybe we should also send men out to forage for more food provisions in the surrounding districts. We must keep the men well fed if we are to keep them with us.'

'You're right,' agreed Adam. 'I reckon this supper is the best that some of them have eaten in weeks. Their loyalty to us will be compounded by full stomachs.'

'I think tomorrow,' said William, as they settled down after posting sentries around the church, 'I will visit William Holland and see if he is as obliging as his brother.' He heard Adam laugh and as he lay listening to the muffled snores and coughs of the men who had answered their call to arms he felt a growing pleasure that they were taking action and were no longer mere victims of their greedy and incompetent overlords.

They roused the men early and sent contingents off to seek weapons whilst others rode in search of more supplies. William sought out his men from Haigh and gathered them around him giving them their orders for the day, and with a good breakfast inside them they set off. The incessant rain dripped off William's hair and trickled inside the cloak that covered his mail hauberk to keep it from rusting. He squirmed irritably. He should have become accustomed to such weather by now, he thought, but he had never been keen on privation, much preferring a warm hearth and good food and wine.

Smoke rose from the chimney of Sir William Holland's house at Haydock and the thought of the man sitting inside, warm and dry, whilst he was out in the wet and cold spurred on William's determination to take as much as they could. The house was flanked by a barn on one side and a shippon on the other. Near the outbuildings there was a vegetable garden, a herb garden and an apple orchard. Beyond that an area of wooded, but uncultivated land.

He reined in the horse and allowed his men to ride up beside him. 'Go to the barn and fill as many carts as you can find with corn and other grain,' he told Harry Palmer. 'Then take anything else that you think may assist us from the house and barn. 'You,' he told another, 'get the cattle and oxen from the shippon and drive them back to Wigan and you, Tom and Leo, go and round up those sheep in yonder meadow. All of them,' he added. 'We have many mouths to feed. And if you meet with any resistance say we act in the name of the king, and if that does not suffice you have my blessing to use whatever force is necessary.' He grinned and the men descended on the manor like crows plundering dead and dying sheep.

Within a couple of hours they had several carts piled high, at least a hundred sheep, about sixty oxen and twelve cows. Sir William Holland was left with nothing but a black eye. And on the return journey they broke into a grange at the house of Sir John de Langton at Newton-in-Makerfield and seized another ten pounds' worth of corn.

Adam had led a party of men to take Halton Castle and by the time William arrived back in Wigan with the provisions he found his friend gloating over his own haul: fifty chain mail hauberks to protect men in battle, a hundred steel helms and a hundred lances to add to the longbows that the men already had.

'We shall be a match for anyone now,' said Adam rubbing his hands together over a fire as William nodded approvingly. 'I feel confident that we will prevail, in the name of the king, against those tyrants Holland and Lancaster!'

★　★　★

Leaving Bella and Amelia in the care of Edith, Mabel put on her outside boots and fastened her threadbare cloak around her to walk to Wigan to witness for herself the excited stories that were circulating in the village. Walking briskly through the dismal autumn day it was about an hour later that she heard the raucous sounds of the gathered army outside the church of All Saints. Smoke rose from myriad camp fires and her mouth watered hungrily at the aroma of roasting mutton. Men were sitting and standing around eating and drinking and the rising voices and laughter conveyed an atmosphere of growing excitement. There were cattle and oxen and sheep in makeshift pens and as she peeped inside the doors of the church she saw more sacks of grain piled up than she had been aware still existed in the whole of Lancashire.

'Can I assist you?' asked a voice almost in her ear, making her jump. Mabel turned to face the flushed faced man, armed with a slightly rusty sword and stood up as straight as she could.

'I am Lady Mabel Bradshaigh. I am seeking my husband.'

'Sorry, m'lady,' mumbled the man. 'But I've been given orders that no one is to enter the church under any circumstances.'

'Not enter the church?' she repeated, 'And what does Father Robert have to say about that?'

'Not much, m' lady. Not with a pike thrust at his chest, anyway.'

'Do you know where Sir William is?'

'Over there.' The man pointed to the far side of the church, under the east window and Mabel hurriedly thanked him and followed the path around the stone wall, stepping over the legs of an outstretched sleeping man, until she caught sight of her husband deep in conversation with Adam Banastre.

'Mab!' he said in surprise when he looked up and saw her. 'What are you doing here?'

'I came to see the preparations for myself,' she told him, glancing around. 'Your men seem well armed and provisioned.'

'We have done our best.'

'So the stories of plunder are true?'

'We have requisitioned much of what we need.'

'Your wife sounds disapproving, Will,' remarked Adam Banastre. Mabel glared at him. She still blamed him for this and thought that there could have been a better way. If William was hurt, or even, though she hardly dared form the thought, killed, she would hold Banastre and his ill thought out rebellion wholly responsible.

'Walk with me, Mab,' said William, taking her arm and gently leading her away from the other man.

'You are afraid I will tell some truths to your so called friend,' she remarked.

'I hope you haven't come to make trouble, Mab,' he said.

'I wish you would give this up,' she said, stopping and resting a hand on his chest. 'You cannot prevail against the force of the Earl of Lancaster.'

'Banastre thinks we can.'

'You know my opinion of him, William. I fear for you,' she said as she glanced around at the preparations for battle. She looked up into her husband's hazel eyes. 'Come home,' she asked, although she could see that he would take no notice of her pleading.

He shook his head. 'I cannot do that. I have sworn an oath and I am committed to this uprising. Besides, I believe that what we are doing is right and necessary. But I would rather go with your blessing Mab.'

She looked again at his earnest face and saw that nothing she could say would dissuade him. 'Then you have it,' she said at last and she clung to him as he leaned to kiss her. 'Come home safely,' she added when he finally released her from his arms.

★ ★ ★

On the following Friday, which was the Eve of All Saints, the army marched for Manchester, helping themselves to several cattle belonging to Henry de Trafford along the way. Once again they took refuge in the church.

'That banner will assist us,' remarked Adam, when he saw the king's colours hanging in the chancel. 'We fight for the king so we should ride beneath his standard. We will say he sent it to us,' he said as he dragged a coffer across the rush strewn floor before clambering up to detach it from the wall and stroke it lovingly with the palm of his hand. He grinned at William. 'We will win, my friend. We will win. Have no fear.'

Behind them the door crashed open and a messenger came in. William recognised him as the young lad that Adam often used to gather intelligence. He could be no more than fourteen years of age and his face had an angelic look that meant he could often overhear the talk of indiscreet men without suspicion.

'What news?' asked Adam.

'My lord, there is an army approaching from the north.'

'We will re-group at Wigan and then head north towards the castle here at Clitheroe,' said Adam pointing to the places on the map that he had spread upon the church's altar. William, Henry Lea, Harry Duxbury and some of the others listened intently as they stood round. 'We should be able to take more arms at Clitheroe and then we will head here to Preston,' he indicated the place with a grubby forefinger, the nail bitten down to the quick. 'The river will give us some advantage and we can take Lancaster's forces here, forcing them to either break up or head for the water. Remember what the Scots did at Bannockburn?' he asked, looking up at them with a smile. 'We shall learn from their tricks and see if we can't drown more of Lancaster's men then they did ours.'

William nodded, but he couldn't quite match Adam's enthusiasm. He had lost some good men at Bannockburn, and the death of young Bryan Palmer still grieved him as much as if the boy had been his own son.

On Tuesday the fourth of November they marched downriver for Preston with their banners flying in the strengthening breeze. For once it was fine and Adam laughed that if it had still been raining the earl's men would never have turned out to fight at all.

Around noon they caught sight of their enemy on flat land near the riverbank. William surmised that they numbered far fewer than the rebels and settled onto his saddle with confident determination that, despite his earlier misgivings, this was a battle they could win easily by sheer force of superior numbers.

'Whose colours are they?' he asked Adam, as he squinted against the low noonday sun.

'Huddleston, Richard de Waleys, Walter le Vavasour,' he replied as he scanned the gathered force before them. 'We can take them easily. Bring up the archers but tell them not to fire until I give the signal. We cannot afford to waste arrows by firing on them before they are within range. Tell your men to do the same, make sure that they wait for the signal.'

William nodded. He knew that battles had been lost by archers too anxious to wait, who thought that it was safer to fire their arrows at the enemy as soon as they saw them. He knew that it was dangerous. The arrows that fell short were easy pickings for an enemy army to return fire.

They advanced slowly. William's horse snickered and tossed its head and he leaned to stroke its chestnut neck to soothe it as he kept it moving forwards. In front of him his archers kept a steady pace and a tight hold on their notched and primed arrows and behind him the men who were mounted rode to the beat of the drums, their lances grasped ready.

Sun glinted on metal armour and the weapons of their enemy. Adam raised his arm and on his signal a volley of arrows took to the air and William's horse recoiled at the sudden noise as they flew towards the advancing men. Gripping his sword tightly he waved the horsemen on. As the wind rushed at his eyes through the gap in his visor and his ears filled with the clash of metal and the shouts and screams of men fighting for their lives, he plunged the blade into a man wearing Walter le Vavasour's colours and watched as he slid slowly from his horse, blood seeping through the hole in his hauberk. William turned and ducked as a lance narrowly missed unseating him and reined his horse around to come up behind the man and plunge his sword again, seeking the unprotected gap under his armpit as he raised his arm to return the blow.

Sweat poured from his body and was soaked up by the thickly padded gambeson under his armour, but the sweat that poured down his face in rivulets made it difficult for him to see and it was the gradual silence that alerted him to their swift success. He peered around him and saw only his own men and, as he cautiously put the visor up and removed a glove to wipe his eyes, he saw what was left of the opposing force running northwards towards the river.

'Shall we give chase, sire?' asked Harry Palmer.

William looked at the man. His face was gashed but he seemed unaware of the blood that ran down his cheek and dripped from his chin.

'Let them go,' he said. 'They have learnt their lesson.'

Adam Banastre led his forces into Preston and William watched as the townspeople shrank into their doorways as they passed. There were no cheers, only fear on their faces as the army congregated in the market square, tired and hungry and thirsty.

'We need provisions,' said Adam. 'Organise men to go house to house and take whatever is necessary to feed the men and horses.

Within the hour the men were settled. The horses were unsaddled and watered and a sheep was roasting over a fire. Bread had been distributed and the men had drunk well from the ale that had been taken from the local brew house. Those who had been injured were having their wounds dressed and William was well pleased with what he saw. He had doubted Adam's ability to lead this rebellion, but as he raised a cup of ale and drank again he began to think that they could indeed succeed.

The shouts of the messengers who rode in from the lookouts they had posted around the town walls didn't concern him until he saw Adam reach for his sword and his helm and order his horse re-saddled.

'What news?' he asked when he had walked quickly across the square towards his friend. Adam's face told him that it was not good.

'Another force, larger, rides from the north,' he said. 'We must get the men harnessed and ready to fight again or they will simply sweep into the town and take us as we are.'

William glanced around at their army, at the men laughing and joking, slapping one another on their backs and arms as they raised their cups in celebration. He looked at the tired horses, their noses to the ground and at those that were too injured to fight again. He knew that it would not be easy to dispel another force, especially if those men were fresh and eager to fight.

'How many?' he asked the white-faced messenger.

'Over three hundred I reckon, my lord.'

'Come, do not look so glum, Will! We have had one victory this day, why not another?'

William glanced at his friend, and Adam's eyes gave a lie to his optimistic words, yet he knew that they could not just sit around and wait for slaughter. He touched his hand to Adam's arm. 'God be with you,' he said before searching the crowd for Harry Palmer to tell him to instruct the men to put down their ale and strap on their harness once more.

The enemy force looked intimidating as they advanced and far outnumbered those rebels who were still able or even willing to fight. William was convinced that many of their own army had mysteriously disappeared at the news of another battle, perhaps into the houses or barns of the townspeople. He had sent trusted men to search the taverns for deserters but they had returned with only a

71

few, mostly too drunk to be of value.

His aching eyes took in the red diagonal cross on the banner of Sir Edmund Neville, the county sheriff.

'The Harringtons, and Sir William Dacre,' said Adam, riding up beside him.

'We cannot win against them,' said William.

'What else can we do but try?' asked Adam. 'Numbers are not everything.'

'No, but they help,' sighed William as he looked around at an archer unsteadily trying to fix an arrow to his bow and prayed that they would not be massacred.

The drink had made the men aggressive. They were keen to fight and not one hung back on the order to advance, but they lacked the discipline of their earlier, more sober, assault and as soon as one let an arrow fly the others followed despite the frantic commands to wait until the enemy were within range.

As William let the riders with lances gallop forwards he saw that they were being approached by another force from the east. Men streamed down the hill towards them and he vaguely recognised the banner of Sir Walter de Strickland as he shouted orders to the men to regroup so that they could defend their flank. But his voice was lost amidst the screams of the dying as the rebel army was cut down like a field of corn at harvest.

William turned his horse as he felt panic rise from the pit of his stomach. He knew he owed it to the men who had supported him to stay with them, but his every instinct was urging him to run for his life, to get away from the oncoming blades that would mean sure death.

'Sir William!' The voice of Harry Palmer jolted him out of his rising terror. 'The men are fleeing. I think we should withdraw.'

William needed no more urging as he saw his men abandoning their weapons and their restrictive helms and tunics of chainmail. Riderless horses were milling around the muddied and blood soaked field whinnying in distress and his own horse, sensing their fear, unexpectedly reared on its hind legs and William felt himself slide backwards. Despite clutching for the animal's mane and for his saddle, he heard rather than saw the ground rush up and he hit the mud with a force that momentarily knocked the breath from him. Struggling to his feet, he felt an arm pulling insistently at his and he offered no resistance as Harry Palmer half led and half supported him towards the fringe of trees at the south of the meadow.

4

The Sheriff of Lancaster

It was still dark when the noise made Mabel jump from her sleep. She sat up in bed, the covers clutched to her and her heart pounding fiercely as she listened again, unsure if something real had woken her, or if it had been another nightmare. She had had so many bad dreams since William had gone, dreams of him being hurt, dead, suffering somewhere out there alone in the dark, unable to reach her except through the mysteries of the night-time. But then, she realised that Calab was barking and growling in the hall and she heard Bella move in her bed. The child's sharp breathing told her that she was also awake and that whatever had disturbed them was real enough. Then it came again. The pounding on the manor house door.

Mabel got up fearfully and pulled a tunic over her head, pausing to cover her long hair as she wondered who was there. Her first thought had been that it was William come home to her, but she doubted that he would have created such a din, unless he had been knocking for a long time and she had been lost in too deep a sleep to have heard him. But she doubted it. She never slept well these days and whenever he was away she seemed to wake often in the night, sometimes getting up to check her daughters were safe, or taking a candle to reassure herself that the doors were locked, the windows shuttered, the fire covered.

Now she crept barefoot into the hall knowing her way instinctively without the need for a candle. She heard the anxious breathing of the kitchen boys and Edith as they cowered on their pallets and Mabel wished that not all the able bodied men had followed William so eagerly. The cold of the floor stung at her feet through the rushes and when Calab ran to her she laid a hand on his soft head and shushed him. When he obeyed she was able to hear muffled barking from the other dogs somewhere outside. She stopped a few paces from the door and stood in the blackness and listened. Outside she could hear horses and men, several men she thought as she listened to the exchange of voices. It couldn't be William. If it had been, she was sure he would have come alone and that Calab would have been wagging his tail rather than making the menacing low growl in his throat that he saved for strangers he distrusted.

Mabel jerked again in alarm as the pounding recommenced. Whoever was there was not going to go away she realised and with shaking hands she fumbled for a candle and flints, taking several strikes to light the wick. With the reassurance of the big dog pressing against her legs she cautiously lifted the beam that secured the outer door and, with the candle held high, pulled it back a fraction, afraid of whom she would see there.

'Ah!' said a voice. 'At last. My apologies for disturbing you Lady Bradshaigh.'

Mabel raised the flickering flame even higher to illuminate the face of the tall man who stood at her door. His hair was long and dark and framed a thin face with an overlarge nose and pale inquiring eyes that were fixed on her with interest. Instinctively she pulled the unpinned neckline of her gown together, allowing the door to swing open. And, as she watched him look her up and down, she wished she had put on her cloak as she feared that the gown was clinging to her shivering, naked body and revealing more than she wanted him to see.

'Who are you? What do you want?' she asked, grasping for an authoritative tone but finding that the words came out as a frightened squeak.

'My name is Sir Edmund Neville. I am sheriff to the Earl of Lancaster. I seek your husband, Lady Bradshaigh.'

In the circumstances she was surprised that his voice sounded so gentle, his tone so conciliatory, but as she glanced outside she saw, in the early morning light, that he had men-at-arms all around both the manor house and the barn.

'My husband is not here.'

'Mama?' Bella's frightened voice made her turn in alarm.

'Go back to your bed and stay there!' she told her daughter. 'There is nothing to trouble you here.' She saw her daughter look at the man who was now filling their doorway and she saw the raw fear on her face. 'Go back to the bedchamber and look after your sister. Close the door behind you.'

With relief she watched as Bella obeyed and she heard the latch click shut. She turned back to Sir Edmund Neville and held the candle up again.

'My husband is not here,' she repeated.

'Then you can have no objection to us searching to be sure?'

'This is my house . . . ' she began as she held out a hand to bar his way. He paused and looked down at her.

'Lady Bradshaigh, if your husband is not here then there is no reason not to admit me and allow me to make sure for myself. If you will co-operate only I will come inside. But if you are unco-operative, then I will be forced to assume that you are concealing him and I will have my men tear the place apart.'

His threat was so at odds with the reasonable tone of his voice that it took a moment for Mabel to comprehend what he had said. Then, glancing at the armed men waiting for a signal beyond the door, she stepped back and allowed Sir Edmund access.

'Wait there,' he told the men, then walked to the centre of the hall and looked around. 'Tie up the dog and light some more candles,' he instructed Mabel, taking the one she held from her hands.

Trembling she slipped a rope through Calab's collar and managed to secure the growling hound to a ring in the wall near the hearth. Then she lit a taper from the glowing embers of the fire, but her hands were shaking so much that she found it impossible to transfer the flame to the wicks. From the corner of her eye she watched as Sir Edmund pulled off his gloves and threw them irritably to the table. She flinched as he moved towards her, but he merely took the taper from her hand and lit the candles and a lamp himself.

'They are all I have!' she burst out as the room filled with light. He looked down at her. 'We are short of oil and wax. We are short of everything,' she told him as if it was his fault.

'I will not be long and then you may extinguish them again,' he told her as he held the lamp up to the walls and turned to survey the hall, confirming to himself that there were no hiding places. 'Where does that door lead?'

'To the bedchamber. But my daughters are sleeping there,' she added as he strode towards it. She caught at his arm but he brushed her aside and pushed open the door and went in. Mabel rushed after him, afraid and also angry at his intrusion. 'There is no one else here.'

She watched as he ignored her pleas. She glanced at the coffer, filled with their valuables, but he didn't touch it. He pulled aside the bed hangings and the covers on her bed and bent to look underneath before holding the light up towards the rafters to check that nobody was concealing themselves up there. Then he turned and held the lamp out towards Bella and Amelia. Mabel saw their stricken faces as they stared up at this imposing stranger; Bella with her arms around her little sister as they cowered together

'Get up!' he told them.

'Please!' begged Mabel. 'They are only children.'

'Get up,' he repeated, and although his voice was gentler in tone none of them could mistake his determination. Mabel nodded and her daughters ran to her. She covered them with her arms as they shook against her, their thin, barely clad bodies shivering with cold and terror as they watched Sir Edmund turn for one last sweep of the bedchamber.

Mabel held the girls close and comforted them as Sir Edmund searched the kitchen and buttery and bake house before he was satisfied. Then he returned and stood in the doorway to the bedchamber and watched her for a moment as she stroked and kissed the heads of her children.

'Has your husband returned here?' he asked.

'No.' She was angry with herself for allowing her voice to quaver as she spoke. Sir Edmund watched her for what seemed like endless time.

'Don't make the mistake of thinking that you can hide him from me,' he told her at last. 'He is a rebel and a traitor and I am determined to bring him to justice. I will come back, and I will keep coming back, until you either show me where he is hidden or tell me where he can be found.'

'I do not know where he is,' she repeated.

'For now I believe you,' said Sir Edmund. 'But they all creep home sooner or later, and when he does he will be mine.'

'And what then?' asked Mabel, though she immediately regretted asking such a question in front of the girls.

'That is for a judge to decide,' remarked Sir Edmund as he met her eyes reluctantly. But Mabel did not need to be told that if William fell into this man's hands it would mean his certain death. 'For now I will wish you good day,' he added, then hesitated. 'And I offer my apologies if I have distressed your daughters.'

Mabel watched as he put out all but the one candle, glanced at Calab who barked at him menacingly and then left, closing the main door behind him. As her daughters clung to her with their small hands she listened as he gave orders to his men and within a few minutes she heard them move away and a tense silence filled the house, punctuated only by occasional barks from Calab.

At last Mabel thought it was safe. She

rubbed the arms and backs of the girls and tried to reassure them. 'It's all right. They've gone now. I'm sure they won't come back, despite what he said. I think he was only trying to frighten us.'

'I am frightened, Mama,' said Amelia and Mabel hugged her daughter and wiped the tears from her pale cheeks.

'There's no need. Come on now. Edith will help you to get properly dressed and the boys will bring some bread for breakfast. And then we must milk the cow and feed the geese,' she encouraged them, trying to make it sound as if life would continue as normal at Haigh Hall, although, deep down, she realised that they all knew as well as she did that their lives had changed irrevocably, and that if William was not already dead then he soon could be, and that they were alone and vulnerable.

As soon as she saw that the girls were calmer and had been given something to eat, Mabel put on her outside boots and her cloak and cautiously drew back the door. Apart from the muddied ground beyond the hall where the men and horses had gathered there was no sign of the visitors, although from the barn came muffled barking and Mabel realised that the other dogs had been shut in. With thoughts of how the rebel army had ransacked the stores of those who were

Lancastrian supporters she ran to the barn door and pulled it open, expecting to find the meagre store of hay and grain gone. The dogs rushed at her wildly, jumping up and barking frenetically. Mabel let them go and they dashed outside growling and sniffing at the flattened grass.

In the pale dawn that crept through the open door she saw that, although the bundles of hay and sacks of grain had all been moved aside and lay strewn across the floor, nothing was missing. She counted to be sure, but not one had been taken and for some reason that she couldn't understand she sat down heavily on the nearest sack and wept.

'My lady?' She looked up as Mistress Palmer came towards her and gently touched her shoulder. 'Are you hurt? They didn't . . . ?'

'No!' She took the woman's hand in hers and squeezed it to reassure her. 'No, they didn't hurt me. He . . . Sir Edmund Neville . . . was very polite,' she said, thinking back to how much respect he had shown her which, under the circumstances, she would not have expected. 'Did they search the houses as well?' she asked.

'All of them,' replied Mistress Palmer.

'Was anything taken? Was anyone harmed?' asked Mabel, suddenly anxious for all the other undefended women who, like herself, had been so brutally awakened.

'No.' Mistress Palmer shook her head, but Mabel saw the hesitation in her eyes.

'What happened?' she asked.

'They pulled old Elmer Andrew from his bed and questioned him quite fiercely,' she said.

'Did they hurt him?' she asked, anger rising in her. Old Elmer was the only man left in Haigh. He was growing old and frail and had not been strong enough to go with William. If he had been harmed and Neville did return then she would tell him exactly what she thought of him, Mabel decided.

'No,' said Mistress Palmer. 'The sheriff shouted a bit and made some threats but in the end he seemed satisfied that no one knows where Sir William is.'

'I will go and try to reassure people that all will be well,' said Mabel. She drew the door of the barn closed and secured it against the wind, then pulled the hood of her cloak around her face and walked down to the village. Smoke was rising from all the houses she saw, relieved that everyone was at least still able to find some warmth, but there was an unnerving silence as she went from house to house to inquire after the wellbeing of her tenants. No children played outside; they clung behind their mothers' skirts looking

84

pale and tired and the women too all looked afraid although Mabel tried as best she could to reassure them. It had made everything worse, she thought, this rebellion of Adam Banastre's. He wasn't here to see the women's faces as they wondered if their husbands were alive or dead or if they would ever see them again — and if not how they would manage to farm the land and feed their children without them.

Returning to the hall, her legs feeling weak and weary, Mabel caught sight of a movement in the trees. Her stomach lurched as she thought it might be Neville and his men come back, but when she heard the soft snicker she called out and William's horse plodded tiredly towards her. It pushed its soft muzzle against her hands and she felt its warm breath as she reached up to stroke the long hard nose, rubbing the small white mark between its eyes.

'Hello boy,' she soothed it. 'You look as if you've come a long way.' She ran a hand along its neck noting the broken, trailing reins and the muddied saddle. There was a drying wound along its flank and blood still seeping down its hind leg from a deep cut. 'Where's William?' she asked, but the horse only pushed its head against her, seeking its own reassurance that it was home and safe.

Mabel picked up the trailing reins and led the horse to the stable where she took off her cloak and, after hanging it over a wooden partition, unsaddled the animal and brought it water and a couple of handfuls of hay before bathing its wounds and brushing what dried mud she could from its coat. Hengist, William called it. They were almost inseparable, she knew. He had ridden the stallion to the Scottish war last year and they had come home safely, and together. Now Mabel worried that her worst fears for William could be true. What had happened to part him from the horse? And if the horse had come home alone where was he now?

She went to draw more water for the few cows and oxen that were left in the shippon, feeding them a ration of hay and hoping that the drying straw would see them through the coming winter months. She checked them carefully for signs of disease then went to see the sheep that had been brought down to pens for the harsh months to come. She counted three dead, but would need to call one of the boys to help her to lift and bury the bodies. She prayed that the men would come home soon; that they were hiding in the forest until they thought it was safe and that they had not all perished. If they did not come home, she didn't know where she would get the help she would need to survive until springtime.

Back in the manor house she put her cloak and boots to dry near the fire and went through the kitchen to the bake house. It was warm and the aroma of fresh bread filled the air. Edith was washing dishes and utensils in the large barrel and Bella was drying them on a cloth and putting them back on the scrubbed table. Amelia was sitting near the oven on a three legged stool playing with a small dough man. For a moment Mabel felt annoyance at the waste, but the concentration on her younger daughter's face quickly dispelled it and she was glad that Edith had made something to distract the little girl's mind from the earlier trauma.

'It smells good. You must have been working very hard,' she told them. 'I think it must be nearly dinner time.'

'I've begun a stew, though it's mostly peas,' said Edith.

'Good,' said Mabel, who was sickened of the sight and smell of peas but knew there was nothing more. How she longed for the feasts they used to have, with three different varieties of roasted meat, poultry and fresh salads from the herb garden. Even the thought made her hungrier than ever and she tried to dismiss the images of filled platters from her mind, though it was not easy.

Later as they sat eating near the oven to take advantage of the warmth, there was a scratching noise and Mabel thought at first that it might be a rat. She was afraid of rats more than ever now that food was short and William had promised to bring a cat for the kitchen — although it would be another creature to feed if it didn't manage to fill itself with vermin. But the scratching came again and Mabel became aware that it was someone or something at the back door. With a glance at the girls, who had all stopped eating and were staring anxiously in the direction of the sound, Mabel called out, 'Who's there?'

'It's me, my lady, Ned Kemp.'

Mabel scraped back the door. 'Come in,' she bade him, taking in the split lip that was turning purple and the swelling to one side of his forehead. 'Do you have news of Sir William?' she asked eagerly.

Her hopes fell as she watched him look down at his filthy boots and shuffle his feet slightly.

'Come and sit down,' she said trying to ease his discomfort. 'Have something to eat. Fetch a bowl of stew,' she said to Edith. And as she turned to do as she was bid, Mabel ached for the girl whose father was also missing. 'Have you any news?' she asked the man.

'I saw Wistan Bennett killed. I have to go and tell his wife.'

'Eat first,' said Mabel as Edith put the bowl down in front of him. Ned needed no further urging as he took up the spoon and ate eagerly, mopping the dregs with a piece of bread still hot from the oven. Mabel poured a generous cup of ale and handed it to him.

'Thank you, my lady. Tis two days since I ate anything at all,' he said. 'The sheriff has his men searching the countryside for those who managed to flee the battle.'

'I know. He has been here this morning seeking Sir William. Have you any news of my husband?' she asked him again.

'I do not know what became of him, my lady,' Ned told her. 'We won the first battle at Preston, but Edmund Neville arrived later the same day with a force that far outnumbered ours. We were already tired and many of the men had been celebrating the earlier victory. We were taken unawares and when a second force hit us side on many men were lost in the mélée. I fought for as long as I could, but then Banastre bid us all run for our lives and I needed no urging.' Mabel watched as he took another drink and wiped his mouth on his sleeve. 'I saw Bennett cut to pieces before my eyes and I fled. I don't know if Sir William survived, though I cannot say with certainty that he is dead.'

The man looked up and Mabel tried to smile. 'Then perhaps we should not give up hope just yet. Did you see Harry Palmer?' she asked, glancing across at Edith. Ned shook his head.

'I'm sorry.'

'No,' said Mabel. 'I am sorry that it has come to this. Please know that I am grateful to you for standing by my husband in this ill-conceived endeavour. Go home to your wife,' she told him. 'She will be overjoyed to see you safe.' But not so Avril Bennett, she thought, or her three young children.

That afternoon Mabel left her own children in Edith's care and walked to the church at Wigan to pray. The stone walls shrouded her in cold as she looked around at the squalid remnants of the army's camp, shocked that they had so defiled the house of God. Brushing aside a moulding trencher of bread she knelt before the chancel steps and her quiet voice echoed around the empty building as she prayed aloud the pater noster.

As she knelt, lost in grief and despair she saw a form move towards her and almost cried out her husband's name until she blinked back her tears and recognised the priest, Father Robert.

'Father, will you hear my confession?'

'Bless you my child. What sins have you to confess?'

'Mostly lack of faith, Father. I pray that my husband is safe, but God does not answer me and I fear He has deserted me in my time of need.'

'God will grant you the strength you need to face each day,' said Father Robert gently. 'But He will not grant your every wish. We mere mortals cannot hope to understand the plans He has for this world and for us. We can only trust that He loves us.'

'But surely it cannot be His plan to take my husband?' she asked.

'He has taken other husbands — and wives and children too. Many have been taken. Why should you expect exemption, Lady Bradshaigh?'

She looked down at her thinned hands, still grasped tightly around her rosary, and she knew the priest was right. She was no different from the poorest villein in God's eyes.

'Forgive me, Father, for my vanity,' she said. The priest laid his hand briefly upon her head and made the sign of the cross on her forehead with his thumb.

'Go home to your children,' he said. 'They

need you, as do the villagers. You are called on to be strong; may God grant you that strength.'

★ ★ ★

Two days later news came that Adam Banastre and Henry Lea had been taken at the house of Henry de Eurfurlong. They had sought shelter, but he had betrayed them for a few paltry marks. Henry Duxbury was also taken, caught in the forest by a party of Neville's men and conveyed to Lancaster to stand trial. Of William there was still no word.

'They say Banastre was hidden in the barn and fought against his captors valiantly,' Siward, another villager who had crept back to Haigh under cover of darkness, told Mabel. 'But he was taken alive and was beheaded at Martinmas on Leyland Moor at the command of Thomas, Earl of Lancaster. Henry Lea also.' Mabel reeled at the news and reached for a stool to sit down. 'You've turned dreadful pale, my lady,' said the man. 'Just praise God it was not Sir William.'

'Indeed,' she managed to say. Adam Banastre may have been a fool, but she would never have wished this for him and she wept again, though not so much for him as for the not knowing what had become of her husband.

5

A Year and a Day

It was fast approaching Christmas and the days were growing ever shorter. Everyone was trying to complete their daytime tasks before the early dusk fell, to save them having to burn the candles that must last them until the longer days returned, and Mabel and her daughters were going early to their beds to try to conserve their meagre supplies of food and fuel.

One dull Thursday, when it seemed to have never come full daylight, Mabel was helping Edith to pour the fresh brew of ale into barrels and secure them when she heard horses approaching. She looked up at Edith whose face had frozen in fear at the sound and, briefly brushing her hand across the girl's arm, she went, wiping her hands on the rough apron that covered her gown, to see who had come.

She immediately recognised Sir Edmund Neville as he dismounted his black stallion and walked across the courtyard towards her.

He was dressed in a thick woollen cloak of the darkest blue that made his pale eyes more intense, and his expression remained as enigmatic as ever.

'My husband is not here,' she told him defensively as he greeted her with a formal but curt bow.

'Though I see that some of the other villagers have returned,' he remarked as he nodded his head towards the houses he had just passed.

'There are menfolk in the village, yes,' she agreed. 'Maybe more than at your last visit, for on that day I think many had left early to go to market — '

'Save yourself the trouble of concocting some story,' he said, holding up his gloved hand to silence her. 'I do not care whether the men were part of the rebellion or not. They are only villagers and villagers must do as their lord bids them. I do not hold them responsible. Neither does my master, the Earl of Lancaster. It is the ringleaders, those who bid them rise up against the noble lords, that the earl seeks to punish.'

'My husband is not here,' repeated Mabel.

'Then perhaps, my lady, he was slain in battle — or died from his wounds soon after,' he remarked with a hint of cynicism. 'I offer you my condolences. It is sad that you do not have the small comfort of burying his body.'

'Until I see his body I will not believe that he is dead,' Mabel told him defiantly.

'You believe he still survives in the forest?' asked Neville with a raised eyebrow.

'I pray that he survives. Though I do not know if it is so,' she replied quickly, worried that her words may have raised suspicions in the sheriff's mind that she knew more than she did.

'May I come inside?' he asked. 'I need to convey to you certain . . . information and I think it would be better for you to hear it within the house than standing here. And perhaps the dog could be restrained,' he suggested, glancing down at Calab who had come to stand beside Mabel and was making his menacing, deep throated growl.

Mabel reached down and tucked her fingers under the dog's collar, though she didn't bid him to be quiet. 'Come in,' she said and led the way into the hall before securing the dog loosely and telling him to lie down.

The dog continued to watch Neville as he strode into the hall and closed the door behind him. He took off his gloves and rubbed his hands at the flames of the small fire as Mabel watched, her arms folded protectively across her chest as she waited for him to speak.

'There has been a hearing at Lancaster into the death of Henry Bury,' he told her at last. 'Certain men, in their absence, have been found guilty of the murder: William Tegg and Stephen Scallard. They have been outlawed and if discovered will pay with their lives for their despicable crime. Henry Duxbury has also been found guilty of instigating rebellion and for being suspected of complicity.' He paused and looked directly at her. 'And for failing to attend as a witness in the case of the Bury murder, your husband William Bradshaw has also been declared an outlaw.' As Edmund Neville watched her Mabel saw the reflected firelight dance in his eyes. 'You do know what that means, don't you?' he asked.

'It means my husband is a wanted man, although he has committed no crime.'

'As an outlaw he is indeed a wanted man,' said Neville. He is outside the law and as such . . . ' He hesitated as he watched her. 'As such it means that he cannot own land. The estates of Blackrod and Haigh are forfeit to the king for a year and a day and he may dispose of them how he pleases.'

'But these lands are my inheritance,' replied Mabel, finding that she was shaking with anger. 'They belong to me. No one can take them away.'

Neville shook his head. 'The lands have

been taken into the protection of the king, and I am granted the authority to seize them in the name of the king until it is decided to whom they should be demised.'

Mabel stared at him. 'And when the time is over?' she asked. 'Will they be returned?'

'A court will decide the ownership. It will depend to some extent on whether or not your husband is found, alive or dead, and the outcome of any trial that may ensue.'

'And what will happen to me? To my tenants? Will Sir Robert Holland take control? He is the mesne lord below the Earl of Lancaster.'

'I am sorry, my lady, I do not know. Until I receive word from the earl about the matter I cannot say more about the outcome or about what decision he may take. All I know is that it is my duty to inform you what the court at Lancaster has decided. The lands are forfeit on William Bradshaw being declared an outlaw.'

'For a year and a day?'

'Yes, my lady. That is correct.'

Mabel turned and looked around Haigh Hall. It was her home. She had been born here. It wasn't possible for her to give it up. And where could she go, she wondered, and what would become of her little girls.

'Sir Edmund, please,' she said, turning to

the tall stranger who was still warming his hands before her hearth. 'Can you not tell me what will happen to me? Will I be forced to leave?' she asked him, thinking that Sir Robert Holland would be unlikely to treat her kindly after the way William had plundered his house and the house of his brother.

'I can only advise you to be compliant with any request made of you. I'm sure that it will be easier for you that way . . . if you do not strive for conflict,' he told her. There was a moment of tense silence between them until he took up his gloves and pulled them slowly over his fingers. 'Have you seen your husband, or heard from him? Tell me the truth, Lady Bradshaigh,' he warned her.

'No,' she replied. 'And that is the truth, my lord. I have had no word.'

'None of your villagers . . . ?'

'None saw him after the battle, though one saw him thrown from his horse. The horse came home alone,' she confessed and, angry with herself for showing weakness in front of this man, Mabel turned away to try to regain control over the tears that threatened to overwhelm her. She was surprised to feel the gentle pressure on her arm and to hear Edmund Neville's voice close to her ear. 'Be brave, my lady,' he said. Then she heard his footsteps retreat and by the time she had regained her composure he was mounted on his horse. As she stood in the doorway and watched him ride away she noticed him glance back at her.

★   ★   ★

Mabel told no one what had been said to her, but every day afterwards she expected Robert Holland to come calling. Christmas drew nearer, but there was little cause for celebration and certainly no prospect of feasting. They would all count themselves lucky not to go to bed hungry on Christmas Day.

Almost every morning there were more dead sheep to bury and as she watched the sacks of grain and sheaths of hay and straw grow fewer and fewer, she imposed strict rationing at the manor house and advised the villagers to do the same.

Illness too continued to take lives. As Advent drew to a close and the dark December days were unrelieved of the mist and gloom, and all-pervading dampness that seemed to creep into the bones and joints of even the most robust of them, Elmer Andrew began to cough up blood as well as phlegm and on Christmas Eve he died in the evening.

'I do not know how much longer I can bear

it,' Mabel told Father Gilbert when the mass for his soul was finished. 'You tell us that God is testing our faith, but surely we are tested beyond all endurance? Why would God see us suffer so?' she asked.

'He will not test you beyond endurance, my lady,' comforted the priest. 'He knows that you are strong.'

'But I am not strong, Father. Every day I would like to give up and not continue. Every night I want to lie down on my bed and sleep and never wake.'

'And what would become of your daughters then?' he chided her. 'And what would become of the villagers who look to you for inspiration? No, you must remain strong, my child. God will grant you the strength.'

'But what of William?' she asked. 'I do not know if he lives or not. He may lie cold and unburied in some forgotten ditch, or, if not, I cannot even bear to think of him starving in the forest, afraid to come home. They say the land is forfeit to the king,' she told the priest. He nodded slowly. 'No one has come yet to turn me out, but every day I fear they will. Do you know anything, Father? You must hear things,' she said.

'I hear many things, my lady, but I can truthfully tell you that I have heard nothing of this matter.'

Mabel sighed and thanked the priest who blessed her, but she walked back to the hall with her thoughts as troubled as ever. Robert Holland had stayed away. She doubted there was much to bring him to Lancashire in these dark, wet winter days, and although she watched each day for the return of the sun, praying for a summer that would bring them food and freedom from the diseases that had plagued them for so long, she also feared the springtime that would thaw the roads would bring him north to claim what she believed was rightfully hers. But she would not give it up, she decided, as she stared up at her home. She would not give it up without a fight.

* * *

At last the darkness abated and the tightly curled buds on the tree branches began to swell with new life as it grew warmer, if not drier. But there was still no news of William, or Harry Palmer, and as each day passed Mabel found it harder and harder to hold onto the hope that they were still alive.

She decided that when the rain stopped she would leave Bella and Amelia in the care of Edith and her mother, Mistress Palmer, and she would take Ned Kemp and go to look for William's body at Preston. If it could not be found she could continue to believe that he lived. And if they did find him, she could bring him home and see him decently buried in the church at Wigan with the blessing of Father Robert upon his soul.

But before she had the opportunity, she was disturbed one day by the sound of hooves approaching from the south. Thinking that it was Edmund Neville come again she reached to untie her apron, took off the woollen shawl she had been wearing for warmth and, pushing stray hair beneath her coif, she told Edith and the girls to stay in the kitchen as she went to greet her visitor at the door of the manor house.

To her surprise the men she saw ride into the courtyard were strangers. One rode a large bay with a wide blaze down its nose. He looked contemptuously down at Mabel from narrow eyes of an indeterminate colour and said nothing until his page came to hold the horse's bridle and help him down. He stood and, as he stretched and flexed his legs as if they were stiff from a long ride, Mabel noticed how short he was, short and squat with his rotund body almost incongruously balanced on his stick thin legs. She watched with a mixture of curiosity and dismay as he glanced up and around the courtyard, as if taking an inventory of the house and outbuildings. Then at last he looked at Mabel and she saw the disdain in his eyes.

'I take it you are Mabel Bradshaw?' he asked in a high pitched whine that reminded her of a petulant child.

'I am Lady Mabel Bradshaigh,' she replied, with more confidence than she felt as she watched him, wondering who he was and what he wanted. Glancing at his companions she saw that they were armed and wore surcoats bearing a spread eagle with a blue beak and claws; it was not a livery that she recognised. Perhaps they were lost, or merely passing by, she hoped, though she suspected that neither explanation was the true one.

He nodded dismissively at her words. 'My name is Sir Peter Lymesey,' he told her. His hard eyes stared at her as if he expected the announcement to mean something.

'You're welcome at my house,' she said uncertainly.

'Your house?' laughed the man suddenly. 'I don't think so Mistress Bradshaw.'

Mabel looked at him, puzzled, not knowing how to respond. The man was not only uncouth, but ill-mannered and a sudden horror seized her that he was the one to whom her lands had been demised.

'Yes, indeed,' he smiled in a self-satisfied way as the recognition of her situation must have become apparent on her face. 'I am your lord and master, and you a mere tenant here, so if you are not going to invite me inside I will gladly take the privilege owing to me.'

'Of course. I apologise. Do come in and take some food and drink,' replied Mabel, quickly gathering her scattered thoughts and fears. She stood back to allow the man to pass into the hall ahead of her, determined to cling on to her position as hostess and not to let him render her entirely powerless.

He swaggered into the manor house and stood looking around as if calculating its worth. Mabel saw three pairs of frightened eyes peeping from behind the kitchen door and she smiled to reassure them before calling for Edith.

'Bring some wine and cakes for our guest,' she said, frowning a warning as she realised that Edith was about to say there were none to spare. 'And what of your men?' Mabel asked him. 'Do they need food? A place to stay? Or do you have other plans?'

'I have no plans that I wish to discuss with you Mistress, except of course the matter of your rents and taxes,' he replied as he pulled off his thick gauntlets, unfastened his cloak and removed his wolf-skin hat, laying them all proprietorially across the largest coffer. Mabel saw that his head was almost bald of hair, except for a few greying strands that barely covered his pink scalp. His chin on the other hand bristled with an untidy beard and along with his slightly protruding ears gave the impression that his head had been adjoined to his body upside down.

She was about to invite him to sit when he pulled William's chair across the hard earthen floor, nearer to the hearth, and lowered himself onto it with an audible sigh.

'You need to feed your fire,' he observed. 'This meagre blaze will not warm me at all and I am chilled to the bone with this damp, northern weather.'

'I will fetch more logs,' said Edith as she put a flagon of the best wine and a filled cup beside him.

'Bring the food first,' he ordered her and with a bewildered glance at Mabel, the girl dropped a curtsey and did as she was bid.

'Keep the girls out of sight and find them some occupation to distract them whilst I attend to our visitor,' Mabel whispered to Edith, catching hold of her arm as she passed her.

'What are you mumbling about?' he demanded.

'I am merely ensuring your comfort, my lord,' replied Mabel. 'I have no wish to seem

unwelcoming. It is just that your arrival was
. . . unexpected.'

He raised his sparse eyebrows as he quaffed
great gulps of the wine. 'Neville did not tell
you to expect me?'

'No. I have neither seen nor heard from Sir
Edmund Neville since before mid-winter.'

Mabel stood before him in the uncomfortable silence and wondered why she had not
been warned of his coming. As she had heard
no more from Sir Edmund she had presumed
that the lands were still under the control of
Robert Holland, and that it would be his
bailiff who would come again to collect rent
from her. And although she had found that
there was less than she had hoped when she
counted the coins in the coffer at the foot of
the bed, she was sure that there was enough
to pay any reasonable demand. Now as she
looked at this avaricious little man who sat
before her fire in her husband's chair, she
couldn't help but wonder if he meant only to
collect money from her and leave. He had the
air of someone with different plans.

'Your house is tolerable,' he remarked with
a slight sneer. 'I have a mind to stay awhile,'
he added, confirming her suspicions.

'I would have thought the house of Sir
Robert Holland would have offered you
better comfort than my humble home,' she

said. 'I presume that you are acquainted with him?'

'Oh yes. Sir Robert however is merely secretary to the Earl of Lancaster, as you no doubt know, whereas I am a knight of the household of his majesty the king.'

'My husband is loyal to the king,' said Mabel, grasping at a hope that the man would after all reveal himself as her ally.

'Your husband was an outlaw, mistress,' he replied with a dismissive shrug of his shoulders. He picked up the cup again and drained it, then took a honey cake and chewed noisily with a slightly open mouth. 'Very good,' he remarked. 'Did you make these?'

'Yes . . . but we are very short of flour and of all supplies,' she burst out in irritation that he should take for granted her ability to place food and wine before him.

'Oh I'm sure your villagers have plenty stashed away. You should squeeze them a little more. They will take advantage of a lone woman you know. Perhaps you would like me to have a word with them?'

'No. That will not be necessary,' she said quickly. 'I'm sure they have paid all their dues. I keep careful accounts.'

'Then perhaps now would be a good time to show me those accounts so that I can judge for myself,' he suggested with a short smile.

'Of course,' said Mabel and excusing herself she went to the bedchamber and unlocked the coffer with the key from her belt. Her hands lingered regretfully on the shining silver coins that she knew she would soon be forced to part with. Then she took out the rolls on which she had written all the payments and expenses of the manor and, after securing the chest, she returned to the hall and gave them to Sir Peter who unrolled them and studied them closely.

'The manor has shown no profit this year,' he observed.

'There has been famine,' she reminded him.

'Well I will still expect a fair rent. I have been granted the income from these lands as a reward for my loyal service,' he said, with a subtle emphasis on the word loyal. 'I cannot afford to be charitable.'

'How much will you require?' she asked. He looked up and studied her for a while.

'I haven't quite decided yet. It depends upon your ability to . . . to make me welcome,' he told her.

A terror struck Mabel as she began to comprehend his meaning. She was sickened and afraid that the kind of payment he was hinting at would be a far greater cost than the hoard of silver. Trying to remain calm she breathed deeply to steady herself.

'I have made you as welcome as I am able,' she replied, her voice shaking. 'But if you would like to stay to supper then I'm sure that we can provide for you . . . and your men . . . though it will be only simple, homely fare.'

He laughed as he rolled up her accounts. 'I'm sure that supper will be a start, and will allow us to get to know one another better.' He smirked as he reached for his hat and gloves. 'And in the meantime I will inspect the barns and shippon to make sure you have no grain or animals hidden away that you have not accounted for. You would be surprised how many tenants are a little . . . creative . . . in their reckonings. But you will find, Mistress Bradshaw, that I am not a man to be duped or cheated.'

'My name is Lady Bradshaigh,' she reminded him in an attempt to keep control of some dignity.

'I think not,' he remarked. 'Remember that you are now merely the widow of an outlaw, without even a strip of land to call your own.'

'I will accompany you,' she said as she picked up the rolls to return them to the bedchamber and collect her cloak.

'No need,' he said. 'I am quite capable of finding my way.' And before she could say more he had left the hall and called for two men to accompany him whilst the page took the horses to be stabled, and Mabel feared that by the time she was rid of them all their precious supplies would have been eaten.

'Have we enough food to provide dinner for so many?' she asked Edith when she found the silent girl cowering in the kitchen with her daughters. Mabel guessed that she had been listening at the door and that, although Bella and Amelia were too young to understand Lymesey's innuendos, Edith understood all too well and probably feared that she might be the next to feel the thrust of the man's attentions.

'We have pea stew,' she said.

'Ah,' remarked Mabel, in an attempt to lighten the mood with humour. 'Whatever we become short of we never seem to be without peas. Do what you can Edith. We have some bread at least and oatcakes. Let us hope they are not too hungry.'

As she came from the buttery after checking the ale she saw her pale-faced daughters watching her and realised that not only were they afraid, but they were vulnerable. If she had to make a payment to

Lymesey of the kind that he had hinted at then it was something she would force herself to do to keep them safe, but it was not an act which she would want them to be under the same roof to witness.

'We may have to offer our guest a bed for the night,' she said, trying to keep her tone conversational. 'I wonder if I should ask Mistress Palmer if you could sleep in her house.'

'But there is plenty of room in the hall,' said Bella, looking alarmed at the suggestion of being parted from her mother.

'I think sleeping at my house sounds a very good idea,' said Edith, perceptively coming to Mabel's assistance. 'Sir Peter has brought many retainers who will need somewhere to bed down and, who knows, they may all snore.'

'Why can't they sleep in the barn?' argued Bella. 'I don't want to sleep at the Palmer's house.'

'I think you should,' Mabel told her firmly. 'I will go and speak to your mother, Edith, and arrange it. No more argument,' she said sharply to Bella and guilt stung at her as she saw the little girl's eyes fill with tears. She knew that neither of her daughters was happy to be out of her company since William had gone and she knew that Bella thought her cruel and unreasonable on this occasion, but she hoped that she would forgive her without ever discovering the real reason she did not want them in Haigh Hall.

6

The Outlaw

William opened his eyes to see a faint light broaching the horizon and as he watched through the entrance to the small den, he saw the stars fading and knew that it was time to face another day of hardship and banishment.

Outside he could see Harry Palmer crouched down and knew that he was coaxing a small fire into life within the circle of stones that served as their hearth. Above the fire, on a framework of sturdy branches that were scorched but too thick to burn easily, hung a pot that they had found and William hoped that they would be able to catch something to cook in it later that day. Despite the famine in the villages the forest teemed with life and the traps they set more often than not provided a hare or some other small mammal for their dinner.

William pushed back the flimsy warmth of the blanket and stood up. The straw-filled sack that was his mattress looked damp in the chilly morning air and he wondered if the sun would shine, and if they would be able to hang their bedding over the bushes to dry out a little.

He shook his boots to remove any insects that were lurking there and pulled them onto his bare feet before pulling on his over-tunic, stolen from a bush outside some village. He ran his fingers through his tangled hair in a token attempt at remaining civilised and went out, stretching and scratching and yawning, to face what the coming day would bring.

At least he was not alone, he thought, as he watched Harry cup his hands around a tiny flicker of flame and gently blow it. The tinder that they had managed to keep dry in a box took hold and soon there was enough of a blaze for them to rub some feeling back into their hands and fingers.

'Is there anything to eat?' he asked as he watched his friend pour stream water into the pot to heat. At first William had refused to drink the water from the stream, saying it would kill them both as surely as the Earl of Lancaster's axe should they be caught, but eventually thirst had overcome his misgivings and surprisingly they had both survived so far, though they had discovered that if the water was first boiled and then left to cool a little it not only provided some comfort but was less likely to send them seeking seclusion

114

in the forest to spew and purge what little food they had found.

'I told you last night that you would regret it this morning if you ate all that was left of the stew,' remarked Harry, and William sighed as he recalled the conversation. 'I'll go and check the traps in a while,' he continued. 'It looks as though it might be a dry day.'

William sat down beside the fire on a stone he had discovered and dragged back to their den. It was smooth and had a small indentation that seemed to fit him snugly and, wrapped in a cloth and heated on the embers of the fire, it also provided him with something warm to take to his bed, though it was a poor substitute for his wife. He watched as steam began to gently rise from the water. Harry threw in a few dried mint leaves for flavour. It was amazing, thought William, how much they had learnt about survival over the harsh winter months.

At last Harry poured the brew into the rough cups and handed one to him. He warmed his hands around it and slowly sipped the contents, feeling the liquid trickle down his gullet and the warmth spread across his chest and into his stomach. He watched his friend through a haze of steam and smoke. The scar on Harry's cheek had healed but was still a vivid red. It made him look fierce, thought William, though he doubted his wife would be impressed by it when she saw him; perhaps it would eventually fade. It was a pity it hadn't been a little lower or his growth of greying beard would have covered it.

Every day he thanked God that Harry had helped him from the field of battle that day at Preston. As he had lain there, winded and confused, it would have been a miracle if he had not been run through with a sword or impaled on a lance if Harry had not seen him and pulled him to his feet and taken him into the cover of the surrounding woodland. For that, he would always owe this man a debt that was too huge to be repaid. He owed Harry Palmer his life.

After Harry had dragged him into the forest and concealed them both in some undergrowth they had waited, straining to hear what was going on around them until it seemed safe enough to come out. Slowly William's breath had returned, though his back and chest had been sore and he'd been glad when Harry suggested that they take off their chainmail armour and dump it in a ditch so that they were less likely to be seen. They had both been afraid that Neville would send dogs to seek them out, but as it had darkened in the late afternoon the men had withdrawn and they had hoped that the sheriff had taken enough prisoners to satisfy him.

Once silence had fallen, apart from two owls disputing their territory and sending their ghoulish cries across the forest, William and Harry had crept from their hiding place and, tripping and stumbling over tree roots, and fending off branches that lashed unseen at their faces, they had made their way cautiously back to the battle site. The iron rich stench of blood pervaded the night air and as a moon rose beyond the horizon William had seen the mutilated corpses of his and Adam's men littering the riverbank. He'd bent to look at the nearest one, a body he had almost fallen over. It was cold and the face was unrecognisable.

'We must take them to the church. Which is the nearest?' he'd asked.

'No,' Harry had argued. 'We cannot do that, unless we want to give ourselves willingly into the captivity of Lancaster's sheriff!' William had stood up and looked around him. The moon had been reflected in the water of the Ribble; an undulating silvery pathway; its beauty at odds with the horror that had lain around him. He had fought in many battles on the Scottish campaign but even there both sides had been given the opportunity to retrieve and bury their dead. 'Neville will see them buried, I'm sure,' Harry had said. 'There is nothing we can do, except . . . '

'Except what?

'For our own survival I think we should salvage what we can whilst we have the opportunity.'

'Yes,' William had agreed, wondering if this was what men meant when they spoke of being in shock. It was usually him who led the men, who made the decisions, who told them what to do, what to think.

Yet here he was, standing as though half dead himself and relying on a vassal to take the lead. 'Yes,' he'd said again more decisively. 'The moonlight is brighter now and there may be things we can use, though I fear my horse is long gone,' he'd said, looking southwards and wondering if Hengist would find his way back to Haigh. He'd worried about what the animal's return might mean to Mab. He'd wished that he could have sent a message to her, to let her know that he was alive, but he knew that Haigh was the first place the sheriff would search for him, and if Mab could truthfully say that she had heard nothing from him and did not know where he was, then it would be easier for her to convince Neville that she genuinely had no

118

knowledge of his whereabouts.

They had stepped over the bodies, retrieving what few weapons were left: some longbows, arrows, a few knives. They had found flints and some pots and utensils from the site where they had camped the previous night, some blankets and a few provisions that they had worked all night to store and conceal in the forest until they could find a safer place to keep them.

'We have enough for a few days. That should see us through,' Harry had said as dawn came, and filthy and exhausted they had settled down once more to await what daylight would bring, wanting to sleep but too afraid, reassured by the silence but dreading that at any moment they would hear horses and hounds coming to hunt them down.

Towards midday they had heard a twig snap and immediately they were both alert. William had drawn his sword and Harry reached for a longbow and an arrow. They hadn't spoken but almost held their breath as they waited, ears straining in the direction of the sound. Footsteps had approached and then another twig had broken nearby and a voice shushed someone as the steps paused. William had slowly straightened his legs to see through the almost bare branches who was coming. He'd exhaled with a sigh of relief and his grip on his sword had slackened as he'd recognised Adam and Henry Lea.

'Will! I'm glad to see you!' Adam had exclaimed. 'I saw you flung from your horse and were sure you must have perished.'

'No. It will take more than that to be rid of me,' he'd grinned at his friend, grasping his hand and then that of Lea. 'I'm glad to see you both alive. Though yesterday was not a good one; many are dead.' He'd waved a hand towards the field and Adam's face became serious.

'I have seen,' he'd said grimly. 'We will make Lancaster pay for this slaughter.'

William had stared at him. 'You can't mean to go on. We are defeated.'

'I will never admit defeat,' he'd replied. 'Henry and I spoke of this last night and we are agreed. We will make our way to the house of de Eurfurlong at Charnock Richard. He will support us and we will raise more men to our cause. Will you come?'

'No,' William had replied. 'I think it may be safer to lay low here for a while, until we can be sure of what Lancaster and his sheriff mean to do next.' At his refusal Adam had silently held out his hand, palm up and grasped Henry Lea's hand to show his palm as well with the livid red line cutting across it.

'I will follow you in a few days,' William had told them, relenting in the face of their combined abhorrence at his breach of their oath. 'It will be safer if we do not travel together anyway.'

Satisfied that he was still loyal to their cause Adam had shared a meal with them in the small clearing near the river where they had set up camp. Then he and Henry Lea had left. It was the last time William had seen them.

He sat now and traced the line that scored his own palm and wondered if he too would have been caught and executed if he had gone with them to the house of the man they thought was their friend, but who had betrayed them. He had heard from a pedlar he'd met on the road of the deaths of his two friends at Martinmas. It was a hard lesson, thought William, to realise that you could trust no one and he wondered how much money it would take for Harry Palmer to be tempted to hand him over to the sheriff.

'You look worried this morning. Does something ail you?' asked Harry. William looked up to find his friend appraising him with a concerned expression.

'I was thinking of Adam Banastre,' he replied, 'and wondering why I ever listened to him. Mab always said he was trouble. I ought to have heeded her.'

'Aye. Lady Mabel is a wise woman. I worry about my wife and daughter, but the thought that she's at Haigh to see them right is a comfort.'

'Yes.' William stood up and prowled restlessly around their small campsite. 'I worry too,' he admitted. 'What was that?' he said suddenly as he caught sight of a movement through the trees.

'Dinner maybe?' said Harry, reaching inside the den for his longbow as his stomach growled audibly in anticipation of food.

William saw something again and reached for the dagger sheathed at his hip as he moved to take cover, glancing behind him to see if the route to the east, his best way of escape was clear, or if they had been fooled in their laxity by an effort to surround them and flush them out. He was fairly sure now that the movement he had seen was a man, crouching as he moved stealthily through the trees.

William saw Harry circle around behind him and silently indicate that there were at least two men. He listened as they closed in but decided that there were no others and that these two could just be opportunist thieves who had been attracted by the smoke from the fire. Then with a sudden thwack

Harry released an arrow and as it juddered into the trunk of a tree one of the men leapt aside with an exclamation of alarm and William recognised him as Will Tegg.

'Hold your fire!' he called out to Harry. 'I know this man. Tegg? What are you doing here? You were lucky not to have your head split into two.'

He watched as Tegg turned to search the trees for the marksman but didn't see him until Harry slowly stood up, a fresh arrow trained on him.

'I'm unarmed!' he called out, raising his hands to show he meant to fire no weapon, 'and so is my companion!'

'Who is with you?' asked William as he saw another movement and the second man stood up, his hands also spread. It was Stephen Scallard. 'It's all right Harry,' he said. 'I doubt these men mean us any harm.'

He hoped he was right. Both Scallard and Tegg were still wanted by the sheriff to answer the charge of the murder of Henry Bury, so another killing would not worsen their fate. And even though he had assisted Tegg, and had hidden him on his own land so that the man owed him favour, he hoped that any price that had been put on his own head did not include a free pardon. That might be enough to tempt Tegg to do him a disservice, and William knew that it was wiser to be cautious.

'What brings you here?' he asked them.

'We heard you were in the forest,' said Tegg, 'and thought that we should make ourselves known to you.'

'Come and sit by the fire,' said William, beckoning Harry to join them as well. 'Though we can offer little in the way of hospitality.'

'A wise visitor brings his own provisions,' replied Scallard, reaching down and then displaying two freshly caught rabbits by their ears. 'I doubt you'll refuse these for your breakfast.'

'Indeed, no,' said William, thinking how quickly the world had been tumbled upside down and how strange it was that a lord of the manor should feel so grateful for a meagre handout. 'I'm indebted to you,' he told them as he watched Scallard begin to skin the beasts and use his stone seat as a workbench to gut and butcher the meat before skewering it onto green twigs to roast over the fire.

'You seem to be managing very well,' remarked William as the aroma of the meat made his mouth water.

'We've learnt many skills in order to survive, Sir William. Though you don't seem to be doing too badly yourself,' he remarked as he looked around the campsite with its partially hidden den.

'Surviving on the Scottish campaigns taught me much about improvisation,' he said. 'My life has not been one of entire luxury, I can assure you. Are you living in the forest?' he asked.

'Mostly, though sometimes we go to the village to hear the latest news. The land there belongs to our master ... well, to our master's widow anyway,' he concluded and William nodded, the unwelcome image of the beheading of Piers Gaveston haunting his mind once more, except that this time the head that rolled away was Adam's.

'And what news of the lady?' he asked, knowing that Margaret Banastre, although Adam's wife, was also the sister of Robert Holland.

'In London these past winter months, under the protection of her brother and where there is food aplenty whilst her tenants starve,' he said angrily. William nodded. He hoped that Mab was finding enough to feed herself and their daughters.

'I don't suppose you have news of Haigh?' he asked.

'I know that Edmund Neville has been asking after your whereabouts,' said Tegg. 'He has sworn that he will find you if you yet live and part you from your head.'

'Then let us hope he thinks I am already dead,' replied William as he took the roasted rabbit and ate hungrily.

★   ★   ★

Tegg and Scallard stayed until late, until it was too dark for them to see their way safely, and it was agreed that they would spend the night at the campsite and that the following day William and Harry would go with them to Chorleigh to discover if there was any more news about the hunt for them or if they had been given up as dead.

William lay awake and worried. With every day that passed his fear for Mab and his daughters grew. What would happen to them if it was thought he was dead? Haigh had been Mab's, but on their marriage it had become his property and now that he had defied the Earl of Lancaster he surmised that the land would be forfeit, which meant that in reality Mab would be in the control of Robert Holland. It was a prospect that alarmed him and he was powerless to do anything about it; even giving himself up would not alter it.

He turned over and over on the uncomfortable straw pallet and wondered if he could creep home in disguise to check on Mab's welfare. Or maybe he should send Harry Palmer, if he was willing to go. Perhaps he would ask him, he thought and eventually drifted into a troubled slumber.

When they woke the next morning there was a strong smell of burning permeating the woodland. William knew that the ground was much too wet for a forest fire to have taken hold and the aroma was so strong that it could not have been just from domestic hearths. His first thought was that it had a connection with the arrival of Scallard and Tegg the previous day, but his suspicions faded when he saw their puzzled faces.

Stephen Scallard climbed to the top of the nearby hill, where the moor rose above the tree line, and came back to report that there was a pall of smoke hanging over the village of Chorleigh.

Harry Palmer looked up in alarm from his cooking pot. 'Do you think something is amiss?' he asked. 'We must go. They may need help,' he said.

William glanced at their two companions, but neither showed any reluctance and he nodded his head decisively. 'But we will need to be careful — in case this has something to do with the sheriff's men.'

After stowing away anything of value that

they could not carry with them they quickly disguised the campsite as best they could and set off to walk the two miles to the village. The small settlement was built on fertile meadowland between two rivers and as they approached William saw that the smoke hung thickly on the still morning air, as if captured in the valley between the houses. It hid them from his sight until he drew near enough to see the devastation. William stared in shock and disbelief at the broken fences, the trampled ground where crops had been growing, the churned and muddied green around the market cross and the smouldering remains of the two rows of houses that had clung to the sides of the main street. The only thing that still stood was the small stone church at the far end of the village, and even the door of that was smashed and hanging half open. Not a dog barked and there was no sign of life; not an ox or sheep or chicken remained and he thought that the village had been completely abandoned until he saw a pair of wary eyes peeping from behind the church door.

Mounting anger seethed in him as his heartbeat quickened and his hand reached for his sword. He hoped that whoever had done this was still nearby so that he could slowly tear them limb from limb for their destruction of this unprotected village. Whoever had done this, he surmised, knew that Adam Banastre was dead and had decided that whatever could be taken would be easy pickings for them; his main suspect was Edmund Neville, the right hand man of the Earl of Lancaster and his sworn enemy since he had taken Adam's oath. He would have revenge, he vowed to himself as he stepped inside the church and looked around in the gloom at about a dozen or so women, some with white faced children clinging behind their skirts, all of them silent with shock.

William turned to the nearest, a young woman with dark hair that trailed in a plait down her back. She looked up at him, her brown eyes wide with fear and her chin visibly trembling as she tried to speak.

'Who did this?' he asked as gently as his temper would allow. The woman swallowed and shook her head as her eyes filled with tears that ran down her face and smudged the ashes that coated her cheeks. William reached down to touch her arm to reassure her. 'Are you hurt?' he asked. She shook her head and looked up at him beseechingly.

'They took my husband,' she whispered as she wiped the tears from her face, smudging the dirt across it and William saw that her hands were blackened and blistered from where she had fought the flames. He looked around at the other women who were all staring at him and at Stephen Scallard who had followed him into the small, bare church.

'The Earl of Lancaster will pay for this, I promise you,' he told them.

''Twas not Lancaster, sir,' whispered an older woman, twisting the hem of her dress to wipe her face.

'The sheriff then, Neville. He has arms of a red cross . . . ' William crossed himself diagonally to show what he meant, but the woman continued to shake her head.

''Twas the Scots,' she told him. 'They took everything . . . food, animals and our husbands, 'cept for those they killed.'

'Go and see!' said William to Scallard. 'But be careful. There may be some who still linger. How long ago was this?' he asked the woman.

'Just before daybreak, my lord.'

'Martha!' Harry Palmer's voice was a mixture of anguish and relief as the woman with the dark hair ran into his arms and clung to him, sobbing uncontrollably. 'Thank God you're safe,' he said as he held her close and kissed her head. 'She is my youngest sister,' he told William, who now realised why his friend had been so grim faced and uncommunicative during their brisk journey up the valley.

'Where is Alfric?' Harry asked her as she brought her tears under control. 'Where are the children?' he demanded taking her arms in his hands and almost shaking her in his desperation to receive a coherent answer from her.

'There,' she said pointing across to where two little boys were sitting, pressed close to one another.

'And Alfric?'

'I don't know,' she said, wiping her face and nose on her sleeve. 'I don't know,' she repeated, and the despair in her voice echoed on the faces of all the other women who sat or stood in stunned horror as if waiting for William and Harry to make everything all right.

William turned as he heard movement behind him.

'Three dead,' said Scallard quietly. 'All men who had fought with us at Preston.'

Survived only to be murdered by Scots, thought William grimly, those barbarians who thought nothing of stealing and pillaging, and murdering anyone who got in their way.

'You had better see if your brother-in-law is amongst them,' he told Harry. 'Then see if there is any food left for these women and children.' He turned back to the villagers. 'Is anyone hurt?' he asked. 'Was anyone . . . ?' He was unsure how to ask the women if any of them had been violated, but the older woman shook her head.

'They told us that if we stayed here and didn't try to stop them that no one would get harmed. But our menfolk weren't going to watch whilst they took everything we had. They tried to stop them, but it was hopeless. There were too many.'

'Don't worry,' said William in an attempt at sympathy, although he knew his words meant little to them. 'We will protect you now. This will not happen again.'

But how could it happen again, wondered William, as he went back outside and looked around him. There was nothing left to take. As he walked amongst the burnt out ruins of the houses he realised that these women had only the meagre clothes they wore and that they were lucky to be alive, lucky that the invaders had only thought of their stomachs and that their hunger had driven other needs from their minds.

Tegg and Scallard came back shaking their heads. 'Everything is gone,' said Tegg. 'I'll kill them if I ever manage to lay my hands on them. War is one thing, but this . . . ?' He shrugged his shoulders as he stared around at the smoking ruins that had been houses.

'We found another body,' said Scallard. 'Should we take them into the church?'

'Let Harry Palmer talk to his sister first,' advised William. 'The women may not want the children to see the dead. And someone will have to go to Croston to fetch the priest for the burials.'

'I'll go,' said Tegg.

'Be careful,' warned William unnecessarily. 'Stephen, you come with me. We'll see what we have in our traps in the forest that might feed people. I think that Harry had best stay here.'

There were three hares in the traps. On another day it would have been a good haul, but it wasn't much to feed four grown men and around a dozen women and their children — especially when there wasn't even a half a sack of grain to make bread or brew ale.

William and Stephen were making their way back to Chorleigh through the royal forest at Heapey when William caught the movement. He put out a hand to stop Stephen and motioned him to be still and silent. Through a gap in the trees he could see the stag, grazing in a clearing. It had not scented them. Moving cautiously he took the longbow from his back and drew an arrow from its quiver. He fixed the notch to the string and drew it back taut, closing one eye to help his aim. Beside him Stephen Scallard stood motionless though William was aware of his rapid breathing as he watched. But William's hand was steady and his aim was true. He let the arrow fly and it whistled through the gaps in the trees and embedded itself with a satisfying thud into the side of the animal which looked round in surprise before staggering forwards and collapsing to its knees as blood poured from the wound.

'A venison supper,' said William with satisfaction. 'If we can manage to carry it back to the village.' He turned and saw his companion's worried face. 'Surely you don't fear to poach a little meat?' he asked him in surprise. 'I thought you were an outlaw?'

'And I . . . I thought you were a lord,' he replied.

'Not any more,' replied William. 'I've become a common man, just like you.'

'What was that?' Scallard spun around and his hand rested on the hilt of his dagger as he listened intently. Above the moans of the dying stag William had also heard something and the two men crept deeper into the trees, each scanning the ground as they went.

'Over here!' called Scallard after a moment

and William ducked under the low branches to where he stood, with his drawn knife, looking down at something.

The man had tried to conceal himself with twigs and grass. His face was white, streaked with black mud and, as he tried to drag himself away from them, William could see that his leg was badly injured.

'It's all right. We're friends. Who are you?' asked William, thinking that the man must be from Chorleigh and had somehow managed to get away from his captors. But the man spat on the ground and swore an oath that although it did not sound English left William with no doubt as to its general implication.

'A damn Scot!' exploded Scallard and raised his blade to finish the man there and then as he stared up defiantly from the ground.

'No!' William was surprised when Scallard obeyed and lowered the dagger.

'Don't you want him dead?' he asked.

'Not just yet. He may have information that we can use.'

'I'll tell ye nothing!' said the man struggling to his feet, though William saw him wince in agony as soon as he tried to bear any weight on his right leg.

'Run away then,' he told him. 'If we don't catch you, you're a free man.'

He saw the man reach inside his jerkin for a weapon, but, as his fist collided with the Scot's jaw, William was satisfied to see him stagger backwards, and as he flexed his fingers against the shock of the blow he saw Scallard remove the knife from the man's grasp and hold the blade to his neck.

'Give me one good reason not to slit your throat right now!'

'I'd rather you left him and finished the stag,' said William. 'Unless you think a Scotsman a more palatable dish.' He felt a prickle of pleasure at the fear on the captive's face at his words. 'You've left us nothing else to eat,' William told him as he placed his boot firmly on the man's chest to pin him down, 'and there are children back in that village I would not allow to starve whilst we buried your vile body in our English soil.'

'Please . . . ' faltered the man.

'That's better,' William told him. 'A show of respect and some co-operation may mean that you're worth something to me alive — as long as you're willing to talk.' The Scot tried to nod as William moved his boot to the man's throat and stood on him with even more of his weight. He watched as the man struggled for breath, knowing that he had the power to end his life right there. But there were answers he would like to hear from this invader before he was finished with him.

With both the Scot and the stag trussed up they made their way slowly back to Chorleigh. The stag, dripping blood, was slung on a makeshift pole that Scallard and William heaved onto their shoulders and William at the front made the limping Scotsman walk ahead of him, prodding him in the backside with the point of his knife every time the man slowed. And, as he saw that walking was agony to the man, William felt a satisfaction that at least one of the murdering mob was being punished, though he knew that it would take all his authority to stop Harry Palmer and the women from ripping this Scot to pieces.

★　★　★

'Why didn't you kill him?' asked Harry, glaring in the direction of the Scot who was bound to the market cross, his hands behind him and his legs tied so tightly as to make him whimper in pain.

'I thought you might like to see him suffer first,' said William.

'No. That's not the reason. There's something more.'

'You're right,' agreed William as he ate a slice of roasted venison and watched the silent children and their mothers eat as if they tasted nothing but the desire for revenge. 'There are four bodies laid out for burial and the other menfolk are missing, probably taken as slaves — or for food,' he said, remembering his earlier threat to the Scot and having to acknowledge that such thoughts would occur to any man if he were hungry enough. 'It's unusual, though, for a Scots raiding party to venture so far south and I would like to know what brought them to this village in particular, and why they didn't take the women and children as well.'

'You suspect it was not a random raid?' asked Harry.

'I suspect that there may be more than one reason for the Scots being here,' replied William, knowing that although the English had been routed at Bannockburn anyone with an ambition to depose the ruling monarch might just be tempted to ally themselves with Robert Bruce.

As the villagers ate and waited for the priest to come to bury their dead, William walked over to speak to the Scot again.

'Loosen my bonds, mon, I beg ye,' he said. 'Ye know I'm unarmed and canna run far.'

'In a little while,' promised William sitting down on the steps of the cross and placing a small slice of venison between them. 'I may

138

even let you eat, but first there are some questions I have to ask you.'

'Ask away, mon. I'll tell ye everything I know.'

'Why did you come here?'

'For food, mon. People are starving to death up yon.'

'So you thought you'd just help yourselves?'

'What would ye ha' done?' asked the man and William's conscience troubled him a little as he thought about the way the rebels had taken supplies.

'You're a long way south,' he observed, taking a small morsel from the venison and placing it on his own tongue as he spoke. 'Was there a reason for that?' The man stared at the meat as William pulled off a second piece and held it between his fingers.

'I just do what I'm told,' he replied slowly.

'Were you told to stay behind and spy?'

'No, mon! If I'd been able to march I'd be halfway back ta Scotland by now. I think they must ha' left me for dead. What'll ye do with me now?'

'If I let you go free these villagers will slaughter you,' said William, 'and I'm not sure I would be able to stop them. I'm not their master and I doubt they will listen to me.'

The Scot looked over towards the church

139

where the bare bones of the stag were all that remained on the spit over the open fire. It was already growing dark, though it was still only afternoon, but the women and children remained huddled around the flames for warmth rather than retreating to the relative safety of the cold church. They needed blankets at the very least, thought William. He would have to try to arrange some supplies for them though he knew that others had little to spare. Perhaps Harry could be persuaded to go to Haigh after all to ask Mab if she could intervene on their behalf.

'What would ye have me do?' asked the Scot, interrupting his thoughts.

'Tell me the real reason why you were so far south into Lancashire and I will protect you,' William told him, still pursuing his guess that the man knew more than he was telling. He put the second piece of meat in his own mouth whilst the man watched hungrily. The Scot glanced across at the villagers, who had gone to greet a loaded cart that was squeaking down the main street between the remains of the houses, and when he looked back at him William was pleased to see the expression of resignation that crossed his face.

'We came south with a message,' he told him.

'For whom?'

'Loosen my bonds mon, and I'll tell ye more. The pain in my leg's scarce bearable.' William looked down at the Scot's white face and relented a little, hoping that he was not being tricked. He bent and unfastened the rope that bound the man's legs to his hands behind his back and pulled tight on his injured thigh. The man barely concealed his yelp of pain as he moved the leg. It needed cleaning and binding, thought William, or an infection would set in and the man would die anyway. And though he had no remorse about running a sword or lance through his enemy on the battlefield, he baulked at the thought of killing this man face to face or even allowing him to die in agony. He tore off another piece from the meat and held it to the man's face where he snatched at it with his teeth and swallowed it almost without chewing.

'For whom?' repeated William.

The Scot swallowed again and glanced across at the crowd of villagers around the cart before looking back at him. 'The sheriff, Edmund Neville.'

'Neville!'

'Aye. He has a house — Middleton Hall — and we've been there afore, but this time his servants said he had ridden south to quell an uprising so we followed, thinking we could pass on the message and maybe find some supplies for ourselves as well.'

William stared down at the man. He looked defeated and his long and unemotional explanation had a ring of truth.

'Who was the message from?'

'From the king, Robert Bruce, though I think Neville is only a go-between.'

'And who do you think Robert Bruce is corresponding with?' asked William, though he was not surprised when the answer came.

'There is talk of a pact wi' the Earl of Lancaster in return for the recognition of the Scottish king and the removal of Edward from the English throne.'

William pulled the knife from his belt and felt a surge of satisfaction at the fear on the Scot's face. He bent to slice through the rope that held the man's wrists and then pushed the remainder of the meat within his reach. 'If you try to escape I will kill you,' he warned and the Scot nodded.

'I thank ye,' he said. 'You've been kinder than I could ha' expected.'

William walked back to the church and saw that it was the priest from Croston who had brought the cart; blankets, tools, a barrel of ale and some bread and grain were being unloaded and stored in the church.

'People have sent what little they can spare,' said Harry.

'I was thinking of sending to Haigh. I thought you might welcome the opportunity to see your wife,' ventured William. Harry put down the sack he had lifted from the cart and drew William aside.

'The priest tells me that Haigh is watched by men belonging to the sheriff,' he said. 'If we go back there we are dead men for sure.'

7

Dicken

Mabel was in the kitchen, overseeing the preparation of the supper, when Sir Peter Lymesey returned from his inspection of the manor. She had sent Edith to her home with an excited Amelia and a reluctant Bella, who had been coaxed into leaving by Mabel allowing her to take Calab. It was better that the dog went with them anyway, she thought. She did not trust Lymesey not to harm it if he got the chance and no matter how often she bid the dog be silent it growled incessantly whenever it saw the strangers.

She heard Lymesey come in through the front door, slamming it closed behind him so that the draft reached the kitchen and rattled the lid of the pot on the trivet over the fire. She waited and listened, wondering if she should go to him, but decided that she would not show too willing to attend to his needs. She watched through the open crack of the door and saw him settle himself onto William's chair once more. It was as if he owned the place, thought Mabel, before reminding herself that he actually did.

She took up a thick cloth and lifted the lid on the pea soup and stirred it with a long handled spoon. It smelt good and she was hungry. She must put some on one side for herself and the kitchen boys before offering it to Lymesey, she thought. She was not going to starve herself for his sake. She replaced the lid, folded the cloth neatly and told one of the boys to pour some clean water into a jug and basin for him to wash his hands. Then she went through to the hall to ask if he was ready to eat. He had thrown his fur-lined cloak, hat and gloves aside and his page had undone the buckles on his muddied boots and was tugging at them whilst he swore at the boy for not pulling them off more easily. At last the first boot parted from his foot and Mabel watched as the boy suddenly staggered backwards.

'Now pull the other one, you young fool, or you'll feel my switch across your backside again!' he roared and Mabel saw by the boy's frightened face that the threat was real and that it would not be the first time he had received a beating. She watched as he knelt and pulled at his master's other boot. He was no more than nine or ten years old and he looked thin and underfed in contrast to his portly master. The second boot came away and the boy dodged a blow to his left ear as he stood up and placed them by the fire to dry.

'Ah!' said Lymesey as he caught sight of Mabel. 'I must say that I am disappointed,' he told her. 'There is very little grain in the barn, the crops in the fields are not growing well and all your animals are sickly. I don't know what sort of master your husband was but it looks as if things have been lax, very lax. But not to worry,' he continued. 'I shall bring the peasants round so that they work hard and turn a profit for me.'

'There has been famine and disease,' said Mabel as she watched her kitchen boy pour water over his outstretched hands. She handed him a cloth to dry them herself.

'As long as there are peasants there will be excuses,' he said. 'But I don't listen to excuses. Now. Is my supper ready?'

'It is, my lord.'

'Then bring it in, woman. I've had a long day and I'm eager for a good meal.'

Mabel returned to the kitchen and instructed the boys to carry through the soup in the best pottery bowl. Without waiting for his men to arrive Lymesey demanded to be served and when she had put a platter of fresh bread before him she poured him a cup of her best wine as if she were a mere servant.

'Is that all?' he asked as she stood back, wondering if he would invite her to eat with him.

'This is all we have,' she replied as he broke off a lump of bread and dipped it into the bowl before transferring it, dripping, to his mouth. He chewed then wiped a dribble of the soup from his beard. 'Not bad,' he remarked. 'Is there no meat?'

'I'm sorry, but all the winter stock of meat is gone. Until we have animals to butcher or we can buy more at market then this is all we have to live on.'

'Well I hope you have enough to fill my men. They have good appetites,' he said as the door opened and the half dozen or so of his retainers came in and looked expectantly at the table. Mabel sent for more trenchers and cups and as they sat on the benches she supervised the ladling of the soup into bowls and watched as they began to eat. The young page hung back, but Mabel smiled at him and beckoned him to the table where she put a bowl in front of him. The boy gazed up at her in surprise and she rested her hand on his young shoulder wishing that she could do more to ease his situation.

'And you can make the bed ready. I'm tired,' said Lymesey. 'My men will sleep in here. I take it you have pallets?'

'You will find sacks and some straw in the barn,' said Mabel, wondering where she was intended to sleep.

'The boy can sleep in the small bed so he can attend me in the night,' Lymesey went on and Mabel was glad that the girls were safe with Mistress Palmer. 'Unless of course you are willing to fulfil my needs.' The men guffawed until he glared them into silence and Mabel saw that they were all watching her to see how she would react.

'As I am a married woman I do not think that would be appropriate in the eyes of God — or man,' she replied. Lymesey studied her as he chewed on his bread and washed it from his mouth with a gulp of wine.

'As far as I am aware you are a widow,' he said. 'And if your husband has not returned after a year and a day, which he will not do, being dead, you will be free to marry again — and I would very much like to make you my wife.'

'You would very much like to retain these lands for yourself you mean,' Mabel told him angrily. He paused and looked her up and down as she felt a prickle of fear that she had provoked him too far.

'Yes, I would like to keep the land, but a comely woman to warm my bed would be a bonus,' he replied.

'Until it is proven that I am a widow I will still consider myself to be a married woman.'

Oh I think you are choosing the harder path, Mistress Bradshaw,' he said, 'which is a shame because you will only arrive at the same destination eventually.'

'Excuse me,' said Mabel, relieved now that he hadn't asked her to join him at table. She walked out with as much dignity as she could to the kitchen where she sat on a stool with her own bowl on her knee. But she found that her appetite was gone. It was unbelievable that she should be treated in such a way in her own home. She could only fume inwardly and try to find ways to keep herself safe until she discovered if there was anyone still alive who was able or willing to protect her. 'Damn you William Bradshaigh!' she said out loud as she put the food to one side. 'Did you never once consider what would happen to me if your rebellion failed?' And as her tears flowed once more she covered her ears to shut out the sound of the men laughing in the hall.

★   ★   ★

'Forgive me Father Gilbert, for I have murder on my mind,' Mabel confessed to the priest as she knelt in the small chapel at Haigh.

'Murder, my child?' repeated the priest. 'Who has troubled you so much that you contemplate a mortal sin?'

'Sir Peter Lymesey,' she said, though she surmised that Father Gilbert would not be surprised at the name. 'Well maybe not murder in reality,' she explained. 'I doubt that I could indeed perpetrate such a thing — though if William were here I would not be surprised to see him raise his sword to the man.'

'Perhaps you had better unburden your mind,' suggested Father Gilbert. 'But you need not do so on your knees, Mabel. Come and sit with me and explain what troubles you. For, in all the years I've known you, I have never heard anything but words of penitence and kindness pass your lips.'

Mabel rose from the cold stone step and followed Father Gilbert to his private chamber where a low fire flickered in the hearth. The priest pulled a stool nearer to the warmth and poured her a cup of wine, pressing it into her cold hands and urging her to drink. She sipped at the liquid and coughed as it stung the back of her throat, then sipped some more enjoying the feeling of warmth that suffused her.

Father Gilbert sat down opposite her and poured a cup for himself. 'I have heard a little of your troubles,' he told her. 'But I urge you not to spill this man's blood. Not only would you damn your eternal soul but your earthly life would be ended in pain and violence also. Think of your children, I beg you. They have lost their father; do not allow them to lose their mother as well. Has the man . . . harmed you in any way?' he asked her gently.

'No,' said Mabel. 'I have managed to prevent that so far, though he continues to hint and threaten that I must go to his bed if I am to be allowed to remain at Haigh.'

'Then perhaps it is time for you to leave.'

'But it is my home, Father. It was my inheritance. Why should I give it over to this vile stranger when I have done nothing wrong?'

'I agree it is hard, Mabel. What of your little girls?'

'They remain in the care of Mistress Palmer but they are not happy. Although Mistress Palmer keeps a neat house it is not what they have been used to. The manor is their home too.'

The priest reached across to take the empty cup from her and then laid his hand over hers as she twisted them on her lap. 'Listen to me Mabel,' he said gently. 'I do not think you can hold onto the hope that the manor will be returned to you. You are in a vulnerable position and soon you will have to marry again for your own protection and for the protection of your children. This man — I do not know him well, but if he extends you his favour, perhaps you should consider what he has to offer.'

Shocked at the priest's words, Mabel snatched her hands from his and stood up, moving out of his reach. 'I do not know how you can suggest such a thing, Father Gilbert!' she told him. 'My husband may still be alive, and even if he is not I . . . I could never give myself to a man like Lymesey. He is vile.'

'But you say that he has not harmed you?'

'No. But it is the things he says; the way he looks at me . . . '

'Some men are diffident when it comes to telling a woman that they admire her,' said the priest. 'The man may just be clumsy in his words and actions. He may mean well.'

Mabel stared at Father Gilbert. How could a man like him, a celibate priest, have any comprehension of the desires of a lecher like Sir Peter Lymesey, she wondered. Whether William was alive or dead, there was no question of her willingly allowing the man to lay so much as a finger on her. But neither was there any question of her willingly giving up the manors of Haigh and Blackrod just because a court of law had outlawed her husband in his absence. None of it was justice. She had expected the priest to support her, to give her words of strength to help her, not to suggest that she give up without a fight.

'You need a husband to protect you, Mabel,' continued Father Gilbert. 'All I'm asking is whether Sir Peter Lymesey is really as bad as you think.'

Mabel looked down into the priest's kindly eyes. She was sure that he meant well, but he could never understand her torment. Although Haigh was rightfully hers she would not marry Peter Lymesey to keep it. Though the only alternative she could envisage was to take her two small daughters and live as an outlaw in the forest herself.

★   ★   ★

'How easy do you think it is to live in the forest?' Mabel asked Ned Kemp as she walked up to the summer pasture with him to see if it was fit to let out the sheep. For all Peter Lymesey's talk he knew very little about farming and despite his boasting about turning a profit he showed no interest in the running of the manor, preferring to hunt or hawk in the king's forest as was his right as a knight of the household. So it was left to Mabel to continue to shoulder most of the work and, as Ned was the most dependable of the few able-bodied men that were left in Haigh, she had come to rely on him more and more.

'Are you thinking of Sir William,' he asked. 'Do you suppose he's out there somewhere?' He paused and Mabel followed his gaze northwards towards the thick forest of Charnock that shrouded the rising hills. 'I would think that the life is hard, my lady, especially for someone used to the privileges of a manor such as this. But I'm sure Sir William could survive.'

'I . . . I was thinking of myself,' admitted Mabel.

'Oh no, my lady!' replied Ned, his disbelief apparent in his voice. 'You could not go to live in the forest! And what of Bella and Amelia? You could not take them to live like animals in the greenwood.'

'You're right,' agreed Mabel, acknowledging that the idea was not feasible.

'Does Lymesey abuse you, my lady?' asked Ned, pausing to turn his weather-lined face towards her.

'He . . . he wants me to marry him,' said Mabel. Ned kicked at a clump of grass and

154

stared back towards the forest.

'Then he does not think my lord still lives?'

'No. He tries to convince me that William is dead. Do you think he is dead?'

'I couldn't say, my lady. But I did not see him killed. And there are outlaws in the forest. Who can say that Sir William is not amongst them?'

'But wouldn't he have come back? Or at least sent a message?' she asked, posing the same questions that she asked herself over and over again.

'It would be too dangerous, my lady, whilst Lymesey is here. If Sir William is found he will surely be executed as a traitor.'

'Yes,' said Mabel, with a sigh. 'I suppose you are right. I do still hope that my husband lives.'

'All the villagers pray for it too,' said Ned. 'None wants Lymesey for their lord. He is a cruel man.'

Mabel nodded in agreement as she remembered that these tenants were her responsibility. If she left them to the mercy of Peter Lymesey she would be letting them down. Her father had always taught her that the tenants deserved respect and consideration in return for their hard work and loyalty. He had been a good and loving lord and Mabel had learnt from him. When she and William had returned to Haigh, her husband had been influenced by her way of doing things, especially when he saw that the villagers worked twice as hard for a lord and lady who appreciated them and treated them fairly. In many ways these people were like a family to her and she knew that she could never leave them.

'I will try to hold out for the year and a day, after which I hope that the land will be returned to me and Lymesey can be persuaded to go,' she said.

'If he tries to harm you, my lady, you need only say a word. There may not be that many men left in Haigh, but those of us that remain would not see you misused.'

'I appreciate the offer, Ned,' she said, laying her hand on his arm. 'But I would not see any of you hanged for my sake, and I think any attack on Lymesey would only bring the sheriff and his men to seek revenge.'

They walked on, up to the summit of the hill and as Mabel paused to catch her breath she looked down at Haigh in the valley below. No, she thought, it would be wrong of her to walk away from her responsibilities. She must find the strength to resist Peter Lymesey, whilst still giving him just enough hope to prevent him turning her out — and when his time was up she must insist that he left and then she would run the manor alone until William returned home to her.

As she turned to look again towards the forest a pall of smoke on the horizon caught her eye.

'Look at that! Something is afire,' she said to Ned.

'That's Chorleigh way,' he replied with a worried look.

'What can have happened?'

'I don't know, my lady. Surely it's too far south for a Scots' raid?'

'Scots? I wouldn't have thought so. Yet . . .' There was lingering doubt in Mabel's mind as she watched the smoke drift on the chill wind. She looked down at Haigh and wondered if they could withstand a raid if the Scots were forced, by their own harsh winter, to venture this far south in search of supplies. Perhaps she had better mention it to Lymesey when he returned from his hunting and ask him what plans he had to protect the village.

'Nonsense, woman! There are no Scots' raids around here,' replied Peter Lymesey when she told him what she had seen. 'Pour me a cup of wine and attend to my supper and leave the manor to those who are able to understand it,' he said. She lingered as the young page boy helped him out of his outdoor clothes in front of the fire that had been made hot and bright in time for his return. The boy looked exhausted, she thought, as she watched him. He was thin too and she suspected that he was not given enough to eat; she must make sure that he had some extra in the kitchen when Lymesey was not looking. 'Wine!' he demanded again. 'Don't just stand there dreaming.' Mabel filled a cup and handed it to him. He drank noisily and then sighed and wiped his mouth on the back of his hand. 'Women are fit only for the kitchen, and the bedchamber,' he said, with a wink that she knew she was supposed to find amusing. 'Don't you worry about the manor. I will take care of it for you.'

'Yes,' she said, tempted to remind him that she had spent the day visiting the villagers and inspecting the pasture as well as helping to brew ale, bake bread and prepare his supper, whilst he had ridden his horse through the forest with a hawk upon his wrist and expected the page to follow on foot and yet still be eager to do his bidding when he returned. She saw the boy stifle a yawn and Lymesey lashed out with a fierce blow to his cheek.

'Take my cloak and brush off every bit of mud if you want any supper!'

'The boy is tired out. Let him rest!' burst out Mabel protectively. 'Why must you be so cruel when he does his best?'

'He is a lazy youth. Get out!' he bawled at the boy. 'And you, mistress,' he said, turning his narrow eyes on Mabel, 'do not reprimand me in such a manner ever again, or I will be inclined to beat you, wife or not!'

'Then do you intend to beat me when I am your wife?' she asked quietly, although her temper boiled within her as she clutched the handle of the jug she held, only just preventing herself from cracking it against his bald head, so pinkly tempting in the firelight.

Suddenly he laughed. 'Of course not, my lady. Do not look so alarmed. Surely you can discern by now when I am jesting with you? Come nearer. You do not need be afraid of me. When you are my wife you will understand my humour better. See, pour me more wine and take a sip yourself and let us get to know one another better.' Mabel refilled his cup whilst trying to avoid the hand that stretched to fondle her. Although she was worried to see how quickly the barrels in the buttery were diminishing she found that Lymesey slept more soundly when he had drunk amply, and even though his snores from the bedchamber disturbed her as she lay on a pallet by the hearth at least she felt safer when she knew that he was sound asleep.

In the kitchen she found Edith skinning the

rabbits that Lymesey had brought home. At least they ate better for his hunting expeditions, she thought, as she watched the girl chop the meat and add it to the herbs in the stew pot, and she much preferred to have him out of the way for most of the time.

★   ★   ★

A few days later, after supper had been served and the boy, Dicken, had been given an extra helping when he brought the bowls and trenchers to the kitchen before assisting his unsteady master to bed; after Edith had been sent home, and Lymesey's men were still drinking in the hall, Mabel was covering the kitchen fire for the night when she heard a gentle knock on the back door. Her heart lurched and she ran to open it, thinking it might be William or at least a message from him, but it was Ned Kemp who stood outside with a dark cloak pulled closely around him.

'May I come in, my lady?'

Mabel stepped back and, with a finger to her lips to warn him to be quiet, she watched as he stepped inside, ducking his head under the low opening, before she quietly closed the door again. She paused, but the laughter from the hall continued and she was confident that they would not be overheard.

'Have you heard from Sir William?' she asked eagerly.

'No, my lady.'

'Oh.' She heard the disappointed in her own voice.

'I'm sorry.'

'No, it is not your fault, Ned. But for a moment I had hope,' she admitted. 'Sit down. There are still some embers to warm us,' she said, drawing two stools nearer to the hearth.

'I do have news that might interest you though, my lady. I was listening to the talk of Lymesey's men as they bedded down the horses. It seems that the smoke we saw rising the other day was from Chorleigh. The village was burned and all the animals and grain were taken — along with some of the menfolk. It seems that it was the Scots.'

'Dear God! That's terrible!' burst out Mabel, before glancing towards the hall door to check that no one had heard her.

'I hate to bring you distressing news, my lady, especially at this time of night,' said Ned, 'but there is something else that I thought might interest you. It seems that the villagers are being assisted by a group of outlaws who are helping them rebuild their houses.'

'Outlaws?' replied Mabel a little unsteadily

as she watched a slight smile play around Ned's eyes.

'Aye, my lady. And Harry Palmer's sister lives at Chorleigh. I know it isn't much news,' he said. 'But I thought you would like to know.'

'Thank you, Ned. The Chorleigh villagers will be in my prayers tonight — and I shall also thank God for the help they have. I've never believed that all outlaws are bad men,' she told him. 'I think most have just been unfortunate.'

'And the law is mostly corrupt anyway,' added Ned. 'What sort of law takes a person's lands from them for no fault of their own?'

★ ★ ★

'Have you heard news of the Scots' raid on Chorleigh?' Mabel asked Father Gilbert after he had heard her confession and given her his blessing. 'I have been thinking that maybe we should send some food, though we have little to spare.'

'The priest from Croston has seen them provided for I believe,' he reassured her.

'What do you think made them come so far south?'

'Desperation. Their winter has been even harsher than ours. Much snow has fallen in

Scotland and starving men will go to what lengths they can to feed themselves and their families.'

'You do not think them evil then?' she asked.

'Their acts are evil, but men are always capable of the redemption of their souls.'

'I wish I could learn to be as forgiving as you, Father Gilbert.' She paused. 'I heard that outlaws were helping the Chorleigh villagers to rebuild their houses,' she said, wanting to hear what the priest knew. Father Gilbert shrugged his shoulders.

'Rumours abound in times like these. You cannot cling to hope because of rumours,' he warned her. 'Have you thought more on what I said about Sir Peter Lymesey? If you are worried now, think how much harder it will be with no man to protect you.'

'I have my villagers.'

'It's not the same, Mabel, and you know it. Villagers do not have the ear of the sheriff or the Earl of Lancaster. You will need the protection of an influential man if these raids continue.'

'And what of Sir William?'

The priest sighed. 'I know you loved him, and that he loved you. It was my pleasure to minister to you both and to baptise your children. But these are hard times, Mabel, and it's probable that Sir William died in battle or soon after. If he had been alive would he not have come home to you?' He took her hand in his. 'You know that I see it as my task to advise you. I promised your father on his deathbed that I would be your friend as well as your confessor, and it is not just your soul that concerns me. I would not see you unhappy, but you cannot manage alone. It's too much to expect you to oversee the manor and raise your daughters without the help and support of a lord and husband. I have made enquiry about Sir Peter.' He paused and Mabel looked up to find him regarding her with a serious expression. 'Sir Edmund Neville speaks well of him. He is highly regarded and a wealthy man. It would be a good match for you Mabel. I urge you to think hard about your future and see whether it would not be better to accept this man as your husband when your year of widowhood comes to an end.'

Mabel pulled her hand from the priest's. She found that she was shaking her head, but words of dissention would not shape themselves on her lips. She had known Father Gilbert for a long time; she had always trusted him and his advice and although she thought he was wrong now she felt unable to say so.

'I . . . I will think on it,' she said at last.

There were men and horses circling the courtyard when Mabel came out of the chapel. Their surcoats bore the emblem of a red diagonal cross and Mabel knew before she reached the hall door that Sir Edmund Neville would be inside.

But it was the white face of Ned Kemp that she saw first as he turned to look at her with a thankful expression. 'Lady Mabel. Thank God you have come,' he said, his voice shaking with fear. Ned's arms were firmly held by two of the sheriff's men. Mabel looked from him to Edmund Neville, who was standing, still clad in his dark cloak, at the far end of the hall. Behind her she heard the door close firmly and saw a man-at-arms move to block the way out.

'What is amiss?' she asked as her eyes strayed towards Lymesey, who sat beside the hearth with a large cloth held to his face — and cowering in the far corner the boy, Dicken, let out an unexpected and audible sob into the taut silence.

'This man stands accused of a serious assault on his lord, Sir Peter Lymesey,' replied Edmund Neville. 'Though it is only through courtesy and personal respect that I reply to you at all, Lady Bradshaigh. You have no jurisdiction in this matter.'

'Neither has she the right to be called 'Lady',' muttered Lymesey. 'Plain Mistress Bradshaw will suffice.'

As Mabel looked across at him she saw that, behind the wet cloth, his left eye was swollen tightly shut and his lip was bleeding profusely.

'I use the lady's former title as a courtesy only,' replied Neville.

'Ned?' said Mabel, looking at the distraught and visibly trembling man. 'What happened?'

'I caught him beating the boy and I hit him,' he told her.

'So you admit the crime? That at least is in your favour,' replied Neville.

''Twas no crime, my lord, twas justice, and justice that's been too long coming in his case,' said Ned, glaring across the hall at Lymesey.

'Hush Ned. You are not making things easier for yourself,' warned Mabel, fearful for what was going to happen to him. She knew that the mere presence of the sheriff meant that Ned would not go unpunished no matter how much Lymesey had deserved the blow.

'Is Dicken hurt?' she asked, though the low sobbing from the corner was confirmation enough.

Mabel pushed past Edmund Neville and went to the boy. She saw straight away that he was naked except for his braies. The dozen or so weals across his back and legs were bleeding and swollen where he had been whipped.

'Dicken!' she exclaimed in horror as she knelt beside him, one hand on his head and the other hovering above him, wanting to hold the boy to her and comfort him, but afraid to touch him and cause him more pain. She turned to look up at Neville. 'Anyone who could do this to a child deserves more than a fist to his face!' she told him. 'It is Lymesey you should have under arrest for his crime, not Ned Kemp!'

She saw that he had the grace to look uncomfortable as she reprimanded him, but then the momentary disquiet faded from his blue eyes.

'It is my duty to uphold the law. A complaint has been made and I must make due judgement.'

'And what is your judgement?' she asked. 'Will you punish Ned for protecting a child against this . . . this tyrant?'

'Ned Kemp has admitted assaulting his lord. I cannot ignore the crime,' he argued.

'Then you are a weak and stupid man who has no right to hold the office of sheriff!'

Mabel told him. 'If Sir William was here he would show you the true meaning of justice!'

'But your husband is not here, my lady, and if he was I would arrest him too. The law must be upheld and it is my duty to uphold it. I cannot pick and choose the parts of it that I prefer!'

Neville's eyes blazed down at her and even when she stood up Mabel felt threatened by his height as he walked towards her, but she resisted the urge to back away from him and held his gaze.

'Look at the boy! Look at him!' she commanded with as much authority as she could muster and was gratified when Neville glanced down at the whimpering child. 'What if he were a son of yours?' she asked.

'You have not asked if the boy deserved it. You have not enquired about his crime.'

'I have no need to enquire. I know the boy has done no wrong. But I have seen him constantly and cruelly abused by this man!' She pointed an accusing finger at Lymesey. 'And whatever so called crime he has invented, I urge you to disregard it for I will swear that it is not true!'

'Hold your tongue woman!' shouted Lymesey. 'Else you'll find yourself and your own two brats sleeping in the forest tonight! Remember that I am the lord of this land until after the next Christmas, and it is only because of my goodwill that you remain here at all!'

Mabel watched as Edmund Neville glanced from one to the other of them. 'Take the prisoner out,' he said at last. 'I will have this case heard before a jury. Let others decide on his guilt.'

'Where will you take him?' asked Mabel as she watched Ned dragged protesting from the hall.

'He will go to the gaol at Lancaster, my lady. I urge you not to interfere and to allow the law to take its course.'

'Sir Edmund, please,' she said, 'do not do this.'

'I have no choice. I cannot disregard the word of a nobleman against a villein. I can only relent if Sir Peter will agree to withdraw the complaint.'

Mabel looked at Lymesey, nursing his injured face, and knew that he would show no mercy.

'I hope the man hangs,' he remarked and spat blood amongst the floor rushes. 'Bring me some wine, woman! And make sure there is some decent food. I will entertain my lord sheriff to dinner.'

She saw Neville raise an eyebrow at Lymesey's attitude towards her but he made no comment. Ignoring them both, Mabel took Dicken by the hand and helped him up from the floor. 'I will tend to this child first,' she replied, defying them both.

Edith jumped back from the door and flattened herself against the kitchen wall as Mabel went in. 'You had better take them some wine,' she said, 'and more's the pity I do not have a poison to add to it, for I would gladly see them both dead! Stand by the fire,' she said more gently to Dicken, 'and I will bathe your wounds. Pour some of the wine in here,' she said to Edith holding out a bowl and then tearing some strips of cloth to dip into it. 'You can water it down for them,' she said, nodding her head towards the door. 'Wait.' She took the jug from the girl and spat into it. 'There,' she said. 'Let's see how they like the taste of that!'

Mabel watched through the kitchen door, but the men took little notice of Edith and once the girl was safely back in the kitchen she set her to preparing food whilst she tended Dicken. The boy had stopped crying but was still trembling with shock and he flinched as she began to wipe the blood from his scrawny back.

'What made him do this?' she asked as she worked.

'I was clearing away his breakfast. There was a piece of bread that I thought he didn't want . . . and I ate it,' Dicken told her. 'He caught me. He said I was a thief and that he would teach me a lesson I would never forget.'

He never would forget it either, thought Mabel, as she dabbed at the lacerations. He would carry the scars all his life from the brutal attack. Her anger mounted alongside her feelings of helplessness. She wanted to do something to protect the boy but didn't know what. She couldn't hide him in the village and if she sent him out into the forest then he might fare worse than being at Haigh.

'Where are your family?' she asked him.

'My father has lands in Hertfordshire. He sent me into the household of Sir Peter to learn knightly skills and courtly manners.'

'And has he always treated you this badly?'

'Not as badly as this.'

'I shall try to send a message to your parents,' she told him. 'I'm sure if they knew how you were being treated they would not want you to remain in Lymesey's household.'

'I have no mother. She died when I was born. I did write once to my father. He wrote back to say I must learn to do as I was told, or take the consequences like a man. He said

I could return to him as a knight, but never as a coward.'

Mabel turned the boy to face her and cupping his wet cheeks in her hands she kissed his forehead, wondering how a parent could love their child so little as to allow this to happen.

She looked up to see Edmund Neville in the doorway watching her. He frowned when she turned the boy to show him his injuries.

'Do you want to hear his crime?' she asked. 'Hunger! The boy was hungry and ate some bread that Lymesey had discarded. Do you think that merited this?' she asked him.

'Lady Bradshaigh,' he began and she was pleased that he still used her title despite what Lymesey had said. 'I honestly regret what has happened here today. I wish that there was more I could do, but I cannot compromise my position as sheriff. I will ensure that your man receives a fair hearing and that the circumstances of his assault are clear. With luck he will be sentenced to a flogging and a spell in the stocks and will not hang.'

'And this boy?'

'He must learn to be more careful. He owes a debt this day to your man who prevented him receiving a worse beating.'

'I wish I had been here,' said Mabel, 'to

prevent any of this occurring.'

'But you were . . . ?'

'At the chapel to make my confession.'

'I'm sure you have no sins to confess, my lady.'

'I think we all sin,' said Mabel, beginning to regret her contamination of the wine, 'though perhaps some of us are in more need of forgiveness than others. Where is my lord Lymesey?' she asked, glancing past Neville into the hall where William's chair was now empty.

'He has taken the last of the wine and his sore head to the bedchamber. I have declined his offer of dinner. I know that you will struggle to feed me and my men so we will not trouble you.' He glanced at Edith who was chopping dried herbs at the kitchen table. 'I hope I have not inconvenienced you?'

'Not at all,' lied Mabel and was pleased to see him look somewhat chided at her sarcastic words.

'I would a private word with you, my lady, if you will return to the hall,' he said, standing aside for her to precede him.

'A moment,' she replied and found a soft blanket to put around the shivering Dicken. 'Pour the boy some wine and add a little of the willow bark infusion to ease his pain,' she said to Edith.

Mabel went and stood by the hearth and watched the fire for a moment before moving the rushes over the bloodstains with her foot. She heard Edmund Neville latch the kitchen door behind them and she looked up. He was an attractive man, she thought, as she studied his profile; not conventionally handsome, his features were too pronounced for that, but there were elements in his face — the strong jaw line, the long nose, the blue eyes — that taken all together had a pleasing effect.

'Lady Bradshaigh, I must ask you about Peter Lymesey.'

'The man is ill-mannered and despicable!' Mabel told him.

'So you do not find favour with him?'

'Does it seem as if I do?' she asked, thinking that what had just occurred should speak for itself.

'No, which is why I am surprised to find you still here, my lady.'

'And where would you suggest I go?' she demanded. 'This is my home!'

'It was your home, my lady, but the actions of your husband . . . your late husband,' he emphasised, 'have resulted in the land being forfeit to the crown. But you know that well enough. You know that Haigh is not yours for at least the year and a day laid down in law. You have no rights here and should have

174

vacated the manor. The fact that you remain led me to conclude that you and Sir Peter had come to some . . . some arrangement.'

Mabel gasped in disbelief. 'Did you think that I had agreed to marry him, that we were betrothed . . . or that I am the man's mistress?' she asked as she began to see how the situation might appear. 'You must understand that nothing is further from the truth! I remain here only to protect my home and my villagers from this . . . this intruder, so that as little as possible will be spoiled until he is gone!'

'Please, sit down,' said Sir Edmund, moving forward to take her arm and guide her to the chair. 'Shall I call the girl to bring you some wine?'

'No. I am quite well,' she replied, even though her heart pounded in her ears and she found that her legs felt weak. She sat down gratefully and looked up at the sheriff.

'Is there nowhere you could go?' he asked. 'After what has taken place today I must say that I am concerned to leave you alone with this man.'

'This is my home,' she repeated.

'Where are your daughters?' he asked.

'They are with Mistress Palmer, in the village. I do not want them to witness anything that goes on here whilst their father is away.'

'That at least is wise,' replied Neville, 'though I would urge you to accept, my lady, that your husband does not live.' He paused awkwardly and turned away from her. 'You are vulnerable, my lady, and Peter Lymesey sees that. I fear that he will press his attentions on you, if only to acquire the land more permanently, if you remain here.'

'And what protection have I now?' she asked him, staring at the broad expanse of his back. 'Now that you have taken the one man I could rely on? Without Ned Kemp my safety here is even more precarious.'

'I cannot ignore his crime, my lady, no matter how much my personal conscience tells me he was not entirely to blame for his actions.'

'And would you have me leave that boy unprotected to be beaten again?' she asked, pointing towards the closed kitchen door.

'The boy is not your responsibility.'

'But I have chosen to make him my responsibility,' she told him. 'This is what you do not understand, Sir Edmund. I feel responsible for every man, woman and child who lives at Haigh. I cannot abandon them because some court of law says my husband is an outlaw and that the manor is no longer mine.'

'Are you saying that you do not recognise

the law?' he asked, looking at her again with a gleam in his eyes. 'That is dangerous talk, my lady.'

'And would you arrest me as well?' she demanded, standing up again to face him. 'For what? For treason?'

'Your husband was a traitor. Why should you not also support his cause?'

For a moment Mabel stared up at him and caught the underlying threat in his voice.

'You would not dare arrest me,' she challenged him.

'Do not press me, my lady,' he warned her. 'What you must accept is that Haigh belongs to Peter Lymesey and that you have no rights here. I advise you to leave. Would you allow me to inquire as to some place where you could go? A nunnery perhaps?'

'No!' she told him. 'I have no intention of leaving.'

He shrugged his shoulders briefly in a gesture of irritation and impatience with her. 'I cannot promise to protect you against him. You do understand that?' he asked. 'As soon as I ride away, you are at the man's mercy just as much as the boy in there. Please God I do not return to find you treated the same — or worse!'

'You need not distress yourself on my

account,' Mabel told him. 'My mind is set and I am sure I can take care of myself.'

'I hope you are right, my lady,' he said. 'But should you change your mind I will be at the house of Robert Holland. There has been some thievery of venison from the king's forest at Charnock that I must investigate before I head north again. Send a message to me there if you decide to leave and I will offer what assistance I can. Now, I will wish you good day.'

Mabel watched as he strode to the door and called to his men. She watched as he mounted his horse and rode off without a backward glance. The only person who looked back was Ned as he was dragged forward, securely tied by ropes between two of the horses. His wife wept on her knees as he was taken and Mabel felt her own tears flow too as she realised that everything was beyond her control.

8

The Scot

The women fell silent as William helped the limping Scot into the church as darkness fell.

'You can't expect us to agree to him sleeping in here, not near our children,' said Martha, looking at the man as though the devil himself had been conjured before her. 'I can't even understand why you have allowed him to live.'

'Tha'll slit ma throat as I sleep anyhow,' whispered the Scot, as William took the man's arm from around his shoulders and lowered him to the cold stone floor.

'I would not allow you such an easy death!' spat Martha as she regarded him with contempt. 'Get rid of him,' she begged William.

'You want him dead?' asked William as he watched the woman. 'Then you kill him.' He pulled the dagger from his belt and turning the handle towards her held it out. 'Go on,' he urged. 'Take it and kill him.'

Martha stared at the weapon and then

looked up at William. Her dark eyes searched his to see if he was serious. 'I will not,' she replied at last. 'I will sully neither my hands nor my soul with his blood.'

'Then bring me some water and a cloth to wash his wounds,' said William, replacing the dagger. 'But do not ask me to leave him outside for the wolves. He will harm no one.'

'How can you be sure?' she asked.

William looked down at the Scot, at his white face staring up at them, at his blank eyes that were resigned to their fate. 'He is too weak and will probably not live through the night anyway,' he said, though he was determined that he would not let the Scot die for want of trying to save him.

When Martha brought water William knelt by the man's side and began to dab at the wound on his thigh. After a moment he felt the woman's hand on his shoulder.

'You will only make it worse like that,' she said. 'Move out of the way.' William stood up to watch as she used the cloth to soak the injured leg in water. 'Cut away his leggings with your knife,' she said as the garment gradually released its hold on the drying blood. She moved aside as William crouched beside her and he heard the Scot curse as the blade pulled at his clothing. But it was the soft fragrance of Harry's sister beside him that filled William's senses. He moved back and watched as her capable, work-worn hands began to circle the wound and, as she worked, the Scot's thigh oozed fresh blood and he lay back on the hard floor moaning. 'Is there a candle?' asked Martha.

'I'll find one,' said William, getting up and searching the supplies stacked near the altar. He lit the wick and held it for her to inspect the wound.

'I will bind it for now, but it needs a poultice to stem the bleeding,' she said. 'Tomorrow I will make one — if you will come with me to the forest to seek the herbs?'

'Yes, of course,' said William, almost forgetting that this woman had been bereaved that day as he looked down into her pretty face and her dark eyes surrounded with thick lashes.

She pressed clean cloth against the wound and bound it tightly. 'It is deep and will take a long time to heal,' she said, 'but if it is kept clean he should recover. I hope he knows how thankful he should be,' she said in a louder voice aimed at the Scot. He opened his eyes and looked up at her.

'Ye are an angel, sent from God,' he whispered. She gave him a look of disgust then turned her contempt upon William.

'I cannot pretend to do this willingly,' she

181

said. 'But if you command me to tend him then I will, for I have reason to be thankful to you for bringing my brother to me this day.'

'Thank you, my lady,' he said and was pleased to see the pleasure that flitted over her face, despite her anguish, as he addressed her as a noble born woman rather than a peasant.

Reluctantly William bound the Scot's hands again in front of him. The man protested, but he didn't quite trust him and thought that the women would feel safer to see him restrained.

★　★　★

'Do you have good reason to let him live?' asked Harry as the church fell silent and the women and children at last drifted into troubled sleep. They had kept one of their precious candles burning in the darkness to offer reassurance and William sat beside the sleeping Scot, partly to guard him and partly because he knew sleep would not come whilst so many conflicting thoughts crowded his mind.

'He told me that they carry messages to the sheriff, Edmund Neville.'

'Neville?'

'Yes, but the intended recipient is the Earl

of Lancaster. He seeks an alliance with Robert Bruce against the king.'

'And that would not be good for us,' said Harry.

'No. Since the rebellion, Lancaster knows beyond a doubt that that I am loyal to the king and not to him. I am his sworn enemy now and I will only be safe when he is dead.'

'But we do not have enough men to fight again.'

'You are right, Harry. But rebellion may not be the only way to rid ourselves of Lancaster.'

'What do you intend?'

'I'm not sure yet,' admitted William, 'but despite your sister's protestations I would like to keep this Scot alive and discover what else he knows. He may be the solution to our problem, or part of it at least.'

'And that is why you guard him?' asked Harry glancing down at the bound prisoner.

'I would not like to find him dead when I wake,' yawned William.

'Then I will share your vigil. Sleep a little, my lord, and I will watch him,' said Harry. William looked at his friend and resisted the temptation to ask if he could trust him.

'Thank you,' he said simply as he gathered his cloak around him against the chill of the night. 'Wake me in an hour or two.'

When William opened his eyes the candle had gone out and he could see the faint light of dawn through the church's east window.

'I told you to wake me,' he said to Harry.

'You were so deep asleep that I didn't like to disturb you. Besides I don't think I would have slept anyway. I'm too angry. I keep reassuring Martha that Alfric will come home, but I know in my heart that he's already dead.'

'You haven't harmed the Scot have you?' William pulled himself up and peered at their prisoner.

'No, although I must say I've been tempted, if only to stop his incessant moaning.'

'I wouldna' be in so much pain if ye'd untie me,' muttered the Scot.

'And what of my brother-in-law?' demanded Harry, seizing the man and making him cry out. 'What about all those dead men? The burned out houses? The stolen food and animals? Don't expect me to show you one scrap of pity. If it wasn't for Sir William here you'd have died yesterday and we'd have roasted your organs for a feast!'

'Leave him Harry,' said William, though he understood and sympathised with his friend's anger. 'Don't waken the children.'

William heard the Scot's head hit the solid

ground with a thud as Harry let him go.

'I had na' choice,' protested the Scot. 'My wife and bairns starved to death and I couldna' sit at home and watch the same happen to other men's families.'

'You had the choice not to kill!' Harry told him.

'And so do we,' William reminded him. 'Show these savages we are better men than that, Harry. Besides,' he whispered, 'if he lives he will owe us favour and we may be able to use him to discover what the Earl of Lancaster is plotting.'

When morning came and they had all eaten some oatcakes and drunk a little ale, Martha came across to William. She was still very pale and her face was tear streaked as if she had cried herself to sleep.

'Can I help you, my lady?' said William as he looked down at her and thought how radiant she would look in fine clothes and jewels. He was about to comment that he did not believe she was sister to Harry Palmer as she was too pretty, until he realised how crass such a compliment would be in her circumstances.

'I have come to see my patient,' she said. 'I may need to dress his wound again, and you promised to accompany me into the forest to look for herbs.'

'I did, my lady. And I will see if I can't shoot something for our supper too whilst we are there — if you are not too squeamish?'

'Why would I object to the sight of food?' she asked and William saw that she had an inner strength that had not been apparent the day before.

'We should check the traps as well,' said Harry. 'And maybe we should set them up closer to the village if we're going to stay here a while.'

★   ★   ★

Stephen Scallard agreed to remain with the women and children and Harry said that he would take Will Tegg to where the traps were and bring them back to Chorleigh. They all set off together, Martha with a basket over her arm and the men armed and wary. They walked into the forest in silence and it was as they were approaching the track that crossed the road north that William put out a hand to stop the others. He listened again and above the tense breathing of his companions he heard the sound of horses, at least two.

'Wait here,' he whispered. 'I will go and see who is coming.' He crept forward as quietly as he could, taking care not to step on any twigs or fallen branches that might crack and give away his presence if there were also men on foot. As he approached the edge of the trees he paused and listened. There were definitely two horses, though they weren't travelling fast. He waited until they came into view and drew a quick breath as he recognised them as sheriff's men. And tied by ropes between them was a prisoner who was struggling to keep pace; probably on his way to the gaol at Lancaster, thought William. As they came closer he saw that the man was Ned Kemp.

William swore under his breath and looked back to where Harry and Tegg were waiting. First putting a finger to his lips to warn them to be quiet, he beckoned them forward and was thankful to see that Harry had the good sense to tell his sister to stay where she was, out of sight. As he waited William drew an arrow and notched it to his bow, hoping that he and Harry could take out the riders without alarming the horses too much. If they bolted then Ned Kemp would be dragged to his death.

As the others crept up behind him, he whispered to Harry to shoot the nearest man and told Tegg that as soon as the arrows were released he must run into the road and grab the horses' reins. It was a risky plan, he knew, but he was not prepared to stand by as Ned was taken away to be punished for fighting with him in the rebellion.

'When I say now, do it,' he told his companions.

There was no time for them to reassure him that they understood. As the riders drew almost level, William stood to take aim at the far man and released the whistling arrow, praying that it would strike its target. With satisfaction he saw the man turn towards him in surprise as he slipped gracelessly from his saddle. Throwing the bow down he ran forward to help grab at the horses. Tegg already had one and was soothing it with steadying words as he raised a hand to its muzzle. William caught the loose reins of the other as he saw Harry pull the second man down, an arrow still protruding from his chest, having pierced his mail at such close range. He handed the reins to Tegg and pulling out his knife he stepped between the skittish animals to where Ned Kemp had been dragged to his knees.

'Hello Ned,' he said to the bewildered man as he sawed through the thick ropes that bound his wrists to the saddles on either side of him.

'My lord!' said Ned, gazing up at him as if he had seen a vision. 'Is it really you?'

'It is,' said William as he put a hand under

Ned's arm and pulled him to his feet. 'Are you hurt?'

'I . . . I don't think so,' he replied, running his hands down his legs and over the torn leggings where he had been dragged several yards along the ground.

'Are they dead?' asked William, looking over to where Harry had the sheriff's men pulled to the side of the road.

'One is, and one soon will be.'

William went to look at them. The man Harry had shot in the chest lay still. The other was wounded and lay groaning as blood seeped from under his shoulder. William hesitated. He could leave the man to take his chances. Someone might find him. But if he lived he would talk and the sheriff would quickly learn of Ned's rescue, whereas if the man died it could be a week or more before Neville discovered that his men and their prisoner had never reached Lancaster. Reluctantly William turned the knife in his hand and bent down. With his left hand he pulled the chainmail hood away from the man's neck to expose the throat, and with a firm stroke he cut the windpipe and then stepped back as the horrific gurgling gave way to silence and the pumping of blood from the body slowed to a steady trickle. Then he stepped aside and spewed his meagre breakfast onto the forest floor.

He looked up to see Martha watching him. Both her hands covered her mouth as she stared in horror at what she had just witnessed.

'Strip them of their clothes and bury them as best you can, out of sight,' he told Harry and Tegg as he wiped his mouth and then bent to clean the blade of his knife on the grass. 'Ned, you'd best ride,' he said, taking the man's arm and leading him towards the nearest horse and pushing him up into the saddle. Then he gathered the reins of both animals and led them towards the track back to Chorleigh. 'Pick up your basket and come with me,' he told Martha. 'You can get your herbs later.'

She looked as if she might protest, but William was relieved to see her follow him without a word. It was not a scene he would have chosen for her to witness. She had already seen more than enough bloodshed, but he wasn't going to waste words justifying what he had done. It had been necessary, though he had taken no pleasure in it.

'Where were they taking you? Lancaster?' he asked Ned.

'I think so. It wasn't easy to ask too many questions.'

'Where did they find you? Have you been

living in the forest?'

'No. I was at home. At Haigh.'

'You went back?' asked William, glancing up at him in surprise.

'I went back just a few days after Preston, my lord.'

'You've been there all winter? And they've only just found you? I thought that Neville had been watching the manor,' said William, wondering if it would, after all, have been safe for him to go home and cursing himself for leaving Mab alone for so long.

'Neville has been watching all right,' he said. 'But it wasn't for rebellion that I was arrested, it was for striking Lymesey.'

'Who's Lymesey?'

William grew more incensed with every word that he heard as Ned explained to him what had happened.

'I hope for his sake that this man has not laid a finger on Lady Bradshaigh,' remarked William as he twitched with anger.

'I do believe that he has hopes of marrying her and keeping the land permanently.'

'Marrying her! How in God's name does he hope to marry her when she is already wed?'

'Everyone believes you are dead, my lord.'

'Even Mab?'

'Lady Bradshaigh refuses to believe it. But

191

what she believes will count for nothing if you are not returned after the year is passed. I doubt that she will be allowed to remain a single woman.'

'Then I will have to return,' said William.

'If you try to return, my lord, it will be you who will be dragged to Lancaster — or taken and beheaded on yonder moor like Adam Banastre. If you go back to Haigh then Lady Bradshaigh will be a widow without a doubt.'

'Dammit! I have to do something!' shouted William, kicking a branch out of his way with as much force as he could muster. 'I'll kill them all if I have to!'

'Perhaps,' said Martha who had been walking beside them in silence, 'there are other ways in which to act?'

'Such as?' asked William.

'The Scot,' she reminded him. 'You said that we might use him. He may know more than he is telling about this message that was brought for the Earl of Lancaster. If we could offer some proof to the king that Lancaster is plotting against him and that he is colluding with the Scots would it not be enough to bring about his downfall? And with Lancaster gone, Robert Holland and Edmund Neville would be powerless.'

'And Adam Banastre had a letter from the king in support of the rebellion,' Ned reminded him. 'The king knows we are loyal to him.'

★   ★   ★

'What was in the letter to the Earl of Lancaster?' demanded William as he stood over the prone man and fingered his dagger. 'I've already killed one man this morning so another will not trouble my conscience, especially if he is a Scot.'

'I dinna know, I tell ye,' wailed the man for the third time as William shifted his foot to put even more pressure on the Scot's injured leg.

'But it was delivered?'

'I dinna . . . aye . . . aye it was delivered,' gasped the man as William increased the force.

'Where?'

'We were to meet up with Neville just west o' here, at a place called Upper Holland.

'And what was in the letter?'

'I dinna know . . . I beg you! No! I'm telling ye all I know!' he cried out as William moved his boot nearer the man's groin. 'It was sealed with the seal of the king, Robert Bruce, and we had to deliver it to Neville. But the letter was for Thomas, Earl of Lancaster. I dinna know what it said!'

'You're sure?'

'It may ha' bin about safe passage . . . to a meeting. But that was only rumour. I could na say for certain.'

William moved his foot away from the man, content that he had extracted as much from him as he knew. A letter from Robert Bruce to Lancaster arranging a meeting would be damning evidence of treason, but they would need the letter; a rumour of what it may have contained was not enough.

'Can I tend his leg now?' asked Martha. William hadn't heard her come into the church and he hoped she hadn't seen too much of what had taken place. He found that he wanted her to think well of him and, as she'd already seen him commit a murder that day, it would not help his cause if she had also witnessed him torturing the Scot.

★   ★   ★

'What troubles you, my lord?' asked Harry as William poked at their campfire with a rough stick later that evening.

'I can't get what Ned Kemp has told me about that man Lymesey out of my mind,' he said. 'I fear for Mab and yet I feel helpless. I want to go home, but I have to acknowledge that what Ned says is true; I would probably be caught and that would not help Mab at all. Yet a man who would beat a boy in the way Ned described may not hesitate to beat a wife as well.'

'I'm sure Lady Bradshaigh will not agree to marry him,' said Harry. 'I'm sure she will not have given up hope of your return.'

'I fear that Mab may not be free to choose,' said William. 'Her lands are worth much and Lancaster will be keen to keep them under his control rather than the king's. One way he can do that would be to see her married to one of his knights.'

'Then we must discredit Lancaster by revealing his plot with the Scots,' said Harry.

'Yes,' agreed William. 'That is our best plan. But how? The Scot has told us everything he knows, but I doubt the word of a Scotsman will convince the king. We need some better evidence. We need one of the letters from Bruce to Lancaster.'

'But how will we get hold of one?'

'I don't know,' admitted William, wishing that Adam Banastre were still alive. Adam would have seen a solution, he was sure.

★   ★   ★

The next morning, William walked down through the forest to the meadowland by the river with Martha beside him. She had said that she needed yarrow leaves to make a poultice to help staunch the bleeding of the Scot's leg and assist in its healing.

It was a fine day with a hint of warmth in the air and William hoped the coming summer would be dry. The priest from Croston had brought some seed that had been spared by the surrounding villages. William knew how generous that was when they were all so short themselves. He hoped that they would soon be able to sow it in the ground where the old crop had been spoiled and that God would send the sun and rain in the right proportions for the plants to thrive and give the women of Chorleigh food for the next winter.

As he watched Martha brushing aside the damp grasses in search of the yarrow, he kept his eyes and ears alert for any creature that might provide them with food. A movement in the sky above the river made him look up and he saw the hawk circling, also looking for prey. He moved slowly down the riverbank as he watched it, squinting his eyes against the sun as he kept them trained on it. This was no random bird. He recognised the broad, pointed wings of a trained falcon and as the raptor plunged to the ground he saw the jessies trailing from its ankles that confirmed his suspicions.

'Someone is coming,' he said quietly to Martha. 'We must go back at once.' He saw her glance at the half filled basket but she didn't argue. As they hurried up the bank she slipped and he reached out to catch her hand and pull her up to the path.

'Did you see the hawk?' he asked. She shook her head. She had kept her eyes downcast, he knew, concentrating on her task. 'There is a hunting party coming,' he told her. 'I think it would be safer for you back in the village.'

They were almost back at Chorleigh when they heard the horses gaining on them. Glancing back towards the sound of the cantering hooves, William knew that they would be seen if they continued along the track.

'I think we must try to conceal ourselves,' he said urgently as he took Martha's arm and led her deeper into the cover. 'Stay silent and still. If the dogs are on the scent of their quarry they may ignore us.'

He pulled Martha down and positioned himself in front of her, laying his bow and an arrow beside him and drawing his knife from its sheath. The rhythm of hoof beats slowed and then voices drifted towards them on the breeze. He did not recognise them and their accent was unfamiliar to him. He tightened his grip on the hilt of the knife as he heard the howling of excited hounds as they pushed through the undergrowth. He wondered how many there were and whether the villagers would eat a dog stew for their dinner.

William was praying that they would veer away in another direction when he heard an animal coming towards them at speed. He crouched in preparation, waiting for it to reach him. His knife was raised to plunge into its throat, hopefully before its fangs sank into him or its barking gave them away.

He saw the grey fur fly at him, but before he had chance to stab at it he felt its paws knock him backwards with force. As he stumbled he swore out loud that the animal had bested him and waited to feel its teeth sink themselves into his unprotected flesh. But it was the rough, warm tongue wetting his face that surprised him and suddenly he was aware of a delighted whining and the thrashing of a familiar tail.

'Calab!' he exclaimed in a mixture of relief and delight as he flung the knife aside and buried his hands in the thick fur. 'Shh!' he warned the dog as he pushed it aside and rolled over and up onto his knees. 'Stay quiet. Good boy,' he whispered as he closed a hand around its muzzle and apprehensively peered through the trees.

'Where did the hound go?' asked a voice. 'It bounded away as if it had a scent of something but there's no sign of it now.'

'It's an ill-trained mutt. I'm sorry we brought it with us,' came the reply. 'I'll give it a beating when it returns. It'll soon learn what's expected of it that way.'

William felt his own hackles rise along with Calab's at the man's words. He turned to where Martha was warily watching the dog and motioned her to stay hidden. With a hand clutching Calab by the scruff he eased his way towards the path to try to catch a glimpse of the huntsmen, suspecting that they were Sir Peter Lymesey and his retainers.

Calab began a low throated growl as they reached the track and a fat little man turned in his saddle. But it was the horse that William recognised as he wondered at the man's audacity in not only hunting with his dogs but also riding his stallion. Still, Hengist was probably far superior to anything the man might own himself, he thought, as he admired the glowing chestnut coat of his favourite mount.

He briefly licked his lips and let out a whistle. Calab began a frenzied barking and the horse spun around with pricked ears before rearing up on its powerful back legs, and William watched in delight as the man slid from the saddle and landed with a resounding thud on the ground.

The men with him looked around in alarm. 'Outlaws!' shouted one and William was pleased to see Stephen Scallard and William Tegg step out from the trees on the other side of the clearing. They too must have heard the commotion as they were inspecting the traps. They had arrows trained on the men, who didn't wait to see if they would release them or not, but quickly turned their horses and fled. The fat little man struggled to his feet, bellowing at them to come back. Then he spun slowly around in a circle as he watched the three men who surrounded him.

William tightened his grip on Calab. 'Stay!' he warned the dog, sensing its eagerness to take a bite or two from the man. 'State your name!' he called out.

The fat man fixed him with a narrow-eyed sneer. 'I am Sir Peter Lymesey, and you will hang, slowly, for this!'

William felt himself smile. So this was the man who thought he could take his wife from him. He let go of Calab and stepped up to him, gratified to find that he could look down onto the top of his balding head. With a clenched fist he punched the man under his jaw and sent him staggering backwards. Before Lymesey had time to regain his balance or reach for anything to defend himself William had followed him and struck again, pleased to see the man completely lose his balance this time and stagger to the ground. He felt the toe of his boot sink a little into soft flesh and, as the man cried out, he pulled back his foot and kicked him again. Lymesey tried to roll over out of his reach and pull himself to his feet, but William grasped his shoulder and threw him down again against a protruding tree root. Then from behind him he saw a flash of grey fur as Calab, unable to contain himself any longer, jumped on the prone man and sank his teeth into his arm. The man screamed a curse, but William did not call the dog off. As Calab pinned the man's arm to the ground William's foot crashed down again, first into his stomach and then as he tried to curl his body into a ball, the side of his head, sending him crashing, breathless and silent, down the slope towards the river as the excited dog leapt back.

'Good boy!' called William and fondled the animal's head and ears as it returned to sit at his feet. He snapped his fingers and Hengist came to him, reins trailing, and pushed his nose against William's shoulder, snickering at his master. William rubbed the horse's soft muzzle at the same time as he patted the dog with his other hand. Then, aware of eyes upon him, he looked across at Scallard and Tegg who had lowered their bows and were staring at him in speechless admiration.

Behind him a branch moved and he turned quickly, but it was Martha. 'Are you safe, my lady?' he asked.

'Yes,' she replied with an attempt at a smile, though he heard her voice break a little in fear.

'I think we should go back to the village in case Lymesey's men have gone for help,' he said as he reached out a hand towards Martha. But as she moved towards him he caught sight of a movement behind her.

'There!' he cried to Tegg and Scallard. 'Another one! Don't let him get away!'

He watched in satisfaction as the two men plunged into the woods and heard Tegg cry out at someone to stand still or die. Moments later he heard their footsteps returning and Tegg came out of the trees, his fist holding the tunic of a young boy.

'Come here lad, I'll not hurt you,' said William as he handed Hengist's reins to Martha. 'And I'll take a bet that your name is Dicken.'

'How . . . how did you know?' trembled the puzzled boy. He was not much older than Bella, thought William, as he held out a hand

and beckoned the child forward. As the others watched, he pulled aside the boy's tunic to reveal the purpled web of scabbing weals across his back. 'I did not know for certain but this confirms it,' he said, wishing that he'd given Lymesey an even worse kicking. 'You are safe now.'

'Where . . . where will you take me?' stammered the frightened boy. William let the tunic drop as the boy shivered.

'Don't be afraid. We are your friends,' he said. 'I'm Sir William Bradshaigh.'

'Mistress Bradshaw's husband?'

'Lady Bradshaigh's husband — though you speak of the same person. I believe she has been kind to you?'

'She has been very kind to me, sire.'

'I would expect nothing less from my Mab,' William told him. 'We will not send you back for another beating. You can be an outlaw now, like us.'

'I . . . I do not think my father would like that,' said the boy.

'A father who would leave you with a man like Lymesey is no father at all,' William told him as he cupped a hand around the back of the boy's head and looked into his anxious blue eyes. 'You may consider yourself answerable to me from now on. Come along,' he said. 'We are going back to Chorleigh. Would you like to ride my horse?'

William watched as a faint smile illuminated Dicken's face. 'Do you mean it?' he asked.

'Every word,' said William as he lifted the lad, who was light as a bird, into Hengist's saddle.

9

Captive

Mabel was sitting at the small scrubbed wooden table in Mistress Palmer's house, eating dinner with her daughters when she heard the shouting. She was already on her way to the door when Edith rushed in. Her hair was escaping from her cap, she had a smudge of black from the oven across her cheek and she had not paused to put on her cloak.

'You'd best come quick, my lady, there's trouble!'

'Stay here!' Mabel told Bella and Amelia. 'You too,' she said to Mistress Palmer as she snatched up her own cloak, pulling it around her shoulders as she ran after Edith back to the manor house.

The men holding the horses outside the door bore the arms of Edmund Neville and Mabel's stomach lurched. Was it possible that William had been found and caught, she wondered, hoping that she might yet see him alive and yet dreading that an execution would follow.

Neville was standing in the hall waiting for her, still wearing his cloak and gloves and with a hand resting on the hilt of the sword at his side.

'Where is Sir Peter?' he asked.

'Sir Peter?' repeated Mabel, momentarily confused by the abrupt question. 'I . . . I'm not sure. He went out to hunt. He's always out hunting,' she added.

'Two of his men have come to me to say that they were attacked by outlaws and that Sir Peter is missing.' He paused and fixed her with inquiring eyes. 'Do you know anything about this?' he asked softly, so softly that Mabel grew far more afraid than she would have done if he had shouted. She felt herself begin to shake beneath his unswerving scrutiny even though she had done nothing.

'Why . . . why would I know anything?' she asked, afraid that her trembling voice would give him reason to suspect her even more.

'As you said he often goes hunting . . . and you may have friends amongst these outlaws.'

'What makes you think that?' she asked, unsure if he knew something or was merely trying to frighten information from her.

He stared at her again for what seemed like a long time without speaking and she felt herself unable to swallow as she stood before him and her fear grew.

'So you did not know that Ned Kemp never reached Lancaster? You did not know that his guards were missing — and you did not know that as my men searched the forest for Sir Peter they discovered two shallow graves with the bodies in them?'

Neville's eyes were so hard and cold that Mabel felt real pain from them. She turned away but her arm was roughly grasped in a painfully tight grip and she cried out in fear and alarm as he pulled her fiercely back to face him. His mouth was inches from her and she could feel his hot breath, smell the masculine scent of him as he held her. 'Answer me,' he said quietly.

Mabel glanced at his face and then down at his gloved fingers which were digging into her arm. He was bruising her, she thought, and then she was aware of the thick silence in the hall as everyone awaited her reply.

'I did not know,' she told him.

'Look at me!'

Mabel raised her eyes and saw the anger on his face. 'I did not know,' she repeated as she held his furious gaze.

The grasp on her arm relaxed but still he did not let her go. 'You knew nothing of Kemp's escape?'

'No. I knew nothing,' she repeated, still watching his eyes anxiously.

'And you do not know what has happened to Sir Peter Lymesey?'

She began to shake her head, but a sound behind her made Neville look away.

'My lord,' said a voice. 'They have found him.'

'Where?' asked Neville.

'In the forest, my lord. But he's in a bad way. It looks as if he's been beaten.'

Mabel felt the pressure of Neville's fingers increase as he asked, 'Where is he now?'

'They're carrying him back, my lord. They'll be here in a moment.'

'Do not move from that spot!' Neville said to her and she rubbed her arm as she watched him stride to the door.

There were voices outside and then they brought Lymesey in. His head was hanging and he looked barely conscious. Blood trickled from his nose and his face was so swollen that she would never have recognised him. He groaned as they carried him through the door to the bedchamber. Neville followed them in and Mabel, not daring to move, looked across at Edith and waved at her to go.

The girl needed no more encouragement. She slipped behind the backs of the remaining guards and out of the door. Mabel prayed that she would stay at home and that

208

she and her mother would take good care of the girls. She was sure that Neville had not believed her when she told him she knew nothing and she was terrified of what he would do. She might even be sent to the gaol herself she thought as her legs became weak and she found herself sinking slowly to the floor.

She sat there, listening to the voices from the bedchamber. One man came out and went to a horse outside and Mabel heard him ride away. Then another came out and after glaring at her he went to the kitchen, returning a moment later.

'Where is the girl?'

'I don't know.'

'There seems to be a lot you don't know,' he jeered and despite her fear Mabel felt angry that he should address her in such a way, but she felt unable to reprimand him.

Edmund Neville came to the door of the bedchamber.

'The girl is not here,' the man told him. Mabel watched warily as Neville looked at her.

'Get up!' he commanded. 'Go and get some cloths and warm water and herbs. You can bathe his wounds whilst we wait for the physician to come.'

Mabel struggled to her feet. She felt

physically sick and was unsure whether she could even walk to the kitchen, but Neville betrayed no emotion as he watched her.

'Do not even think of running for the door. I have men positioned front and back,' he warned her as she passed him.

In the kitchen Mabel removed her cloak and took a few deep breaths. Whatever was going to happen to her she must face it with dignity, she thought. She must not let them see how frightened she was.

She reached for a bowl, for some dried rosemary flowers to sprinkle onto the warm water and two clean linen cloths then she walked to the bedchamber and went in.

Edmund Neville stood at the foot of the bed, staring down at Peter Lymesey, who lay still moaning and muttering. Mabel put the bowl down on the coffer beside the bed and as she soaked and wrung a cloth in the water she looked in horror at the man's injuries.

His face, which had barely recovered from Ned Kemp's assault, was twice its normal size. One eye was shut fast, the other barely a slit. Lymesey cried out and lashed at her with his hand as she touched his nose to wipe away the blood.

'Be careful!' burst out Edmund Neville.

'I . . . I cannot clean his wounds without touching him,' she said, feeling tears in her eyes as her voice broke. She dabbed again at his face, trying to be as gentle as she could but Lymesey swore oaths, words that made the blood rush to her face when she heard them. 'His . . . his clothes will need to be removed,' she said. 'He is more hurt than just his face.'

She moved back as Neville came around the bed. He took off his gloves and cloak and she cringed as his arm briefly touched hers as he leant to cut Lymesey's tunic and silk undershirt from him. Beneath his ribs were covered in swollen red marks.

'Someone has given him a kicking,' observed Neville, turning to glance at Mabel for a moment. 'These outlaws are vicious thugs. He is lucky to have escaped them with his life.' She didn't reply. 'I will find who did this and see them punished,' he told her. 'Perhaps you had better pray that your husband is truly dead. A death on the battle field is nothing compared to what is in store for an outlaw who attacks a lord like this!'

Mabel squeezed the bloodied cloth in her hands, wanting to reply but finding that she was unable to speak. She brushed a tear from her face as she felt his harsh gaze on her and was only saved by the arrival of the physician from Wigan.

'Wait for me in the hall,' said Neville. 'Do

not go anywhere. I have not finished with you.'

Mabel crept from the bedchamber. It had been a happy room once, she thought, but now it had been defiled and spoiled by these strangers who had come to take everything away from her. She stood in the hall, at a small window with the shutters open and tried to breathe, waiting to hear what Edmund Neville intended to do with her. Although she had been gladdened by the news that Ned Kemp had escaped his guards, she realised that Neville suspected her of collusion and that it was unlikely her protestations that she knew nothing would make him change his mind.

After a long time she heard the chamber door open and the physician came out with a grim face and though she had prayed every night for his demise, Mabel now prayed that Peter Lymesey was not dead. It was bad enough that two guards had been killed, but to kill a nobleman was a worse crime. She touched her neck, in fear for her own life, even though she had done nothing but try to protect her lands from the usurper.

Neville came to the door of the chamber. His face was impassive and she was unable to judge what he was thinking.

'He is sleeping now with the help of a draft

from the physician,' he said at last. 'But before he drank it he expressed a fear of being nursed by you. He believes you betrayed his whereabouts to the outlaws. He says that you will either poison him or bind him by witchcraft if you remain under the same roof.' Mabel waited, hoping that he would say that he was going to arrange for Lymesey to be moved. 'So you had better gather a few of your possessions,' he said.

'Where am I to go?' she asked as she realised that she was the one who must leave.

'I will take you to Robert Holland's house, where you will be confined until I have enquired into your part in this matter,' he told her. 'You had better bring something warm to wear.'

'What about my daughters?'

'Where are they now?'

'They are in the village with Mistress Palmer.'

'Then they can stay there. I will send a message to explain where you are,' he said and Mabel was thankful for that small kindness.

Whilst he waited she gathered a few of her things from the kitchen. 'I have some clothing stored in the bedchamber,' she said, uncertainly, thinking of the coffer by the bed with the money in it.

'I cannot allow you to go in there. You will have to make do with what you have,' said Neville shortly and Mabel felt his fingers close around her upper arm again as he escorted her to the door. Outside a few of his men were milling around with horses and she waited, afraid that she would be bound for the journey. 'See this lady onto a horse, but keep tight hold of its reins,' instructed Neville. 'She will return with us.'

Mabel barely noticed what was happening as a large, dark horse was led forward and a man lifted her roughly into its saddle. Clutching her bag in one hand and the saddle with the other, Mabel turned to see Edith holding the hands of her daughters as they watched her go. She was too far away to reassure them and she wanted to ask Edmund Neville to allow her a moment to say goodbye, but he urged the horses forward and she was led out of the courtyard without knowing whether she would ever be allowed to return. The manor house at Upholland was well built from stone. It looked well protected and impossible to escape from, thought Mabel. They stopped in an inner courtyard and she was told to get down. Then Neville grasped her arm again and took her inside. She expected to be led straight to some prison but instead he took her into the hall where servants were lighting candles. A fire blazed in the hearth and there was an appetising smell of food coming from somewhere beyond the chamber.

'Wait there,' instructed Edmund Neville as he pointed towards a bench near the hearth. Thankfully Mabel sat down and waited as he took off his outdoor clothes and handed them to a page.

Dicken, she thought, and felt appalled that it was only now that she remembered him. He had accompanied Lymesey as usual on the hunt that morning, but had not returned. Where was he, wondered Mabel, hoping that the boy had come to no harm.

'Do not look so afraid, Lady Bradshaigh. I do not mean to harm you,' said Edmund Neville.

Mabel looked up as he stood over her. 'I was not thinking of myself,' she said. 'I was thinking of Lymesey's young page boy who went out with him this morning. Has no one seen him?'

A shadow passed over Neville's face. 'I had not thought about the boy,' he admitted. He walked to the door and called to someone, exchanged quiet words and then came back to the fire. 'I have given orders that if he is found in the forest, or with the outlaws, he is not to be harmed but is to be brought here.'

'Thank you,' said Mabel, surprised at his consideration.

He paused and then said, 'I was appalled at what Lymesey did, but I could not ignore the assault of your villager. I hope you understand that I did what I had to do?'

'Yet I suppose that you are still searching for Ned Kemp, to bring him to what you call justice,' she replied, thinking that she may as well speak her mind whilst she had the chance, before she was taken to be locked away in some cold, dank dungeon.

Neville frowned. 'I do my job,' he said. 'And my job is to uphold the law. I would not remain a sheriff of the Earl of Lancaster for very long if I were to pick and choose who I brought to the courts. When Sir Peter made a complaint against Ned Kemp and the man admitted that he had struck him, then it was not for me to choose whether he was brought to justice. It was my job to send him to the court for others to judge him. And now that I find he has escaped his guards, and those guards have been murdered, I cannot choose to do nothing. Neither can I choose to ignore the vicious assault on Sir Peter. That would not be justice, would it?'

'And what of the assault on the boy, Dicken?' asked Mabel.

Neville sighed. 'That is something I could

do nothing about. If his father has given the boy into Lymesey's care then Lymesey is within his rights to punish the boy as he sees fit.' He paused. 'You cannot blame me personally for the shortcomings of the law, Lady Bradshaigh,' he told her.

'But I would expect you to use some discretion,' she replied.

'And why do you think you are here rather than on your way to a dungeon in the castle at Lancaster?' he asked her. 'There is much that points to your involvement in this. You have refused to give up Haigh to Sir Peter when he has a legal right to be there. As Ned Kemp was taken north he was rescued and his guards murdered by men who cannot have been there simply by chance. And now Sir Peter has been attacked and left for dead. I cannot believe that it is all coincidence.'

'You have no proof that I am involved!' she protested.

'But I have enough circumstantial evidence to send you to trial.'

'And is that what you mean to do?' she asked, her heart beating faster as her fear grew.

'No,' he said. 'But I do mean to keep you here so that you will have no more opportunity to send messages to these outlaws. And I will find them, Lady

Bradshaigh. And they will be brought to justice for their crimes both old and new.' She looked up to find him studying her closely. 'You are an enigmatic woman,' he said. 'I do not know whether to believe your protestations that you know nothing or whether you are a very convincing liar.' He held up his hand to silence her as she began to speak. 'But if I discover proof that you have been in communication with these outlaws then I will not hesitate to see justice done,' he warned her.

'I have done nothing wrong!' she told him, afraid that she would be accused of crimes for which she could not prove her innocence. As he had said, the circumstances made her appear guilty even though she was not.

'In the meantime,' he continued. 'I am having a chamber prepared for you and you are welcome to warm yourself at my fire, and I hope that you will share some supper with me.'

She was about to tell him that she would rather starve than sup with him, but the food smelt good and she was very hungry. Besides, she told herself, it would be foolish to antagonise him when her future lay within his control. So she nodded her agreement and he seemed satisfied.

'Will you take off your cloak?' he asked.

Whether it was because he was concerned for her comfort or because he wanted to deprive her of its warmth should she seek to escape, Mabel was unsure, but she unfastened it and handed it to him.

Servants came in with cups and platters and laid them on the table. Then, once they were seated and had washed their hands in scented water, a platter with a roasted chicken was brought in. It was a long time since she had eaten any meat and Mabel watched, feeling her mouth water as Edmund Neville sliced generous portions and laid them in front of her before filling her cup with wine.

'Eat,' he said. 'I'm sure you must be hungry.'

She tore off a piece of meat and placed it in her mouth. It was tender and moist and tasted better than anything she could ever remember eating before. Hungrily she tore some more then took some of the freshly baked bread and tasted the heady fruitiness of the wine. It was very different from the meagre portion of bean stew and oatcakes she had had for her dinner at Mistress Palmer's house.

When he seemed satisfied that she had eaten enough he stood up.

'Will you allow me to escort you to your chamber?' he asked.

'I take it my choices are limited,' she said. Although she had been glad of the food she felt suddenly guilty now as she thought of Bella and Amelia and hoped that they had not gone to bed hungry. She considered asking him how he had come by the food and if he would send some to Haigh, but she was wary. For all his apparent hospitality she was still more than a little afraid of him.

'You do have some choices,' he replied in answer to her question. 'You can do as you are bid and I will treat you as a guest. But if you make trouble, I will treat you as a prisoner.'

Mabel stood up and placed the tips of her fingers on the arm he offered, feeling the sumptuousness of the quilted sleeve. He led her up a winding stone staircase until they came to a door which he held open for her to enter. She stepped in and looked around. It was only small but there was an adequate bed with blankets and thick hangings, a stool, a low coffer with a single candle burning beside a bowl and a pitcher of water, and a fire had been lit in the small hearth.

He walked across to the shuttered window to check that it was secure.

'There is only a sheer drop beneath,' he told her. And with a nod of the head he closed the door with a final thud and Mabel heard the key scrape in the lock. It may not have been a dungeon, she reflected, but there was no doubt that Sir Edmund Neville intended to keep her securely confined.

She pulled the low stool closer to the smoky hearth and sat down, reaching her hands towards the flames. She was better fed than she had been for a long time, the room was growing warmer and the bed looked clean and comfortable, but she was a prisoner and she was at the mercy of Sir Edmund Neville whom she knew little about except for his reputation as a conscientious sheriff. Now that his anger had abated he had shown her courtesy and consideration. He had neither threatened to hurt her nor to seduce her as Peter Lymesey had, but there was still something about him that made her cautious.

As she sat watching the flames she hoped that Bella and Amelia were not too worried about her. She knew that Mistress Palmer would comfort them as best she could, but her daughters had never been completely parted from her before and Mabel knew that they would find it upsetting. She wondered too about Dicken and hoped that he wasn't alone and afraid in the forest. She prayed that someone had found him and was taking care of him and that they would never send him back to Lymesey. Yet she prayed for

Lymesey's life too. If he died there would be even more trouble for her. Suspicion was bound to be directed at her because everyone knew how incensed she was that he had been given her lands.

She was considering what to do when she had the idea of asking Edmund Neville if she could see Father Gilbert to make her confession and receive his blessing. It might make Neville think that she had something to hide, but it would at least be a way of getting some news that might not otherwise be forthcoming. Mabel decided that she would ask him. He might refuse her, but she knew that even prisoners in gaols were allowed a priest, though maybe that was only if they were to be executed, she thought with a frown.

When the flames had burned down to no more than hot ashes and the candle was flickering its death throes Mabel slowly took off her shoes and gown and slipped into the bed. She doubted that sleep would come, but at least it was warm. As she lay there, reliving the events of the day she suddenly realised that it was not just Dicken who had not returned home. Lymesey had been very impressed with William's horse and had decided to ride it. She remembered watching as one of his men had heaved his squat little body up into the saddle and thinking how ridiculous he looked, perched on the huge stallion that did not look pleased to be ridden by anyone but its master. And they had taken Calab with the dogs as well, despite her protestations.

'If I am to feed the animal then it must earn its keep,' Lymesey had told her. 'It isn't a pet.'

Mabel had been afraid that he would lose patience with the dog, which was devoted to William, and harm or kill it. A tear crept down her cheek at the thought.

But Hengist, she knew, would always come home. She doubted that Lymesey would have been willing or able to kill the stallion and she knew that if he had fallen or been dragged from it then the horse would have simply trotted back to its stable. Maybe the outlaws had caught and kept it, she reasoned. It was a beautiful and valuable animal.

She turned over in the bed as the thoughts raced around her mind. Was it possible that William was one of the outlaws who were causing so much trouble? She hoped he was, though if it was true she couldn't understand why he hadn't sent a message to her to reassure her and let her know that he was alive. Of course if he had done she would have had to lie to Neville, but if he didn't believe her anyway what difference did it make?

★ ★ ★

When she woke, she couldn't understand why everything looked strange. Then she remembered where she was, and why, and a despondency fell over her that she couldn't shake off, no matter how often she tried to convince herself that everything would eventually be all right.

She pushed back the covers and shivered as she put on her clothes and used the pot that had been provided, feeling ashamed, and pushing it quickly back under the bed when she was done. Then she waited and after a long time she heard footsteps and the door was unlocked. A man she didn't recognise stood guard at the door as a girl brought in bread and ale on a tray and placed it on the coffer before hurrying out again without speaking. Then the man slammed the door shut and locked it. Mabel sighed. Was this to be her life from now on?

★ ★ ★

On the third day, in the afternoon, Sir Edmund Neville came to see her. He closed the door behind him but didn't lock it and stood beside her fire, fiddling with the key, as he scrutinised her.

'Are you well?' he asked. 'Is there anything that you need?'

Mabel looked down at the floor, ashamed of her unkempt appearance, her grubby gown, her unbrushed hair and the smell that she knew must make the small unaired chamber almost unbearable.

'I am well, thank you,' she replied. 'How is Sir Peter?'

Neville raised an eyebrow. 'You're concerned for him?' he asked.

'I enquire after his health as a matter of courtesy only,' she told him and found herself annoyed to see the man smile. He looked so fresh and clean, she thought. He had shaved his face and his slightly wavy dark hair was neatly brushed, falling almost to his collar on either side of his thin face. His dark tunic looked new and his hose fitted well to his muscled thighs and calves.

She looked back to his face and met his pale blue eyes.

'Sir Peter is much improved, though very sore and bruised in many shades of purple and vermillion. He will live, you may be relieved to know, but has sworn vengeance on the man who attacked him. He says he would recognise him again with ease and has given me a detailed description — fair hair, hazel eyes, medium build — all of which could, I am told, describe your late husband.'

'I'm sure there are many men who fit that description,' she said.

'Lymesey also said that the dog he took appeared to know the man and that the horse he was riding unseated him at a given signal.'

Mabel watched Neville's face carefully. Inside her she could feel an excitement growing, a belief that William was alive and in the forest and that he was the one who had given Lymesey a good kicking. But what if Neville was playing some game with her, she wondered. What if he was telling her these things to see how she would reply, to see if she would reveal any knowledge that would condemn her? She realised that she needed to be very careful what she said.

'Indeed?' she remarked, after a moment. 'Perhaps he needs to make an excuse for why he didn't get the better of his attacker.'

'So you think he invented a story?'

'Perhaps.'

She flinched as Neville closed the short distance between them. He stood so close that they were almost touching and she hardly dared breathe as she felt him watching her.

'The dog,' he said almost conversationally. 'Was it the same dog you had at the hall that barked and snarled at me so fiercely?'

'We have many dogs at Haigh.'

'This one was a hunting dog. A big animal with grey fur.'

'What of it?'

'I searched the barns for it when I was there this morning. There was no sign of it, or the horse that Lymesey spoke of.'

'Well,' said Mabel, looking up to meet his eyes with a show of confidence, 'the outlaws must have kept them. Perhaps they butchered and ate them, for they must be as hungry as the rest of the peasants.'

'Even after they have feasted on the king's venison?'

Neville held her gaze and Mabel was the first to look away.

'My daughters will be sorry if the dog is dead,' she told him. 'They were very fond of it.' She hesitated. 'Did you see my daughters?' she asked.

'They are well,' he reassured her. 'Lady Bradshaigh, would you have supper with me — in the hall?' he asked. Mabel hesitated, wondering if this was some new ploy to wear her down. 'I will not insist if you prefer to stay here in your chamber. I will see that ample food and wine are sent up. But I would enjoy your company for a while. I . . . I would like to get to know you better,' he said.

Mabel glanced up again at his well-presented demeanour and she wondered what he intended now.

'I beg your indulgence, my lord,' she said warily, 'but I am very tired and I fear I would not be the best company tonight.'

'Tomorrow then,' he said and she nodded briefly as she realised it was not a question but a statement of intent. 'And is there anything else I can provide you with, my lady?'

She hesitated for only a moment before asking for the priest. 'I would be grateful if you would allow me to see my confessor, Father Gilbert,' she said.

Neville watched her curiously. 'You would like to make a confession?'

'I would like the comfort of my priest's blessing.'

'Very well,' he agreed. 'I will arrange it.'

★　★　★

Mabel was relieved the following morning when she saw the familiar face of Father Gilbert.

'Father!' she exclaimed getting up from the low stool as the door was closed and locked

228

again behind him. 'I am so glad you have come to me!'

'Are you well, child? No one has harmed you, have they?' he asked as he closed his warm fingers around the hands she held out to him.

'No, I'm not harmed. I am well looked after, although I am confined to this chamber — and I apologise for the condition you find me in.'

'You look well enough to me,' he reassured her. 'Just tired and afraid. Though Sir Edmund assures me that he keeps you here only for your own safety and well-being.'

'He keeps me here because he suspects me of collusion with outlaws, and with my husband,' she whispered as she looked beyond him towards the door and wondered if Neville was there, with his ear pressed to the wood, trying to hear what she confessed.

'But that is not true? You have not seen Sir William? Or heard from him?'

'No,' sighed Mabel. 'But you know that the outlaws rescued Ned Kemp? Neville thinks that I sent them word of his being taken to Lancaster gaol. And he thinks that one of the outlaws may be William and that it is he who attacked Peter Lymesey. Father, do you think that William really is alive and in the forest?' she asked.

'Mabel, my child,' soothed the priest. 'How often must I advise you not to excite yourself with false hopes.'

'But Lymesey told Neville that Calab recognised the outlaw and that Hengist threw him off at a signal. Neither has come home and they would have come home, unless they have found William.'

'Mabel . . . Mabel, hush! Come and sit down with me near the fire and we will speak calmly of this,' said the priest. 'I know how much you loved Sir William and I know it is hard for you, child, but you must look into your heart and admit to yourself before God that your husband is dead. Only when you have done that will you be able to find any peace.'

Father Gilbert patted her hand as he spoke to her in the gentle way that she recognised as the tone she used to comfort Amelia if she woke from a bad dream, holding her and reassuring her that none of it was real, just a figment of imagination.

'But what if this outlaw is William?' she pleaded, looking into his kind yet concerned face.

'And do you think that your husband would dwell so closely by and not send you a message to tell you that he was safe?' asked the priest. 'And I have seen Sir Peter's injuries. I would never believe that Sir William did that. It was a cowardly attack on a man who only wanted to enjoy a few hours hunting in the forest. It was the work of thugs and scoundrels.'

'William has a temper when roused,' argued Mabel, not wanting to believe the priest. But Father Gilbert was still shaking his head.

'You are making yourself ill with this,' he told her, reaching out a hand to her head. 'It grieves me to see you so distressed. You must stay strong, Mabel. You must pray for strength and God will grant it. You owe it to your daughters to be strong and not to torment them with the hope that their father will return.'

Mabel pulled her hands away and the sobs began to convulse her body unchecked and uncontrollable. She had thought that when he heard what she had to say that Father Gilbert would agree that William lived. But his mind had not been changed and she began to think that he might be right and that she was deluding herself and holding onto a vain hope rather than facing the truth . . . the truth that when her year of widowhood was ended she would have to marry again.

She felt Father Gilbert's hands on her shoulders as he tried to comfort her.

'Do not cry, child,' he said. 'God will comfort you in your loss.

'What will become of me, Father? Must I be forced to take Peter Lymesey as a husband?' she asked, unable to contemplate how horrific that fate might be, especially if the man believed that she had tried to have him killed. She thought of the weals that she had seen across Dicken's back and she shivered convulsively.

★   ★   ★

Father Gilbert had given her his blessing and left. Alone again, she had thought about the future that awaited her. She could accept it, as the priest recommended or she could try to avoid it, though how she wasn't sure. Even if she could escape her imprisonment she had nowhere to go. Her mother was dead and she doubted that William's brother would welcome her at Bradshaw Hall. And she had Amelia and Bella to consider. If she ran and took them with her, how could she feed and protect them if they were forced to wander homeless through the forest with the sheriff's men hunting them down? And if she chose to leave them behind in the care of Mistress Palmer there was the risk that Lymesey might decide to take Bella as a bride instead, to gain possession of the land — and Mabel knew that she would rather submit to him herself a thousand times than allow that to happen.

As it drew dark and she heard the church bell ring out in the distance, her door was unlocked and a servant girl told her that Sir Edmund Neville was awaiting her in the great hall. Having made herself as presentable as she was able, Mabel went down the stone steps to where he was standing, waiting to greet her.

'My lady,' he said with a slight bow. 'I am pleased you are well enough to keep company with me this evening.' He took her hand in his firm grasp and led her towards the fire. Servants were busy all around, bringing warm water, platters and wine for the meal and once again the smell of roasting meats from the kitchen tempted her appetite despite her anguish.

'I wish that you could send some of this food to my daughters at Haigh,' she told him as the meats were brought in and placed before them and he reached out with his knife to carve some for her.

'I am not surprised that you are concerned for your daughters' welfare, my lady,' he said as he laid the meat on the trencher before her. 'A villager's house is not the place for such well-born girls.'

'I will not have them beneath the same roof as Lymesey.'

'And what will happen if . . . when you marry him?'

'I will not marry him!'

'Is that wise?' asked Sir Edmund. 'After all if you were Sir Peter's wife I would feel less inclined to distrust you. I would certainly not be able to keep you here.'

Mabel stared at the meat before her and knew that if she tried to eat it she would choke. 'Are you saying that I must marry him to be released?' she asked quietly.

'I didn't say that, my lady.'

'But you inferred it.'

'Perhaps you misunderstand me. Eat your supper,' he urged, pouring some wine for both of them. 'But what alternative do you have' he asked her as he placed the flagon on the table.

Mabel met his blue eyes and remained silent for a long time. 'I could remain a widow,' she said at last.

'The Earl of Lancaster will not allow it,' said Sir Edmund. 'As your lord, he has the right to compel you to marry a husband of his choosing. If he decides that you are to marry Sir Peter Lymesey and Sir Peter is willing to take you as his wife then you have no choice in the matter. It is the law,' he added, glancing at her as she sat in a sickened silence.

'Did you make your confession to the priest?' he asked her after a moment.

'Yes.'

'And did Father Gilbert offer you any guidance?'

'We spoke . . . about my future,' she said.

'Lady Bradshaigh, there is another solution,' he told her. Mabel said nothing, but looked up to see that he was carefully studying her reaction. 'The earl could be persuaded to nominate someone else as your husband.'

'Who?' she asked.

He reached out to take her hand. 'Lady Bradshaigh . . . Lady Mabel . . . would it be more acceptable to you to become my wife?'

10

An Audience with the King

The Scot was outside the church chopping logs when they got back. William frowned at the sight of the man with an axe in his hand and wondered who had given it to him.

As they approached, Harry Palmer hurried towards them from where he and Ned Kemp had been hammering stakes into the ground to make the framework for a new house. Martha dropped her basket and ran to him.

'What's happened?' he asked as his arms closed around his sister and he glanced from William to the small boy perched on the horse and then back again.

'We ran into a hunting party,' said William briefly. 'Who let the Scot out and gave him a weapon?' he demanded, looking past Harry to where the man had paused and was watching warily.

'I thought it was time he earned his keep,' said Harry. 'He'll do no harm. But what of these hunters? Are you all right?' he asked his sister who nodded her head as she regained

236

her composure. 'And where did you find your horse?' Harry asked in surprise as he recognised the stallion. 'And Calab?' he added, staring at the hound that stood beside William.

'Well if Sir Peter Lymesey thought that he could ride my horse and hunt with my hound, this day has proved him wrong. We came across them in the forest and I took back what was rightfully mine,' he explained.

'And the boy?'

William glanced up at the thin figure clutching the pommel of the saddle and reached to lift him down. 'This is Dicken,' he said.

'Dicken, lad!' exclaimed Ned Kemp as he came up. 'I'm pleased to see you safe! You'll not send him back?' he asked William, who shook his head as he ran a hand over the boy's hair.

'I will not. The boy is in my care now.'

'What happened?'

'Sir William saw a hawk circling and realised there was a hunting party,' explained Martha. 'We tried to get back but they caught up with us. Then the dog recognised Sir William, and the horse tipped off his rider who turned out to be Lymesey.'

'Surely he wasn't alone?'

'His men ran when they saw Tegg and

Scallard,' laughed William. 'They thought it was an ambush and probably expected another dozen outlaws to leap out from behind the trees.'

'And Lymesey?' asked Ned Kemp with a frightened look. 'Where is he?'

'Lying where I left him I should think,' said William.

'You killed him?'

'I don't think so. But I gave him a beating he'll not quickly forget.' His laughter faded as he saw Ned's concerned face.

'They'll come looking for you,' he said. 'They'll not let that go unpunished.'

'They have been looking for me for months and have not found me yet,' boasted William, though he did not feel as confident as he tried to sound. The beating of Peter Lymesey had been done in anger and he had not been able to stop himself. On reflection it may not have been the wisest thing to do, he had to acknowledge. If it brought the sheriff's men to Chorleigh then he would have done a disservice to the women and children and those who were trying to help them. It was not unlikely that the rebuilding would be broken down again as an excuse to search for outlaws and that the few stores they had gathered from the generosity of the surrounding villages would be plundered.

'The forest is already full of the sheriff's men,' said Stephen Scallard as he came up. 'I doubt it will take them long to find us.'

'Perhaps,' suggested Harry Palmer, 'it would be better if we were not all in the same place.'

'A good point,' said William. 'But you must stay here with your sister. Ned you can stay if you like, but it may be safer for you and Will and Stephen to keep moving rather than wait to be run to ground here.'

'And you?' asked Harry.

'I will stay to give you what protection I can, for a while at least,' said William, though it was the Scot he was watching. He was not prepared to let the man get away until he was sure he was of no further use. 'I have my horse, and Calab will give warning if anyone comes near so I will have time to escape. But the others on foot will need a head start and it may be safer if you go now and keep moving through the forest.'

He watched as Scallard looked at Tegg and he nodded his approval. 'I'd rather take my chances out there than sit and wait for the bastards to find me here,' he said.

'Ned?' asked William. 'Will you go with them?'

'If I go with your blessing, my lord, for I would not like to be taken by them again.'

'Then make haste, and take whatever you might need,' said William with a backward glance down the track, as if he expected to see armed men coming even as they spoke.

'And the boy?' asked Ned.

'Dicken stays with me,' said William firmly, his hand on the boy's shoulder. It was partly because the boy was so young and partly because he had made him a promise that he would care for him. But as he looked down at the frail youngster beside him he knew that it was mostly because Mab had cared for the boy, and that he felt he would be letting her down if he didn't take personal responsibility for him now.

With a brief nod, William Tegg and Stephen Scallard gathered more arrows, some food and blankets, and taking Ned with them they crept off into the forest. William prayed that they could outwit the sheriff's men and that they would stay safe until things changed enough for them to go safely to their homes and get on with their lives.

'And take the axe off that damn' Scot!' he cried in irritation as he led Hengist away in search of some shelter for the stallion. 'And feed the child!' he said as Calab followed him and Dicken stood and stared at the strangers who surrounded him in bewilderment.

'Douglas?' asked William staring at the boy in genuine mystification a few days later. 'Who the heck is Douglas?'

'The Scot,' explained Dicken and William wondered why he had never thought before that the man might actually have a name.

'Didn't I tell you to stay well away from him?' he reprimanded the boy and immediately regretted his harsh tone as he saw the boy cower, as if preparing himself to submit to a blow. 'All right,' he said more gently. 'What did he want?'

'He wants to talk to you,' explained Dicken. 'He says he has something that might help you.'

'Has he indeed?' asked William, wondering what trick the Scot was up to now. As he had recovered, the man had begun to exude an unexpected charm to which only William seemed to remain immune. Even Martha, who had been adamant that she wanted him dead on the first evening of his capture, seemed to have been taken in by him, allowing him to assist with the rebuilding of her house and allowing him to handle hammers, nails and all manner of implements that would suffice as weapons should the man prove unfriendly after all. William had argued that he should be kept restrained and confined but the women had said that as there were so few men he should help with the rebuilding of the village to prove that his words of regret at being one of those who had burnt it down were genuine. Even Harry, whose good judgement William had always relied upon in the past, had quickly trusted the word of the Scot and unbound his hands to allow him to work.

'Go to Martha and see if your supper is ready,' William told Dicken with a gentle push and then he walked around to the back of the church where the Scot was sitting on the ground with his back against the thick stone of the wall waiting for him. He struggled up when he saw William. The wound to his thigh obviously still pained him although he no longer complained. He had not shaved and several days' growth of beard showed a sandy red colour over his face and throat. He was only short, even when standing, and his fierce blue eyes looked up at William who waited to hear what he had to say.

'Whoever would beat a bairn like that is beneath my contempt,' he said at last and turned to spit on the floor to show the depth of his feelings.

'You mean Dicken?' asked William.

'Aye. I had a bairn about the same age.' He hesitated. 'The boy showed me his back. I'd kill a man who did that.'

'I did my best,' replied William. 'But I've heard they found him alive and he still lives.'

'Lymesey,' said the Scot as if it were a foul taste in his mouth. 'He's one of the Earl of Lancaster's men?'

'He is. He's been given my lands since I've been declared an outlaw,' said William.

'Then who do you fight for?' asked the Scot.

'For the king,' he told him. 'For right; for justice. I fought against the Scots for many years. I fought at Bannockburn and saw many of my fellow Englishmen cut down.' He paused as he saw the Scot shake his head. 'You deny it?' he asked, feeling his temper rising and his fist clench.

'Nay, it was a sorry battle, but a man must fight for his own country. You'll not argue with that?'

'What is it you want?' asked William impatiently. 'I've better things to do than discuss the finer points of patriotism with you. No!' His hand closed around the Scot's wrist as the man reached into his tunic. He should have made sure the man was thoroughly searched when they first took him, realised William. Stephen Scallard had relieved him of one knife but that did not mean he hadn't concealed a second.

William glared at the man as he leaned all his weight into him and pinned him against the wall.

'If ye'll let me go I'll show ye the letter,' breathed the Scot.

'Letter?'

'The letter I carry for Sir Edmund Neville, for Thomas, Earl of Lancaster — signed and sealed by king Robert the Bruce of Scotland.'

William did not relinquish his grasp but continued to hold the Scot firm. 'That's a pretty attempt at trickery,' he told him. 'Do you think I look that stupid?'

'Then take it for yourself. It's concealed in a pouch sewn inside my shirt.'

William hesitated. He didn't really want to slide a hand inside the Scot's clothing, but if what he was saying were true then it would provide him with the proof he needed of Lancaster's treachery.

'And why did you not show it to me before? Why did you say it had been delivered?'

'Because I hoped to escape and deliver it and warn Edmund Neville that you were still alive. Ye make the simple mistake of thinking that I am either deaf or sleeping when ye talk,' grinned the man. 'You should learn to

244

guard yer tongue. I know who you are, Sir William Bradshaigh, and I know that you're a wanted man. In fact I expected to reap quite a bonny reward for your capture.'

'I should have cut your throat that first night,' growled William in return. 'I show you compassion and this is how you repay me?'

'Compassion? Nay, Sir William. You kept me alive to use me, no more than that.'

'And now I have used you? What good are you to me now? If I cut your throat I can take either letter or knife from you with ease.'

'And what will ye tell the bairn, wee Dicken?'

William relaxed his hold on the Scot just enough to allow him to slip a hand inside the man's clothing. Sure enough it closed around a hidden pouch and he ripped it out, leaving a strip of the Scot's torn woollen undershirt to hang tattered over the top of his tunic. With one hand William shook it and a rolled parchment fell to the ground. He bent to retrieve it and in the twilight saw that the Scot was telling the truth. It was held by the Scottish seal that it would have been impossible for the man to fake.

'What does it say?' he demanded.

'It says what I told ye before. Tis a safe pass for the Earl of Lancaster to meet with Robert

Bruce to discuss a joint assault on the English king, Edward.'

William quickly pushed the letter inside his own shirt and searched the Scot thoroughly for any hidden weapons. The man stood with his back to the wall and offered no resistance.

'What's in this for you?' asked William. 'You must realise that I won't run the risk of letting you leave here to betray me.'

'Then kill me and finish it,' said the Scot. 'My wife and bairns are dead, starved or struck with the fever. And if I canna go back then at least I can go ta God knowing that I've done some good, for I'll not support a man who'd allow a bairn to be beaten.'

William drew his knife from its sheath and held it to the Scot's bare throat. 'You spin a fine tale,' he said, 'but it's a tale that changes its shape to suit your purpose ... ' He stopped as he heard soft footsteps behind him.

'Sir William?' said Martha. 'What do you mean to do to Douglas?'

After a long moment William lowered the knife and heard the audible sigh of relief from behind him.

'You wanted me to kill him not many days past,' he remarked to her.

'And you showed him mercy. Show him mercy once more, I beg you,' she said. 'He

246

has proved himself to us by his hard work and sorrow for what was done.'

'But did you know that he still harboured a letter for the sheriff and that he meant to betray me for a reward?' asked William, still glaring down at the Scot.

'How do you know this?' she asked.

'He has just told me.'

'And would he have told you if he meant to carry through his plans?' she reasoned.

William looked around at Martha's worried face, illuminated by the gentle golden light of sunset and he stepped away from the Scot. 'On your conscience be it, my lady, if he betrays me!' he snapped as he walked past her, brushing against her arm and wishing that he did not keep giving her reason to dislike him.

William found a quiet place inside the church, sat down on the cold stone step and lit a candle which he placed beside him. Gently, he unrolled the short letter. It was what the Scot had said: a letter that would give Thomas, Earl of Lancaster, and up to thirty knights permission to ride into Scotland to meet with Robert Bruce. William re-rolled the parchment with a wry smile and stowed it back in his own clothing. This was the evidence he needed to persuade the king to raise an army against his traitorous cousin.

He went to seek out Harry Palmer and found him sitting around a fire with his sister, the Scot and young Dicken where the outline of Martha's new house was gradually taking shape.

'How would you like to go to seek out the king with proof that Lancaster is a traitor,' he whispered in Harry's ear with a grin, expecting him to be brimming with similar enthusiasm. He was puzzled and disappointed as he saw the frown flicker across his face.

'I cannot leave my sister alone with . . . ' he nodded to where Martha and the Scot were in deep conversation. 'Besides the other women need a man to protect them now that Tegg and Scallard have gone — and at least I'm near my own family at Haigh. I hope to get a message to them soon.' He looked across at William with a worried expression. 'I'm sorry, my lord. I will go with you if you command me,' he added, dutifully.

'No,' said William after a moment. 'I am no longer your lord to command you and even if I was I would not press you. I should not have suggested it. Of course you must stay here,' he said, patting Harry's shoulder reassuringly. 'I will go alone,' he said and then he noticed Dicken watching them and listening. 'Unless you would like to be my squire?' he asked with a raised eyebrow. 'It will be hard — but I vow not to beat you.'

'And we'd really go to see the king?' asked the boy in wide-eyed awe.

'We would indeed.'

'He'll need a horse,' said Harry, ever practical. 'And it's a pity we threw off our armour as we fled the field at Preston. It would have been useful to you now.'

'We'll manage well enough,' said William. 'There's the mail and the cloaks we took from the sheriff's men and if I ride Hengist the boy can have one of their horses. The other I will leave you, for we'll have no use for a baggage animal, and if you can condition it to the plough it may prove its worth here.'

* * *

Early the next morning, William settled himself into the familiar saddle astride his stallion and picked up the reins. He leant forward to pat the muscular neck and watched the animal's furry ears twist this way and that, eager to please his master but excited at the prospect of an adventure. Beside him Dicken was seated on a slightly calmer bay and William was pleased to see that the boy looked an assured and competent horseman.

'Take care of yourself and your sister,' said William to Harry. 'And watch that Scot. Do not trust him too far. And if you can,' he added, circling the impatient horse around in a tight circle, 'try to let Mab know that I am alive and beg her not to marry some Welsh knight whilst I am gone.'

He looked around the village that was beginning to grow again from the ashes and cursed every Scotsman to hell. Then he raised a hand in farewell to the assembled villagers as he winked at Dicken. 'Ready?' he asked.

'I am, my lord!' replied the boy.

'Then let us away,' said William. 'The king awaits us and the fate of Thomas, Earl of Lancaster, will be sealed.'

Although there had been a week or so of spring sunshine that had filled them with the hope that this year the crops would grow and the animals would thrive, they had only been riding south for a couple of hours when the clouds began to veil the face of a weak sun and before long they were being soaked by the overfamiliar drizzle. Calab ran ahead of them, sniffing at every tree root along the road. His grey fur was saturated and clung closely to his thin body showing that he was not such a huge hound after all, but the horses didn't seem to mind the rain and when William saw the smile on Dicken's face he realised that the boy couldn't have been happier despite the weather.

'How long will it take us?' he asked as they splashed through the puddles side by side.

'Around five days to a week. It depends on the weather and how quickly we ride, though I do not plan a leisurely excursion. Do you think you can keep up?' asked William as he pushed Hengist to a lengthening canter. Looking back he was pleased to see Dicken kick the bay to a similar pace. Although it seemed lazy, Dicken was not allowing it to take advantage of him, thought William, as he watched the boy's face become serious as he settled to the horse's stride. He was a good boy and William was glad that he had brought him.

Calab loped ahead of them, turning his head now and then to make sure that they were still following and William felt confident that they would make Langley before too many days had passed. It was the favourite palace of the king and queen and he hoped that they would be there. The thought of meeting the king lifted his spirits beyond the gloomy weather and for a while he felt happy. But, as William reminded himself that evening, happiness was often a fleeting and fickle emotion and more often than not there was some misfortune awaiting in the none too distant future to even out the balance.

Towards dusk on the second day they reached an inn far enough to the south for William to decide that the risk of being recognised was small. The temptation of a hot meal, water to wash and a decent bed after all the months living rough was too much to resist. He and Dicken saw the horses stabled behind the Rising Sun and were sitting warming themselves by the blazing fire, eating broth with herb dumplings from huge wooden bowls, when some other travellers came in and began to talk.

'We saw two outlaws captured today,' said one conversationally as he spooned the hot broth into his mouth by the light of the guttering tallow candles.

'Near here?' asked William, trying to sound a little indifferent as he poured himself another cup of ale from the pitcher on the scrubbed table.

'To the north. They put up a fierce fight. One got away.'

'You can't help but feel some sympathy for them,' remarked his companion. 'With so many going hungry and so much venison roaming the forest you can hardly blame a man for helping himself.'

'Aye, but the new sheriff of Lancashire, Edmund Neville, has vowed to purge the forest of lawlessness. The man is making it his mission.'

'The Earl of Lancaster has chosen a wily one there,' agreed his companion. 'He's not like Robert Holland who barely shows his face on his lands from one year end to the next. Neville means to do business.'

'Did you hear what the outlaws did to Sir Peter Lymesey, the new lord of Haigh?' asked one, passing the bread basket to William.

'I heard he'd taken a tumble whilst out hunting,' said William with a warning hand to Dicken's knee beneath the table.

'Tumble?' laughed the man. 'He took a beating and was lucky to live from what I hear. They say he will return to his lands in the south, not being tough enough to survive our harsh northern ways!' Both men laughed and William joined them but his humour was feigned and he wanted to know more about the men who had been captured, fearing for Stephen Scallard and William Tegg and Ned Kemp.

'And these two who were caught?' he asked, trying to sound nonchalant. 'Were they the perpetrators of the crime?'

'I dare say they'll hang for it whether they were or not. Sir Edmund Neville will be keen to prove himself,' replied the man as he dipped his bread into the remains of his meal to wipe up every last drop.

'But still, I felt sorry to see them taken,' added his companion, 'especially when they fought so well.'

The men chatted on for a while until William bade them goodnight and he and Dicken climbed the steep wooden stairs from the courtyard to their room.

'Do you think the captured men were your friends?' asked Dicken when they were alone.

'There are many outlaws in the forest,' replied William. 'I wouldn't worry. Get yourself to bed. We have another long ride tomorrow.' But, as William lay and listened to the steady breathing of the sleeping boy beside him, he couldn't dismiss the feeling of disquiet that made him suspect that two of the three men he had last seen the day before at Chorleigh were now in the hands of the sheriff.

★   ★   ★

At last they approached Langley and followed the course of the river Gade, past the two small islands with their mills, which were slapping idly at the water, and on through the parkland where William caught sight of a deer and was tempted to shoot it for their supper, but thought that it would be an inauspicious beginning if he were to be dragged before the king for poaching.

As they rode up towards the high flint walls that surrounded the palace and the priory church, the houses lining the road became larger and their owners looked a little more affluent, though none of the villagers who were farming their strips of land and tending their thin animals paid them much attention. William reined in Hengist and stared through the steady rain at the array of buildings partly visible in the distance through the open gateway. Some looked newly built and it seemed that there had been a recent transformation of what had been an impressive manor house into a lavish palace.

'I've never been inside a real palace before,' said Dicken beside him. The boy's eyes were shining beneath the dripping fringe of his wet hair and William hoped that he would not be disappointed. Calling Calab to his side, he touched his heels to the stallion's flanks and they trotted forward towards the causeway that spanned the moat and led to the gatehouse where the portcullis was raised. William slowed the horse to a steady walk as two men-at-arms with pikes came forward to bar his way.

'State your business!' said one. William looked down at the man whose royal surcoat was stuck fast to his chain shirt by the rain. Water ran from his helmet onto his neck and he looked surly, cold and bored.

'I am Sir William Bradshaigh. I seek an audience with the king.'

The guard looked at him suspiciously for a moment then waved them through into the Court Wick. William looked around the crowded courtyard where servants and villeins were busy with their tasks. There was a second gateway which was more closely guarded, and here he stated his business again before he and Dicken were allowed through to the Great Court. It was surrounded by the usual range of buildings — stables, a well house, cellars and barns; and from a building on the far side of the court came the appetising smell of roasting goose, which was making Calab sniff the air in appreciation.

'Wait in there,' said a man, indicating the wide door to the stables. 'I will send your name to the chamberlain.'

William slid down from Hengist's back and, telling Dicken to follow him, he led the way out of the persistent rain. Several grooms looked up as they came in and one showed them a couple of empty stalls where they could tether and unsaddle the tired mounts. William took some silver coins from the purse at his waist and exchanged them with a groom for some handfuls of hay to feed the horses and some straw to bed them and to dry them off so they wouldn't catch a chill.

He took off his cloak and spread it over a wooden partition to dry, telling Dicken to do the same. As they worked, and the pale faced boy gazed curiously around, William realised that it was a long time since they had eaten and that if there was food to be had here it was a good opportunity to fill their bellies. He considered following the aroma of the roasting meat across to the kitchen to see what he could beg, buy or charm from the cooks, but he was reluctant to disappear until he was sure that someone had sent his name to the king and secured him an audience.

He was mentally debating what to do when a man in the king's livery came to the door.

'Are you Sir William Bradshaigh?' he asked. William nodded. 'I have been sent by the chamberlain to ask your business.'

'My business is with the king,' said William.

The man rolled his eyes and shook his head dismissively. 'We have a hundred people come every week saying they have business with the king. We cannot possibly grant them all an audience or His Grace would be over-whelmed. Tell me why you need to see the king and I will pass your request to the chamberlain.'

'My business with the king is as private as it is vital!' William told him angrily, whilst trying to keep his temper in check.

'If you will not tell me why you need to see the king then your request cannot be considered and I must ask you to leave.'

William clenched and unclenched his fists. He had thought that riding south without being apprehended would be the biggest challenge, but now he saw that had been the easy part. It had never occurred to him that he would not be ushered straight into the king's presence and, not for the first time, he wished that Adam Banastre, with his charmed tongue, were still alive and in his company.

'I have information for the king regarding a threat from the Scots.'

'You need to be more precise than that,' said the man and turned to leave.

'The news also concerns Thomas, Earl of Lancaster.' The man hesitated and William saw that he had his interest. But it wasn't enough. 'I have a letter,' he said as his hand felt for the pouch at his waist, 'that was intended for Lancaster.' He paused. 'It is signed and sealed by Robert Bruce, the so-called king of Scotland.'

'Wait here,' said the man with no show of

emotion, but William saw from the way he hurried back across the yard in the rain that it wasn't just the weather that made him fleet of foot. Within minutes he was back. 'Come with me,' he said.

'Come on then. What are you waiting for?' said William to Dicken and, calling Calab to heel, he followed the man to the wooden steps that led to an upper door in the main building. In a small antechamber to the great hall another man dressed in crimson cloth of gold, trimmed with fur, was waiting to greet them.

'Sir William? Welcome to Langley. I am Hugh Despenser, the king's chamberlain. I am told you seek an audience?'

Irritably, William gave the man a stiff bow and explained once again why he needed to see the king.

'Wait there,' said the chamberlain at last and pointed to a bench near the doorway. With a sigh William sat down and Dicken settled beside him with Calab at his feet. He wished that he had had the foresight to deal with their hunger and thirst before they approached the palace because now he dared not leave in search of sustenance, and he doubted that it would be the correct etiquette to give Dicken some pennies to go and fetch a slice or two of the roast bird that was driving him wild with its mouth-watering smell.

After waiting for most of the afternoon on the hard bench outside the king's chamber, William was told to tie Calab to an iron ring and, after being relieved of every knife and weapon that he carried, he was at last admitted with the letter in his hand.

King Edward was sitting on a carved wooden chair on a dais and his chamberlain, Hugh Despenser, stood to one side, near enough to whisper into the king's ear to guide and advise him. William pulled off his hat and went down on one knee before his sovereign, pulling the overawed Dicken down beside him.

'Sire, I am grateful to you for giving up your valuable time to see me,' he told him.

Even though William had fought at Bannockburn, he had only caught distant glimpses of the king before. Now, he could see that Edward was as handsome as people said, with his wavy fair hair and candid eyes. The king assessed William carefully for a moment and then his features relaxed into a wide and disarming smile.

'Arise, arise,' he said, with an encouraging wave of his hand. 'My lord Despenser tells me that you carry a letter from Robert Bruce?'

'I do, sire . . . though you are not the intended recipient.' The king frowned slightly as he awaited William's further explanation. 'It is a letter that reveals the treacherous villainy of your cousin, Thomas, Earl of Lancaster.'

'Are you one of Lancaster's men?' asked Edward as William stepped forward with the parchment only to be intercepted by Despenser, who took it from him and looked at the seals before handing it to the king.

'I was, sire. I was there when Piers Gaveston was executed at Blacklow Hill. I am sorry,' he added as he saw the sorrow and anguish on the king's face.

'Poor Piers,' he said quietly as he shook his head and gazed into the distance. 'If he had taken my advice he would never have fallen into the hands of the earls. And you, Sir William?' he asked, looking at him again. 'Are you no longer in Lancaster's household?' he asked.

'Sire,' said William, with a glance at the chamberlain, who was watching him shrewdly. 'I have been living as an outlaw for my part in Adam Banastre's rebellion against Lancaster.'

'Banastre,' repeated the king. 'I know that name,' he said, turning to the chamberlain.

'Indeed you do, my lord. We sent him a

261

letter of support in the hope that he could raise enough men to defeat Lancaster, but the rebellion unfortunately failed and Banastre was caught and executed.'

The king frowned, then turned his attention back to William. 'Were you his friend?' he asked.

'I was,' said William. 'I was deeply saddened by our failure and by his death — and by what the Scots have done to his lands. Although that is how I came into possession of the letter.'

He waited as the king read it and then passed it to his chamberlain. Hugh Despenser examined it carefully, looking closely at the seal and the signature as well as the content.

'It seems genuine, my lord,' he said. 'I think that we may have more of a problem with your cousin than we first thought.'

'And what should be done?' asked the king.

'With respect, I find that this is proof of treason, my lord. Which means there is only one option. Lancaster must be brought to trial.'

'And executed?' asked the king.

'If it be your will, my lord.'

'It is my will,' said the king as he brought down his fist on the arm of the chair. 'I have long wished to avenge the death of my brother, Piers!' He paused and for a moment

William thought that he was going to weep, but he regained his control and managed to smile again. 'Will you fight for me?' he asked William.

'My loyalty to you has never been in question, Your Grace,' he said, going down again on one knee. 'I am yours to command. I would only ask one thing.'

'And what is that?' inquired the king as he moved forward on his chair.

'My lands are in your possession,' he explained. 'When I was declared an outlaw they were forfeit to the crown for a year and a day. The lands were the inheritance of my wife, the Lady Mabel de Haigh, and I beg that they be returned to her.'

'What do you know of this?' the king asked his chamberlain.

'I will make enquiry if you wish it, my lord. I cannot say who is in control of the lands at present.'

'It is a Sir Peter Lymesey,' said William and felt Dicken flinch even at mention of the name.

'Lymesey?' The king turned again to his chamberlain for advice.

'He is one of your household knights and his family have lands at Pirton, around a day's hard ride to the north.'

'Ah. I thought I knew the name. Make

enquiry will you, Hugh? And see that the lands are returned to Sir William's wife as repayment for his loyalty to us.'

'I am in your debt, Your Grace,' said Sir William and bowed low as the chamberlain moved forward to indicate that the audience was finished.

'See that Sir William and his page have food and a bed for the night,' said the king as they left.

'This man Lymesey,' said William to the chamberlain as he showed them where they could sleep and called a servant to bring pallets and blankets for them. 'It was not the king who directly granted my lands to him?'

'No. The king has not the time to embroil himself in every detail, and neither do I. There are more important matters to take up our time.'

'Then who?' asked William as he watched the straw mattresses being unrolled and green, square-rimmed jugs placed on the trestles in preparation for their long overdue meal.

'Lancaster, or more probably his sheriff, would deal with it,' he told him.

'I see, thank you,' replied William as the man hurried off. And as Dicken stood in wonderment and gazed around at the walls which were decorated with a huge mural of knights on their way to a tournament, William realised that the gift of his lands had been in the control of Sir Edmund Neville.

11

The Adulteress

Sir Edmund Neville did not press Mabel for an answer to his proposal of marriage. She realised that he was well aware that a choice between himself and Sir Peter Lymesey would be an easy one for her, and that she had, by uttering no outright refusal, given him to understand that she was agreeable.

He had seemed concerned that she had no appetite for her supper that evening and when she had complained of a headache he had escorted her back to her chamber. He had wished her a goodnight, only indicating by a brief raising of her hand to his lips what his future intentions were.

Mabel had lain awake and fully clothed. Although she had been more relieved than she could have imagined to be spared Lymesey for a husband she could take no pleasure in the alternative. She loved William. Nothing had happened to change that and the thought of any other man taking her to his marriage bed filled her with revulsion.

The next morning the servant girl brought copious pitchers of warm water for her to bathe and provided her with scented herbs, a clean silk kirtle and stockings more expensive than any she had owned before. Her fire was built up to a roaring blaze, the food was plentiful and extra candles were brought as darkness fell, together with a thick woollen gown of a beautiful blue to keep her warm.

Mabel knew that she was being rewarded and courted by Sir Edmund and when he sent a message asking her to come down to supper she realised that she was expected to obey or lose her newfound privileges.

He smiled when he saw her. 'Good evening, my lady. I must apologise for leaving you alone all day but I have had various tasks to attend to. Come and sit near me,' he smiled. 'I have news that I think will cheer you. Sir Peter's health is much improved,' he told her as he arranged a cushion on the bench beside the fire. 'In fact he is feeling so well that he has decided to travel home to his lands in Hertfordshire. He should be gone within the week.'

'I am glad to hear that news,' she replied.

'And I have made more inquiries into the circumstances surrounding the attack on Sir Peter,' he went on, 'and it pleases me to say that I can find no evidence whatsoever that you had any communication with the outlaws.'

'I am relieved to hear that I am exonerated,' she told him as he sat down beside her, too near for comfort.

'And so there is no reason for you to remain under my care — unless you wish to do so?'

'I would prefer to return to my home, to care for my daughters.'

He frowned slightly. 'Haigh will remain in the possession of Sir Peter until the year and a day are passed,' he said. 'He will continue to enjoy any revenue from the lands — and to ensure that he receives his dues I have promised him that I will install a bailiff to oversee the villagers and the farming. You will not be concerned with the management of the manor,' he warned her.

'But they are my villagers,' she protested. 'I have always had a say in the running of the manor.'

'Not for the present time,' he replied firmly. 'Do not defy me in this matter, Mabel,' he warned. 'Or I may have to reconsider allowing you to return there.'

She met his eyes and saw that it would be useless to argue.

'I hope you have someone honest and hard working in mind,' she said. 'I shall keep a close watch on him.'

After a moment of hesitation, Edmund Neville laughed softly. 'You are a proud and independent woman,' he said. 'I like you for it and I will enjoy coming to know you better. Now,' he said, 'let us eat our supper. Tomorrow I will introduce you to your new bailiff so that all your concerns will be allayed. Then, when Sir Peter has gone, I will arrange for Haigh to be prepared for your return. And in the meantime I hope you will be happy to remain here . . . as my guest.' He gestured to a servant to pour wine and then handed the cup to her himself. 'And I hope that we will soon be able to announce our betrothal,' he added with a smile.

'It seems that my future is all mapped out for me,' she replied.

★   ★   ★

Bella and Amelia tore their hands from Edith's grasp and came running to meet her before she had even got down from the horse. Mabel opened her arms wide and then pulled her daughters closely to her, kissing their heads in turn and thinking that she would like to hold them forever and never let them go again.

Amelia clung tightly to the folds of her

gown and wept copiously, whilst Bella eventually drew back but remained white-faced and silent with her hand firmly in Mabel's.

'Are you well?' asked Mistress Palmer as she came up behind the girls. Mabel saw her look of concern and was quick to reassure her.

'I have been treated as an honoured guest,' she reassured her. 'And Lymesey? Is he really gone?'

'Yes, my lady. He went off the day before yesterday in a covered litter, muttering that the north was an evil and a hostile place and that he wished he'd never set foot in it.'

'A sentiment I can only agree with,' said Mabel as she looked across to the open door of the manor house.

'We have scrubbed everything, my lady,' said Edith, 'especially the bedchamber. And the bed is made up with all clean coverings,' she reassured her.

'Thank you,' said Mabel. 'It's good to be home.'

She took the girls inside and as Edith had promised all trace of Peter Lymesey had been removed. The shutters had been opened despite the chilly weather. The floors had been swept and fresh rushes laid and there was the aroma of baking bread from the bake house oven and stew from the kitchen, prepared with meat that Sir Edmund had sent from his own stores.

'Dinner is almost ready,' said Edith.

'I hope you haven't gone to too much trouble,' said Mabel.

'It's a homecoming,' replied Mistress Palmer. 'What better cause for a celebration?'

After they had eaten, all sitting together at the trestle table in the hall, Mabel put on her cloak and walked out in the drizzle to thank her villagers for their support and forbearance during Lymesey's tenure, but also to discover their opinions on the subject of the new bailiff. His name was Fossard and he had come from Edmund Neville's own estate at Middleton Hall. When Sir Edmund had introduced him to her, Mabel had, despite her misgivings, taken a liking to the short, red-faced man who looked as if he would have been a plump and jolly character in better times. As it was, he had been deferential and assured her that he would take good care of the manor, but it was the opinion of her villagers that Mabel valued most on the matter of the man's capability.

'It's good to see you, my lady,' they told her at every house as they plied her with food and drink which they could ill afford to share. And at each table Mabel took a little, knowing that a refusal would offend them.

'How do you find the new bailiff?' she asked each one and was reassured that, although they expressed the opinion that no one could better Harry Palmer and that they would be glad when both he and Sir William came home, there were no complaints and the man seemed fair and knowledgeable.

Later that night as she lay once more in her own bed and listened to the steady breathing of her daughters as they slept nearby, Mabel tried to convince herself that things were improving. Lymesey and his entourage were gone and, although she could see no immediate way out of her agreement with Sir Edmund Neville, she decided that she would refuse to wed him until given absolute proof that William was dead — in the hope that her husband would return.

★   ★   ★

Mabel and the girls were sitting in the bedchamber sewing when they heard the horses approaching. As always, Mabel hoped that it might be William and she put aside her work and went quickly to the door. In the courtyard were Sir Edmund and two of his men. He handed the reins of his horse to one and came across to her.

'My lady,' he greeted her, taking her hand and kissing it. 'You are well, I hope?'

'I am well,' she replied as she watched him, suspecting from his solemn expression that this was more than a courtesy visit.

'May I come in?' he asked.

'Of course,' she said, pleased that he had asked her permission rather than taking it for granted that he would be admitted.

He followed her into the hall and, as was his habit, he stood and took off his gloves to warm his hands at the fire even though it was not particularly cold outside.

'I have more news concerning the attack on Sir Peter Lymesey,' he told her after a moment.

'Oh,' said Mabel, looking towards the bedchamber where she saw Bella straining to overhear their conversation. Sir Edmund followed her glance and silently indicated that she should close the door.

'I think that what I have to say should be for your ears only, my lady, for the present time.' He hesitated again. 'Perhaps you had better sit down,' he said, and catching the note of concern in his voice, Mabel's heart raced. He spoke like a man who was the bearer of bad tidings.

She sat down on William's chair, clutching the arms until her knuckles showed white as she waited to hear what Sir Edmund had to say.

'I have two outlaws in custody,' he began, without meeting her eyes. 'Their names are Stephen Scallard and William Tegg. Both were tenants of the rebel, Adam Banastre. Do you know them, my lady?' he asked, looking directly at her.

'No.' She shook her head as she held his look to convince him that she spoke the truth. She knew that Tegg was the man who had killed Sir Henry Bury and that William had hidden him in their barn. She was sure that her blatant lie would be obvious on her face, but Sir Edmund seemed to believe her. He looked away again, studying the flames intently and she wondered what was to come. That the men would be found guilty and would hang seemed without question, but she felt that there was something more that he was about to tell her.

'I have interrogated them,' he went on and Mabel gripped the chair more tightly. 'They have both admitted to the murder of Sir Henry Bury, and of my two guards on the road to Lancaster, and of the attempted murder of Sir Peter Lymesey.' Mabel released one hand to cross herself and she said a silent prayer for the salvation of their souls. 'They swore an oath that everything else they told me was also true,' he said. 'I'm sorry, my lady, if this is news that will distress you.' He paused again and Mabel watched his face as he hesitated, seeming to be unsure how to phrase what he wanted to say. 'The men both swore that your husband, Sir William Bradshaigh, is dead. I am sorry, my lady.'

Mabel heard herself gasp and, as Sir Edmund continued to study the fire, she began to pace the hall, not wanting to believe what he had said, but not knowing how to argue against it.

At last she stopped and clung to the back of the chair, almost able to see William sitting there with Calab at his feet.

'How did it happen? What did they tell you?' she asked as she felt hot tears begin to flow down her cheeks.

Sir Edmund looked uncomfortable as she wiped her face on her sleeve.

'They said that he did not survive the battle at Preston, my lady. They said that he was knocked from his horse and died soon afterwards.'

'And his body?' she asked, hearing that her voice was shaking.

Sir Edmund took her arm and pushed her gently towards the chair. Then he crouched down in front of her and took her trembling hands in his and held them firmly. 'Mabel, please believe me when I say that it gives me no pleasure to bring you this news.'

'His body?' she sobbed again, watching his blurred face through her tears.

'He must have been buried in the mass grave with all the other dead. I'm sorry. If I had known I would have ensured that his body was brought home for burial.'

Mabel was vaguely aware of him standing up and going to the kitchen. Then she felt Edith touch her shoulder and press a cup of wine into her hands, steadying them as she drank.

'I will have to tell Bella and Amelia,' she said, wondering how her daughters would cope with the news. Like her, she knew that they had believed that William was still alive.

'Later,' he said. 'When you are calmer. For it will do them no good to hear it from you like this.'

William, she cried silently as she rocked herself in his chair. William. How can you be dead? How can you be gone? What am I going to do without you?

It wasn't until later that evening, after she had comforted her distraught daughters and seen them to their beds with a sleeping draft that would numb their grief for a little while, that Mabel began to realise the full implication of the situation. Mistress Palmer had tried to press a draft on her, but Mabel had refused and sent her home, only wondering afterwards if the outlaws had also revealed the fate of her husband, Harry, and regretting that she had been so embroiled in her own grief that she had omitted to inquire of Sir Edmund on her friend's behalf.

Now, as she sat on William's chair and watched the embers of the uncovered fire, a blanket wrapped around her shoulders for warmth, she realised that it would be impossible to hold out against Sir Edmund Neville and that when her period of mourning ended she would have no choice other than to become his wife. But as the night wore on and the bell of the church rang out matins and then prime she thought of one last thing that she could do for William. She would argue that Sir Edmund must prefer to marry the widow of a knight rather than the widow of an outlaw. She would ask him to arrange a pardon for Sir William before the marriage went ahead.

He came to visit her again the next morning and expressed concern at her pale face.

'Shall I send for Father Gilbert to offer you some words of comfort?' he asked.

'In a while. I think that I may try to sleep a little,' she whispered, having to admit that exhaustion was threatening to claim her senses completely. 'But first there is a favour I must beg from you.'

'Tell me. I will do whatever I can to comfort you in your sorrow,' he promised.

'If it is true that my husband was not involved in the murder of Henry Bury then can the verdict of the court that outlawed him for non-attendance at the trial be over-turned?' she asked. 'For how could he attend if he was already dead? Surely he can be granted a pardon now?'

She waited, hearing only her own breathing and the flow of the blood past her ears as he considered her request in silence.

'Yes,' he said at last as he shifted his weight from one leg to the other. 'I think that you are right. Of course it is not within my power to grant such a pardon, but I will present your petition to the court and I am sure they will find in Sir William's favour.'

'Thank you,' she said, looking up at him with genuine gratitude.

He smiled. 'Try to sleep,' he said, 'and I will send for Father Gilbert.'

The sun was shining in through a gap in the shutters when Mabel woke and pushed aside the bed hangings. She could hear people moving about outside the window and then the sound of soft voices from the hall. A moment later there was a tap on her door and Mistress Palmer opened it slightly. She smiled as she saw Mabel smoothing down her gown.

Are you feeling better?' she asked. Father Gilbert has come. Shall I bring him to you?'

'Yes, please,' said Mabel as she plaited her long hair and reached for a plain linen cap to cover it. She pulled the hangings closed around the unmade bed and was opening one of the shutters when she heard the door open and close again as the priest came in.

'Mabel, my child, may God grant you succour in your loss,' he said and made the sign of the cross over her as she knelt at his feet. 'I will pray for William's soul.'

Mabel covered her face with her hands in an effort to keep a check on her grief. She felt Father Gilbert's hand rest on her head for a moment. 'Compose yourself, my child,' he told her as he waited for her sobbing to subside. 'Come, sit down and let us talk.'

The priest took her arm and helped her to stand and then drew a stool nearer to her. She sat down and he reached for another and seated himself opposite to her, his long gown trailing onto the floor. 'It was expected,' he said at last, 'but it is always a shock when word comes. I know that you were clinging to hope.'

'I never felt it, Father,' she said. 'I never felt

his loss here,' she told him as she clutched a closed fist to her heart. 'And I loved him so much that I thought I should feel it if he had gone.'

'It is because his spirit survives and still watches over you,' said the priest.

'But if he is watching over me how can I give myself to another man?' she asked.

The priest remained silent as he met her eyes and Mabel could see that he was searching for a reply that would give her some comfort. 'Mabel,' he said at last, taking her hand between his. 'When a soul leaves this world it ceases to be concerned with the physical and is concerned only with spiritual wellbeing. As William looks down on you from above, he will not be jealous that your body lies with that of another man, but will be gladdened to see that you and Bella and Amelia are cared for and safe.'

'Is that true, Father?'

'Why would I tell you so if it were not?' he asked gently.

Mabel looked down at his hands holding hers. 'What must I do?' she asked.

'I have spoken to Sir Edmund Neville,' he said. 'He tells me that he has offered to make you his wife and that you have accepted him. Is this true?'

Mabel could only manage to nod her head.

She wanted to explain to the priest how afraid she was of what would come, but could find no words to adequately explain her fears. She was, after all, no innocent virgin; she understood well enough the duties of a wife and although she had feared beatings at the hand of Peter Lymesey, Sir Edmund had shown her kindness and consideration.

'Sir Edmund has asked me to conduct a betrothal ceremony,' said Father Gilbert.

'So soon?' exclaimed Mabel.

'You will not be married until your mourning is over.' No, thought Mabel, but a betrothal was as binding as a marriage.

She had expected it to take place in a day or so, but when Father Gilbert led her from the bed chamber she saw Sir Edmund get up from where he was waiting, in William's chair beside the fire, and she realised that the ceremony was to take place that day.

Mistress Palmer and Edith were called as witnesses and Mabel saw Bella and Amelia standing wide-eyed, watching but not really understanding. She moved to go to them but Sir Edmund's hand closed around her arm. 'Later, my lady,' he told her firmly.

Almost without comprehending what was happening, Mabel found herself standing beside Sir Edmund at the chapel door as Father Gilbert prompted the vows that she should repeat. As if from a distance she heard her shaking voice saying the words 'I will take you to be my husband.' Then Sir Edmund took her hand in his and was about to push a ring onto her finger when he saw that she was still wearing the one which William had given her. He hesitated and there was a long awkward moment until Mabel reluctantly twisted and pulled it from her finger. She held it tightly and wept as the new one was put on in its place and the priest blessed the union.

She managed not to flinch as Edmund Neville leant towards her and she felt his lips press briefly against hers. 'As soon as your mourning is over, we will be married,' he told her.

Sir Edmund stayed to take supper with them, to celebrate the betrothal, but he took his leave soon after, telling her that he might be away for a while as there were many matters around the county that needed his attention. He kissed her cheek, nodded his head to Bella and Amelia, and, as she watched him mount his horse and raise a hand in brief farewell, Mabel leaned against the door post and sighed a long breath of pure relief. He had agreed that they should not be married until the following year and she still clung to the hope that something might change as the seasons turned one by one.

Another difficult winter followed. Their barns were less than half filled, although she had to acknowledge that the bailiff, Fossard, was quick witted and able. And, thankfully, there were no more deaths at Haigh, even though snow covered the ground for many weeks and the streams and woodlands were spangled with ice and hoar frost.

Sir Edmund celebrated Christmas at Middleton and Mabel was not sorry. It meant that she and her daughters could walk alone through the snow to the church at Wigan to hear the Christ's mass and to say special prayers for William's soul. Afterwards she provided the usual dinner for all the tenants in the hall. The food was meagre but there were minstrels to play on horns and lutes, evergreen branches had been brought in for decoration and the villagers danced and sang, although Mabel couldn't help but compare the day with all the Christmases past when William had been there.

Amelia and Bella were subdued as well, perhaps catching her sorrowful mood. They had said little about their father since the day she had struggled to find the right words to tell them that William was dead. They had cried and she had cried as she comforted them. They had all clung in each other's arms for a long time, drawing what strength they could from the physical union, whilst knowing that something precious had gone from their lives that could never be replaced. Haigh would never be the same again without William.

Just after Epiphany, Sir Edmund Neville came to visit them. He arrived with only a couple of hours' warning, having sent a messenger on ahead through the snow. He would not spend the night, he said, but would be glad to take a meal with them if possible. They had rushed to prepare and, by the time food was being cooked and the hall had been swept and tidied, Mabel barely had the chance to attend to her own appearance or that of her daughters before she heard the horses come up to the door.

She curtseyed to him as he came in, wrapped against the cold in his dark cloak with his reddened cheeks intensifying the blue of his eyes. He kissed her hand in greeting to his icy lips before going to warm himself and Mabel felt unaccountably angry when he sat down, uninvited, in William's chair.

After he was warmed he took off his cloak and picked up the bag he had unstrapped from his saddle and brought in. Mabel watched as Bella and Amelia were presented with gifts — fine leather gloves and a length of cloth each to sew new gowns. Then Sir Edmund handed her a parcel wrapped in linen. Mabel sat down on the bench and carefully drew back the folds. Inside lay two neatly folded lengths of sarcenet — one blue and one white and a pair of silk stockings with garters.

'For our wedding, my lady,' he told her. 'I hope that my choices please you?'

'They are very fine. Thank you,' she replied as she realised that the marriage she had tried so hard to dismiss from her mind would come about, and that she would be married to him wearing a wedding gown sewn from the cloth he had brought. And when she glanced up at his face she saw in his eyes that he would take pleasure in the removing of the clothes as well as in seeing her wear them. Her stomach contracted as fear flooded through her. When William had looked at her like that she had felt desire and excitement, but now all she felt was apprehension — and as she took the cloth away to stow it in her coffer in the bedchamber, she was thankful that it was only his gaze that followed her.

He stayed to eat with them, providing his own gifts of food and wine to supplement their meagre stores. He remained polite and asked no more familiarity from her other than being allowed to take her hand. Yet it was a hand that bore his ring, a symbol that bound her to him and Mabel knew that it was only because he was sure of having her that he was content to bide his time.

In the spring he sent builders to make repairs to the roof and to add another bedchamber for Bella and Amelia, on a mezzanine floor above the back of the hall. Mabel was grateful for that as she had worried about what would happen after the wedding. The girls were growing older and Bella knew well enough what went on between the ram and the ewes before the lambs were born, and Mabel was shamed to even consider that her daughter might overhear the similar attentions that she would be forced to endure from Sir Edmund.

The springtime of 1318 had been sunnier and warmer than that of the two previous years and, as Mabel walked around the village to visit the tenants one day towards the end of May, she was thrilled to learn that two of the women were with child again. She prayed that these babies would be delivered strong and healthy.

She had just finished congratulating the blacksmith's wife on her good news when she heard horses approaching along the Wigan road and, as she watched, she saw Sir Edmund coming towards the manor house. She excused herself and walked to greet him.

'My lady.' He took her hand in his firm grasp and kissed it, allowing his soft lips to linger for a moment on her skin. She did not pull her hand away, but waited anxiously to hear what he had to say. 'Are you well?' he asked.

'Quite well,' she replied.

He smiled warmly. 'Do not look so worried, my lady. I am the bearer of good news. I have a writ that exonerates your late husband of any crime.'

He placed a hand under her elbow and ushered her inside as his squire led the horses away to the barn. Then, standing in his usual place by the fire, he showed her the signed parchment that pardoned Sir William Bradshaigh.

'Now there is only one more obstacle between us and our marriage,' he told her. 'I have also brought a writ which asks for an inquiry into the ownership of Haigh and Blackrod, though it is a formality only.'

★ ★ ★

On the Monday after midsummer, Mabel watched as the local noblemen were shown into the newly decorated hall to sit before Sir Henry Dalton who was to hear the inquiry.

The jurors agreed that because of Sir William Bradshaigh's pardon the lands were no longer forfeit to the crown and that Sir Peter Lymesey had no claim. On the death of Sir William, the lands had reverted to Lady Mabel Bradshaigh, and Sir Robert Holland gave her wardship to Sir Edmund Neville to whom she was already betrothed.

The documents were then signed and witnessed and seals were pressed into hot wax. The visitors drank cups of the best wine and ate all of the little honeyed cakes that had been handed round on platters. Then, after expressing their best wishes to her and Sir Edmund, they called for their horses and rode away to their homes.

'Are you content, my lady, now that both your land and your late husband's reputation are recovered?' asked Sir Edmund when they were gone. She saw that he was hoping for gratitude and possibly some show of affection

'More content than when William was called an outlaw,' she told him.

'Lady Mabel.' He stopped and she watched as he tried to find the right words to say something. 'Mabel,' he repeated. 'I understand that you loved Sir William. But I hoped that, if you were given time, you might come to have some feelings for me.'

'Feelings are not something that can be put on or taken off like a gown,' she replied. 'I cannot force myself to feel something for you.'

He frowned in disappointment. 'Perhaps,' he said, 'when you are my wife you may speak differently.'

Mabel turned away. She had heard many people comment on Sir Edmund's appearance and it was true that he was an attractive man, but she could conjure no love for him. She supposed that this was what marriage was like for many women and that she had been fortunate to have experienced a love match with William. But she would do herself no favours to anger him and her marriage vows alone would force her to be meek whatever her true emotions were. She supposed that she would not be the first wife to resort to a little pretence to keep her husband sweet.

'I will try, my lord,' she promised and she saw that her words pleased him.

★ ★ ★

A month later the marriage was celebrated in the church at Wigan. Bathed and perfumed and dressed in her new gown, Mabel walked the last few steps to the grey porch of the church as if a penitent, her eyes on the ground and her spirits low despite the blessing of sunshine. The previous day, Father Gilbert had become unusually severe as she had once more poured out her fears and misgivings to him as he heard her confession. He had urged her to make the best of her situation and reminded her that she was better off giving herself compliantly to Edmund Neville than risking him changing his mind and finding herself with Peter Lymesey instead. At his direct words she had nodded and seen the sense in it but, as the swallows swooped in to their nests in the tower and she saw Sir Edmund awaiting her at the church door, she could only remember a similar day when she had looked up to meet William's hazel eyes and been glad because she had loved him.

Sir Edmund smiled at her and she did her utmost to return his smile, though she felt it fleetingly fail as a sigh of regret and resignation escaped from her lips instead. She saw Father Gilbert frown slightly and, in a last attempt to fulfil her promise to him that she would not weep and wail her way through the ceremony, she gulped back the tears and placed her cold hand into that of her betrothed and repeated the wedding vows in a tremulous voice.

After the brief ceremony, Sir Edmund kept her hand gripped in his as if he feared that she might take sudden fright and run off into the forest — a thought that had tempted Mabel as they had come out of the stone-cold church into the sunlight. His horse was waiting, decked out with bells on its harness and ribbons in its mane. He loosed her hand to grasp her around the waist and lifted her easily into the saddle for the procession back to Haigh.

The warm sun shone down on her head. The wedding and the summer weather should both have been a cause for rejoicing, but the villagers of Haigh were subdued as the couple seated themselves at the top table that had been set out on the green. The servants and retainers brought by Sir Edmund came forward with a roasted swan and other fowls, a salmon and pies filled with meats and fruits and sweetmeats. There was claret and burgundy wine and best ale, and as the guests ate and drank and were entertained by musicians and minstrels and jugglers and acrobats they began to talk, and then to laugh, and finally to dance and sing.

Mabel remained mostly silent, a taut apprehension growing within her as the time to go to the bedchamber with her new husband drew closer. Sir Edmund was attentive. He made sure that her platter and her cup were filled, though she barely touched the food and wine. He kept a watchful eye on Bella and Amelia too. The girls were dressed in new gowns and wore new shoes. Amelia threaded some daisies together and hung them around her neck and Sir Edmund told her that she looked like a fairy princess. He was kind to her daughters, thought Mabel, and though he could never replace their father they had warmed to him as he had tempted their affection with his generous gifts.

Had he tempted her affection, she wondered, as she noticed the way his dark hair fell in waves to the collar of his dark blue tunic. The hand that rested on the table was strong and clean and the nails were neatly trimmed. He smiled when he caught her looking at him and the smile masked an expression she recognised as desire. He had kept himself in check up until now, but she knew that he would not wait much longer. The sun was already beginning to sink in the reddened sky and a freshening wind was creeping from the east, making the cloths on the trestles flap irritably. Sir Edmund reached for her hand.

'You look chilled, my lady,' he said. 'Shall we go inside?'

Mabel nodded and cast a warning look towards Mistress Palmer. She had forbidden her to indulge in any of the traditional marriage bed superstitions, where family and friends would escort the couple to their chamber. She had also told a slightly shocked Father Gilbert that she wanted no blessing of the bed, for it had been blessed when she married William and that it was only her union with him that was fitting in the sight of God. The priest had tried to change her mind, but she had been adamant, and if Sir Edmund was surprised that they were not accompanied as he led her inside the manor house he made no comment.

Outside, the villagers laughed and shouted as they cleared away the remains of the feast. There was still music from the minstrels and the sound of clapping hands echoed on the evening air as the dancing went on.

'I think they will dance until dawn,' remarked Sir Edmund.

'You provided a sumptuous feast. It's a long time since they ate so well. No wonder they are happy,' said Mabel, wondering if he really thought that it would only take a few roasted fowl and kegs of wine for him to win the approval of his tenants at Haigh. She knew that their support had been for her and that they all wished her happiness, though most knew that this marriage had not been her own free choice.

She looked around at the windows where Sir Edmund was closing the shutters against the night air, at the precious beeswax candles that he had provided, the fireplace with its bright fire, the table, the benches — William's chair. She went to touch it, remembering the times he had sat there until late and she had gone to him, draping her arm around his shoulders and kissing his rough cheek and whispering in his ear that it was time for bed. He used to look up with mischievous eyes and smile and she would go to the bedchamber to check the little girls were sound asleep before he came to her.

Tonight Bella and Amelia would stay with Mistress Palmer. Even though their new bedchamber was ready, Mabel did not want them to be in the manor house. She did not want them to hear her cry out if she found that her resolve to be meek and compliant was weak.

Too soon the servants were sent to their own beds, the fires covered and the house made secure. Sir Edmund held out his hand for hers.

'Are you ready?' he asked. She nodded, avoiding his eyes. He took her through to the bedchamber and closed the door firmly. The bed had been made up with fresh linen sheets and Edith had sprinkled dried herbs across the covers and over the floor, filling the room with the scent of flowers. Mabel watched as Sir Edmund unlaced the blue tunic and shook it from his arms before laying it over the coffer that had once held all her wealth. He pulled off his leather shoes and rolled his hose down his muscular legs as he sat on the edge of the bed. Then he took off his linen undershirt to reveal a surprisingly broad chest, dusted with freckles and fine hair. Wearing only his braies he looked across at her.

'Do you mean to come to me still wearing your wedding gown?' he asked. Mabel shook her head and began to untie the cords of the jewelled and embroidered belt that circled her slim waist; his wedding gift to her. Her fingers shook and she was aware of him watching her as she struggled with it. She slipped the blue gown and the white kirtle from her shivering body and folded them neatly into her coffer. Then she removed her shoes and peeled off the silk stockings, grasping at the wall to help keep her balance rather than sit beside him on the bed.

She kept on the embroidered chemise, but she knew that it was so finely woven that her body was revealed beneath it, and she felt ashamed and humiliated as he looked at her for a long time.

'Come to me,' he said at last and, like a prisoner going to the block, she walked slowly across the chamber to stand before him. He reached out and his hands on her hips were hot as he pulled her close, between his legs. She closed her eyes so that she couldn't see him admiring her breasts as they pressed against the thin fabric. His arms encircled her and she placed her hands reluctantly on his shoulders, feeling his hard muscles as he pressed her tightly against him. Warm lips kissed her neck and throat and as his hands began to move over her she felt the betrayal of her body as it responded to his touch.

He lifted the chemise and stripped it from her then pulled her down with him onto the bed, rolling her over until she was beneath him. His mouth covered hers, gently seeking the pleasure of her lips and against her will she found that she did not resist him. His slow and gentle caresses kindled desires in her that she could not control, and when his warm hands parted her thighs and his weight held her against the mattress she didn't struggle. She closed her eyes tightly and clenched her fingers into fists as she felt him push inside her. She tried hard not to think about William, but the sensations she felt within her made her yearn for him even more.

When Sir Edmund had finished and parted from her she turned away and lay curled on her side with a blanket clutched to her as she tried to contain her tears, afraid that her response would make him angry. But as she lay trying to stifle her sobs she felt him move and his hand touched her arm.

'Mabel? Did I hurt you? You should have told me.'

She shook her head in the darkness as she fought to control herself. 'You did not hurt me,' she told him, wishing that he would leave her alone and go to sleep.

'Then why do you weep?' he asked in a puzzled voice. 'I hope it is not because you find me unkind.'

'I do not weep, my lord,' she told him, wiping her eyes and nose on the blanket as she struggled to make her voice sound even and controlled. She moved away from him in the bed and a moment later he withdrew his hand, though she could hear by his breathing that he did not sleep either and they both lay very still and quiet, waiting for the morning to come, the silence only disturbed by the laughter of the last villagers making their way home.

12

The Battle of Boroughbridge

At last, with their empty stomachs filled, William and Dicken lay down on their pallet beds. Sleep was a long time coming for William as he watched the flickering night candle and listened to the groaning of those who had shown even less restraint than he had at the supper table.

Beside him young Dicken was lost in the easy slumber of childhood and William smiled as he watched the slow rise and fall of the boy's chest. He loved his two daughters without question, but he had always yearned for a son and, although Mab had never been reluctant to bear one, they had not, so far, been blessed. The famine hadn't helped, he thought, as he lay and luxuriated in the unaccustomed feeling of having overeaten, although a pang of guilt plagued him as he remembered Mab's stick thin body the last time he had lain with her and he hoped that she and the girls were safe and fed.

At least she would approve of what he'd

decided to do about Dicken, he thought. The boy had told him that his family home was not far distant, but when he had offered to take him there a look of terror had seized the boy's face.

'Do you not want to go home?' William had asked him, finding it strange that the boy seemed reluctant.

'They will send me back to Lymesey.'

'No. I'm sure they won't. Not when they hear how he treated you and see your scars. They'll be more likely to go and knock him down again,' said William, absently flexing the fingers of his right hand as he remembered the pleasure he had gained from punching the man.

But Dicken still shook his head. 'My father thinks that the discipline is good for me,' he explained quietly. 'If you take me home and tell him that I have had a beating, he will give me another for bringing shame on him.'

William had reached out to the frightened child and, with an arm around his thin shoulders, had drawn him closer as they sat side by side. 'Then I will not take you back,' he had promised.

'What will happen to me now?' Dicken had asked after a moment.

'You can stay with me,' he'd told him. 'You can join my household and be my squire, and in a year or two I will teach you to be a knight.' He had smiled in satisfaction at his decision. The king had suggested that he join the forces that were going north for another assault on the Scots. It would be useful for him to have a boy to clean his harnesses and run errands and generally attend to him rather than riding alone. Besides, he liked young Dicken and enjoyed his company.

William reached out an arm and fondled Calab's ears. The dog whimpered obligingly and William heard his tail thud a few times on the floor. If only it was Mab lying beside him, he thought, as he turned over again and tried once more to sleep.

The next morning he went to the priory church and, having dipped his fingers in the holy water and made the sign of the cross, he went up to the chancel and the magnificent tomb that the king had erected over the body of Piers Gaveston. It was ornate, with twisting vines of flowers and fruit adorning the panels and on the top, chiselled from the finest white marble, was an effigy of Gaveston in full armour that bore such a striking resemblance to the man that William shivered in the dank church — both with cold and with the revulsion he still felt at the murder by the Earl of Lancaster. He owed Lancaster nothing he thought, shaking off the years of loyal service that he had given in return for the lands at Haigh and Blackrod. He could not support a man who had committed such an atrocity and who had betrayed his cousin to the Scots. He touched a hand to the tomb in a gesture of regret and an appeal for forgiveness. There had been nothing he could have done to save Gaveston, but he could repay the man by remaining loyal to Edward and helping him to wreak his revenge.

A week later, warmed and fed and rested, William took his leave of the king who had given him armour, a cloak, new clothing for both himself and Dicken, a tent, a packhorse to carry their belongings and a well-filled purse. He had bowed gratefully from Edward's presence after thanking him for his generosity and now, with a letter of introduction to Sir Andrew Harcla carefully stowed in his bags, he and Dicken rode out across the causeway, away from Langley and headed north again.

They had not ridden far when William heard the sound of an approaching party. He reined back Hengist to make way for them to pass on the narrow road when he saw that it was a horse litter coming towards them.

'Move off the road!' cried an outrider and William urged his stallion onto the wet grass at the side of the rutted track.

He sat and watched as the party approached and it was only when Dicken whispered urgently, 'My lord! It is Lymesey!' that he realised the danger. To run would attract attention, he decided. The best they could do was to keep their heads down, as if in obeisance, as the man passed and hope that he did not recognise either of them.

From the corner of his eye William saw the curtain of the litter twitch, but Sir Peter Lymesey only glanced and then looked away, having reassured himself that whoever was on the road had stepped aside for him.

As the sound of the hooves faded away into the distance William turned to Dicken and relieved smiles spread over their faces until they were both laughing uncontrollably. Then, still chuckling at the near escape, they heeled the horses back to the track.

'Will we stop at Chorleigh on the way?' asked Dicken as they rode with a feeble sun on their backs and an icy wind in their faces. The boy had voiced the question that William had been pondering over for a day now. It was to Haigh that he really wanted to go, and with his pardon secured inside his tunic he ought to have been free to do so, but he was uncertain whether the sheriff of Lancaster would extend him much of a welcome and he decided that it might be better to keep his head low until the earl had been dealt a final blow. They could perhaps call at Chorleigh though, he thought. There might be news of Mab and it might be possible to get a message to her.

'We'll stop a night at Chorleigh,' he replied, turning slightly in his saddle so that his words were not whisked away on the wind. 'But I don't want to linger long. We have a duty to the king in exchange for all he has given us.'

Dicken nodded with an enthusiastic grin. He looked happy, thought William, who had felt the tension ease from the boy with every pace away from his family home and from Sir Peter Lymesey.

On the third day they reached a roadside inn just before darkness fell and William reckoned that if they spent the night there and set off early then they could reach Chorleigh by the following nightfall. Dicken was rubbing down the horses with some handfuls of straw and William was about to go inside to enquire about beds and supper when a figure approached him out of the shadows. It was because Calab gave a sharp bark of recognition rather than his throaty growl that William looked at the man more closely.

'Ned?' he asked the bearded figure who shuffled into view wearing a patched and threadbare cloak with hay sticking to it as if he had been sleeping.

'Aye, my lord. It's me. And I'm glad to see you looking so well.'

William could see that Ned Kemp was not so fortunate though, even if he had so far escaped capture by the sheriff.

'I'm pleased to see you with your liberty,' he replied. 'We heard that two outlaws had been captured and I feared for you.

'Scallard and Tegg were taken, my lord, but I managed to get away. Twas a close run thing though. I evaded the sheriff's men and managed to hide away from the dogs in the forest until they called off their hunt. But I dare not go home or to Chorleigh. Edmund Neville has eyes and ears everywhere, my lord.'

William patted the man on the shoulder in sympathy. He was more sorry than he could say about the other two, but he was glad that it was Ned who had got away. He didn't need to ask what had happened to them. They would be dead by now, he knew, on one charge or another. Tegg's days had been numbered since he'd killed Henry Bury, but William had liked the man, and Scallard too. They had been good, brave men who had fought hard at Preston and helped him in the forest.

'Come into the inn with us and I will buy you some supper and a cup of ale. I've been more than amply rewarded by the king,' William told Ned, seeing that the man was in dire need of a good meal.

'I'm pleased your journey was worthwhile, my lord,' said Ned as they settled by the warmth of a roaring log fire. 'Where are you headed now?'

'We are on our way to the borders. There is a new assault on the Scots planned. But we intend to stop off at Chorleigh along the way to see how the rebuilding is progressing.'

'I wouldn't, my lord. Not if you value your head,' Ned told him. 'Edmund Neville has posted men-at arms all around. He says it is to protect the women against another Scots raid, but the true reason is that he has vowed to rid the county of every last outlaw. I daren't go back and I know that Harry Palmer has gone to the den in the forest and had to leave his sister.'

Ned was right, thought William, as he filled his mouth with bread and stew. It would be safer to ride straight for Carlisle and sort out the Scots and the Earl of Lancaster for good so that he could go home with no fear to claim back his land and his wife.

'Come with us,' he said to Ned. 'You're nifty with a sword and it has to be better than playing hide and seek with Neville's men in the forest.'

'I have no horse, or armour, my lord,' said Ned, though William saw from his expression that he yearned to come. He shook the purse at his waist with a smile.

'I will supply whatever you need,' he told him. 'I'm sure we can find a horse for sale somewhere.'

But it turned out that horses were as rare as a four-leafed clover and Dicken had to give up his mount to Ned and ride the pack-pony instead after they'd shared its burden amongst them.

At last they arrived at Carlisle and rode up to the castle where William, having explained his identity several times and waved the letter with the king's seal under the curious noses of the guards, was at last allowed through the gates to see Sir Andrew Harcla.

Sir Andrew and some other men were studying maps spread out across a trestle. He looked up when William was announced and appraised him for a moment, obviously impressed by the quality of his armour. Then he opened the letter and nodded his head as if in concurrence with the words before rolling it decisively and looked again at William.

'You are welcome,' he said. 'I need loyal

men who are prepared to fight.' He beckoned to one of his knights. 'Find a place for this man to pitch his tent,' he said, 'and see that he gets something to eat.'

'Thank you, my lord,' replied William with a courteous bow. Although Sir Andrew was in appearance an unprepossessing man, he was something of a legend for having held Carlisle against the Scots in 1315 and William was more than happy to serve under him.

* * *

Mabel woke as Edmund Neville gently touched her in the early morning gloom of the shuttered bedchamber. She turned away from him. She had begun to bleed again in the night. It was a sure indication that she still did not carry the son that he wanted. She pushed his hand away and shook her head.

'It is my time again,' she told him and quickly got up to dress herself. She didn't look back at him. She knew that his eyes would be reproachful, as if it were her fault that his seed didn't quicken in her womb.

She went into the hall and began to kindle the fire herself rather than waken the kitchen boys who still slept, sprawled untidily across their pallets. As she watched the flames take hold she rubbed her aching back and wondered if she would ever be able to give Edmund the child he wanted. He had been kinder to her than she had deserved in the first weeks of their marriage and now, despite her earlier reluctance, she wanted to do her duty and be a good wife.

Later, whilst she was supervising the cheese-making in the dairy, she heard a messenger come and after a while she could no longer contain her curiosity and went across the yard to the hall where Edmund was reading a letter with a serious expression. He looked up at her and she hesitated. She and William had always shared everything, but she worried that Edmund might think it prying if she asked what news had come. She waited a moment not knowing what to say, but he spoke first.

'The Scots have broken the negotiated peace and recaptured Berwick,' he told her, 'and laid waste to much of Northumberland, even the port of Newcastle. Last month they stayed three days in Ripon and spoiled much of the countryside around, but thankfully took a thousand marks not to bum the city. But they have sacked and plundered and burned Knaresborough and Skipton and taken cattle and prisoners, both men and women.' He tossed the letter angrily onto the table.

'Then the wars with the Scots begin again,' she said, wondering if he would be called away to fight.

'Did they ever finish?' he asked. She shook her head, thinking of what she had been told about the pillaging and burning of Chorleigh, though thankfully there had been no more raids on Lancaster's lands. 'The king is too weak and pays too little attention to affairs here in the north as he pursues his common pleasures in the southern counties,' said Edmund. 'If he will not or cannot commit enough resources to beating the Scots then he should do as the Earl of Lancaster wants and make agreement with them. It is not right that people should lose everything, even their lives, whilst he does nothing. The life of everyone along the borders has become untenable and there will be no peace for them, no chance for them to rebuild their homes and farm their lands, until Edward either defeats the Scots, of which he is incapable, or recognises Bruce as their king and makes the best of it.'

Mabel stared at his furious face. William had always believed that the Scots should be crushed and taught a lesson they would never forget. He had seen the fragile truce as a weakness, forced on the king by poor advisers such as Lancaster himself. She was shocked at Edmund's contrary opinions and yet, as she considered his words, she could see that his point of view also had its merit.

'Why must men fight amongst themselves?' she asked, more of herself than of him. Edmund shook his head.

'It does not help that there is so little food because of the bad harvests and this continuous appalling weather.' Mabel jumped as the wind rattled at the shutters and blew one open as if to demonstrate the truth of his words. 'When men are desperate they will fight amongst themselves for scraps,' he said as he went to secure it.

'And what will happen now?' she asked. 'Will you go away to war?'

'I will fight for Lancaster if he sends word that he requires my service,' Edmund told her.

A few months ago the words would have filled Mabel with relief. She would have been pleased to have him removed from her bed, from her manor and from her life for a short time at least. But she had grown used to his company.

She looked at him as he bent over the table re-reading the letter. His dark hair needed cutting. She went across to him and hesitantly placed her hand on his arm. He looked up in surprise at her gesture.

'What troubles you, my lady?' he asked gently.

'I am afraid for you,' she confessed. 'I have already lost one husband in battle. I . . . I would be sorry to lose another.'

He stared at her and Mabel was suddenly sorry that she had spoken and turned to leave, but he caught hold of her wrist.

'Don't walk away from me,' he told her. She didn't pull against his restraint and he drew her closer to him and held her with a strong arm around her waist so she could not escape. Mabel breathed quickly. It was unusual for him to touch her at all outside the bedchamber and she was concerned that Edith or one of her daughters would come in. 'Don't look so dismayed,' he said as she glanced towards the kitchen door. 'What are you afraid of? I am your husband.'

'Yes, my lord. But it is not seemly,' she said. 'My daughters . . . '

'Are busy at their tasks,' he replied as he held her firmly. 'I thought that you only tolerated me,' he said as their eyes held for a moment. 'Yet now you admit that you would be sorry if I did not return.'

Mabel pressed her hands against the cloth of his grey tunic. 'I spoke only out of concern for you as my husband,' she told him, as she tried to push away from him.

311

'No,' he smiled. 'There was a ring of truth in your words, my lady, as clear as a church bell. If I were a betting man I would take a wager that you were beginning to like me.'

Mabel knew that he spoke the truth. Lately, no matter how much she tried to keep her memories of William fresh in her mind, she found that her previous life was fading and that the only place she could now clearly see his features were in the echoes of his face when she looked at her daughters.

'Do you think you will ever come to love me?' Edmund asked her, quietly.

'Maybe,' she said. 'Given time.'

'Then let us pray that we are given time,' he replied, releasing her as the kitchen door opened behind them and Edith came in with fresh logs for the fire.

★　★　★

It wasn't until July of the following year, 1319, that William saw Berwick again. He had last been in the town when the king had mustered troops in readiness for their foray into Scotland before the disastrous rout at Bannockburn. Now, with Dicken and Ned beside him, he stared up at the hilltop castle behind the steep ramparts and stone walls that surrounded the fortified town. An armoured roof had been built at the base of the outer wall and a team of miners was already busy digging at the foundations in an attempt to bring it down. From above, the Scots were trying to prevent the attack by hurling large stones from a trebuchet onto the protective covering. They had already succeeded in exposing some of its timbers and, as William watched, he saw a crane swing out over the city wall and drop a huge incendiary bale of wood and tar held together with iron hoops. The smell spread on the prevailing wind and William coughed as the stench caught at the back of his throat. He pulled the hood of his cloak around to cover his mouth and nostrils as more and more blazing bales fell to the ground around the terrified men, who had thrown down their picks and spades and were running for their lives as the fire took hold.

William looked in the other direction, at the tents of the English army stretched almost as far as he could see. There must be around ten thousand men, he thought, at a quick estimate. But what use were they if the walls could not be breached? Most sieges failed eventually for lack of food, but the Scots had been holding Berwick for over a year now with no sign of hardship or surrender and

William had to admit to a grudging admiration.

As he searched for a decent and still vacant spot to set up camp William kept a weather eye open for any men bearing the three lions of the Earl of Lancaster. He doubted that anyone would recognise his face after all this time but, as an extra precaution, he had exchanged his own surcoat with its three martlets for the single bird of Sir Andrew Harcla's emblem.

Sir Andrew had told them that Lancaster had declared the capture of Berwick a national disgrace and eventually the king had agreed to meet with him the previous August near Leicester, where they had made a show of reconciliation. Now Lancaster had accompanied the king to Berwick to try to end the siege and take the town back into English control, but from what William had just seen it didn't look as if it was going to be easy.

Once they had the tents up and the horses unsaddled, Dicken asked if he could go back to watch what was happening. William could see from his bright eyes that he had been fascinated by the crane and the catapult and was eager to take a closer look.

'Don't get too near, and don't get in the way,' William told him. 'And don't get lost!' he shouted after him as the boy sprinted off.

One tent looked much like another, he thought, and even though the boy was quickly growing towards manhood, he still felt unaccountably protective of him.

Leaving Ned to make sure that everything was secure he wandered out to where men were sitting around a roaring fire, drinking and talking. Someone moved up for him and a cup of ale was thrust into his hand as he was recognised as 'one of Harcla's men'.

'Lancaster won't be at all pleased when he hears that the king means to give the governance of Berwick to Hugh Despenser,' said one man.

'Who told you that?' asked another.

'The men who came with the king and Despenser are boasting of it openly. Mind you Lancaster's men are calling them filthy liars, and worse, and there's been a scuffle or two broken out already.'

'Men are eager to fight,' commented another. 'If they can't fight the Scots, they'll fight each other.'

'And do you think the siege will hold?' asked someone.

'All sieges break in the end,' remarked another. 'It's just that some take longer than others.'

William, sitting listening to the conversation but not joining in, was the first to hear the horns of the heralds as they ran through the camp. He turned to see men jumping up from firesides all around him in agitation. Hands and arms were being waved as they stared at one another in disbelief and as he jumped up, spilling his drink in his eagerness to discover what was amiss, his companions fell silent to hear what the approaching messenger had to say.

'My lords,' panted the herald, having run the length of the field to impart his news. 'The Scots have invaded! They rode south plundering and burning everything in their path and then headed for York.' The silent men stared as the messenger briefly related, probably for the umpteenth time, how the Archbishop of York had hastily raised a force of local citizens, farmers, priests and monks to defend the city. They had bravely marched out to battle with the Scots and engaged with them at Myton on Swale, but these untrained men had stood little chance against Robert Bruce's army and many had been slaughtered.

'Where are these Scots now?' asked someone as the shock of what had happened took hold.

'On their way to Pontefract. And my lord of Lancaster is rallying his men to head them off.'

In the ensuing turmoil the siege of Berwick was forgotten as earls and lords rounded up their men ready to ride home to protect their own properties. Back inside his tent William's thoughts were all for Haigh and for Mab and he was discussing the implications with an equally worried Ned when the flap was lifted and Dicken crept inside.

'I couldn't find the right place,' he said, shamefaced. 'Everyone is shouting and running about and people are taking down their tents and preparing to leave.'

'The Scots have killed many priests and monks in Yorkshire,' William told him and felt the boy shiver in his arms. 'And the lords will ride home to protect their manors. Tomorrow we will return to Carlisle with Sir Andrew to defend that city should Bruce decide to pay it a visit on his way home with his plunder. I pray to God that the Lady Mabel is safe,' he said out loud.

'Amen,' whispered Dicken.

If it had been William then Mabel would have lifted her skirts and run to meet him as soon as she heard the horses, but even though she restrained her desire to do the same for Edmund she could not wait inside, but stood outside the hall door watching for him. It was a sultry summer's day with a hint of thunder building on the horizon. It would rain again before nightfall, she surmised, as she watched him turn his tired horse into the courtyard and give orders to his men to tend to the needs of the animals and stow away the armour and weapons and other accoutrements of battle.

She walked shyly to meet him and curtseyed as he came towards her. She was always surprised at how tall he was. William had been a head smaller, but with Edmund she needed to rise on tiptoe even when he bent to kiss her. William would have taken her up in his arms and lifted her from her feet and whirled her around before kissing her lingeringly on the lips and been damned to who was watching, but Edmund only took her hand and raised it briefly for a perfunctory kiss.

'Are you well, my lady?' he asked. His shrewd look reassured her that his concern was genuine — or maybe he was just hoping she would tell him that she was, at last, with child.

'I am well,' she said and gave a small shake of her head in response to his raised eyebrow. He said no more, but she knew he was disappointed.

They went inside and she poured him wine, but he asked for ale and drank thirstily, still standing. Mabel called for Edith to bring water for him to wash and, after allowing his squires to help him off with his armour, he dismissed them and said he would go to the bedchamber to change the rest of his clothes and bathe.

'Come with me,' he said to Mabel and she followed him, obeying his instruction to close the door behind them.

'Have there been any raids by the Scots?' he asked her.

'None,' she said and watched as the relief crossed his face.

He pulled off the undershirt that was sticking to his skin with sweat and grime and then plunged his face into the basin and rubbed hard before standing back to watch as the dirt discoloured the swirling water. As she looked at him, standing wearing only his braies, Mabel wondered why she was always surprised to discover that she found him handsome. He plunged his face again and when he stood up for a second time, with the water dripping from the ends of his hair, he began to relate to her what had taken place whilst they were trying to break the siege at Berwick.

'So all the lords rode home in haste to defend their lands,' he told her. 'Lancaster withdrew to Pontefract, but as far as I've heard none of his estates have been raided.

The king and Despenser fled but the queen was almost captured by the Scots, though now she is safe at Nottingham. Hugh Despenser has claimed that Lancaster betrayed her and that he is in the pay of the Scots and has given them secret aid.'

Mabel watched as he rubbed his face on a linen towel.

'Is it true?' she asked. He paused then dropped the towel onto the bed, ran his fingers through his hair and looked at her.

'It isn't true that he betrayed the queen, but he has met with Robert Bruce to discuss a way of ending these constant troubles.'

'That is treason then!'

'Treason against an incompetent king, in an effort to promote peace. If Lancaster had had the governing of this land we'd all have been better off,' he told her as he held out his hand for the clean undershirt she was holding.

★　★　★

The strained relations between the king and his cousin, Lancaster, eventually broke down completely. But although Lancaster's reputation had been damaged by talk of his involvement with the Scots, there were still many who supported him. Hugh Despenser

320

had grown ever more powerful and craved not only power, but wealth as well. He'd begun to gather territory in Wales by whatever means he could, which had endeared him to few apart from the king. His acquisitiveness had particularly alarmed the Marcher Lords and, as the earls and barons split into factions, civil war threatened England and Wales, and those who hated his influence over the king began to look towards the Earl of Lancaster for leadership.

During the late spring and early summer of 1321, Lancaster began to gather supporters with the intention of bringing about the downfall of Hugh Despenser, although many of the greatest northern families, who were still paying protection money to the Scots, held themselves aloof from him, still suspecting him of involvement with Robert Bruce.

In July, Parliament sat at Westminster and the Earl of Hereford and others who opposed Despenser occupied the city, cutting off the king from his military supplies in the Tower of London. At first the king resisted, but when they told him that they would utterly renounce their homage and set up another ruler in his place he was persuaded by the Earl of Pembroke to submit and in August Hugh Despenser was banished from the kingdom.

In October, Queen Isabella went on a pilgrimage to the shrine of Thomas a Becket at Canterbury Cathedral and on her way home she sought a bed for the night at Leeds Castle. The governor of the castle, Lord Badlesmere, had been a supporter of Lancaster against Despenser and, although he wasn't in residence, his wife saw fit to refuse the queen admittance and she was forced to take refuge in a nearby priory instead. When the king discovered this enormous insult he was furious and his justifiable anger won him strong support in the south-eastern counties where many of the barons rallied to his call for Badlesmere to be punished. But as Lord Badlesmere rode to raise support for his own cause, Leeds Castle fell after a week long siege and Lady Badlesmere was imprisoned at Dover.

This success renewed support for the king and as Badlesmere fled northwards King Edward pursued him, intent on finally destroying his cousin Lancaster and his supporters and at last wreaking revenge for the murder of his beloved Piers Gaveston.

★ ★ ★

William stood beside Sir Andrew Harcla in his tent as he addressed a group of knights.

322

They had just returned from Coventry where Sir Andrew had sought a meeting with the king to beg him to take decisive action against the continuous Scottish incursions which they were failing to keep in check.

'The king has ordered me to treat the Scottish menace as of only secondary importance,' he told them. 'Instead, we are to join with his forces to put down the rebellion by the Earl of Lancaster. We are to intercept him as he marches north to seek to ally himself with the Scots. So go to instruct your men and tend to your horses and ensure that you are all prepared. Much may be asked of us and I expect every man to do his duty and fight to his last breath for his sovereign king.'

As the sombre men filed out of the tent William heard Sir Andrew call him back. 'Do you know Sir Robert Holland?' he asked.

'I do indeed, my lord. I lived under him at Haigh. Why do you ask?'

'What manner of man is he?'

William paused, not sure what response was required, but he knew that Holland was one of Lancaster's supporters so saw no reason not to speak the truth. 'He is a man who will always look to his own back,' he said. 'I would not trust him.'

Sir Andrew nodded, apparently pleased with William's assessment. 'I have received word that he has betrayed the Earl of Lancaster,' he told him. 'The earl sent him home to Lancashire to raise men to fight, but rather than taking them back to Pontefract he has taken them to the king instead. But I will bear in mind your words. Thank you.'

Dismissed, William ducked out from the tent and paused to let out a whistle of surprise. If Holland had turned against his master Lancaster, and Lancaster could be defeated by the king's army, then it would be safe for him to return home, thought William. He could go back to Haigh, back to Mab and his girls. He smiled at the thought and found that he was rubbing his hands together in anticipation of the battle to come.

Two days later on a cold March afternoon one of Sir Andrew's spies galloped into their camp at Ripon to say that Lancaster's forces had been seen heading up the Great North Road. Immediately, Sir Andrew ordered them to strike camp with all haste and march south towards Boroughbridge. Here Lancaster and his men would need to cross the river Ure by either the bridge or the ford and Andrew Harcla told William that he was confident that if they reached the town first they could hold the bridge and stop them.

* * *

With snow flurries adding to the white covering on the distant hillsides, the mounted men quickly covered the four miles south to secure the bridge before their enemy arrived, leaving the archers and baggage train to follow behind. As soon as these arrived and they had made camp a little distance from the river, Sir Andrew called his commanders to his tent to discuss tactics. William was impressed by his plan. His admiration for Andrew Harcla had grown during the eighteen months that he had served under him. The harsh lessons of Bannockburn had been well learned, thought William, as he listened to how Sir Andrew planned to copy the best of the Scots' tactics to outwit Lancaster. To set men on foot against men on horses seemed rash at best and foolhardy at worst, but they had all come to trust his judgement and William acknowledged that it could work in their favour.

As they were studying the roughly sketched map a scout came to the tent flap to say that the Earl of Lancaster had arrived in the town and was arranging lodgings for his men.

'How many?' asked Sir Andrew.

'Fewer than us,' grinned the scout with satisfaction. 'And he has not yet realised that we hold the bridge.'

'Well I doubt he will remain uninformed

for long,' he replied as he turned back to his men. 'Let us prepare for a battle before darkness falls,' he said grimly.

* * *

After firmly telling a resentful Dicken that he must stay by the tent for his own safety, William rode down the incline to the riverbank and looked around. Knights and pikemen were deployed to guard the northern end of the wooden bridge that was only wide enough to be crossed on foot. Further upstream, at the ford, more pikemen were in a defensive formation with their spears pointing outwards to ward off any mounted attack. They were supported on both flanks by bodies of archers who had been instructed to fire as fast and relentlessly as they could once the enemy came within range. William was confident that they would hold both the crossings.

As he sat astride Hengist, listening as the impatient stallion chewed on its bit, he heard the rhythmic marching of an oncoming force and, out of the late afternoon, he saw two columns of men approaching from the town, one of cavalry and one of infantry. He recognised the colours of both the Earl of Hereford and Roger de Clifford as they approached the bridge leading the foot soldiers. The column of horsemen, under Lancaster's command, was heading for the ford.

William watched as Hereford and his standard bearer led a running assault on the wooden bridge at the head of his men. But before the force was even half way across there were sharp cries of pain and dismay as a quill of sharpened spears suddenly stabbed upwards from beneath the planking making men jump and turn in alarm as if they were performing some new and energetic dance.

One of the soldiers thrust his spear upwards in a lucky strike that impaled the Earl of Hereford from below. For a moment he looked stunned as he gazed at the torrent of blood that flowed unchecked from his bowels, across the bridge, and began to drip into the swirling water of the river below. As if intending to pray he sank slowly to his knees and with an expression of disbelief he fell over sideways, dead. His standard bearer lay motionless beside him, his hand still clutched around the fallen banner and Clifford, nursing a gaping wound to his forehead, ordered a retreat.

The men, who would have followed their leaders had they crossed the bridge, suddenly became a whirling, frenzied mass as they all tried to turn at once to flee. The pikemen were eager to give chase, but Sir Andrew called them off as the enemy ran for their lives. William looked upstream to where the archers had inflicted heavy casualties on the mounted assault. Having seen the defeat of his foot soldiers, Lancaster was also calling them to pull back.

Minutes later a lone rider in Lancaster's colours approached them with a white cloth tied to a stick. William watched with narrowed eyes as Hengist fidgeted, eager and excited by the events. The messenger handed a note to Sir Andrew and waited as he read it. William saw the amusement light his face.

'Tell him no!' he said to the messenger. 'Though, as the afternoon darkens, I will grant him a truce until the morrow.'

They watched as Lancaster and his men turned and withdrew back into the town.

'He offered me a bribe to let him cross,' laughed Harcla as he passed William. 'I'd rather have his head on a platter to present to the king.'

$\star$ $\star$ $\star$

During the night Sir Simon Warde, the governor of York, arrived by river with reinforcements and at first light a confident and expectant royalist army awaited Lancaster and his men.

'If he thinks I will wait here until his Scottish allies arrive to give him aid then he is a bigger fool than I first thought,' grumbled Sir Andrew as the weak March sunlight breached the horizon. 'I'll not wait in this chill wind an hour longer,' he added to William. 'Come, let us find the damned earl and finish this, then we can all enjoy a good dinner.'

With an eager smile, William nudged his spurs to his stallion's sides and they trotted off towards the town of Boroughbridge to engage with their enemy. But there was no sign of Lancaster's forces and they met up with a scout who told them that most of Hereford's and Clifford's men had deserted and that Lancaster himself had taken refuge in the chapel.

As they reined in outside the small stone building William glanced across at his lord, wondering what he would suggest they do. It was obvious that Lancaster had taken sanctuary in the hope that the Scots would arrive and, if he could not be compelled to come out and give himself up, then the victory that had seemed certain might not be assured.

William heard Sir Andrew shift irritably in

his saddle, making the harness creak under his weight.

'Be damned to this!' he exploded. 'What say we go in and fetch him out?'

'If you are not afraid of being struck down for violating sanctuary then I am more than willing to follow you in, sire,' said William, already half out of his saddle.

Sir Andrew ordered a group of men to take to the chapel door with a battering ram in the shape of a sturdy fallen tree trunk. William watched the door shudder and shake under the onslaught until it finally splintered with a resounding crack and flew open, causing the men to fall over themselves in a heap. With sword drawn he clambered in over the top of their prostrate bodies with Andrew Harcla close behind him.

Lancaster, clad in his chain hauberk covered with a surcoat bearing his own heraldic lions, was kneeling before the crucifix. He turned in alarm, his eyes momentarily meeting William's with a vague glimpse of recognition. Then the earl crossed himself.

'Good Lord, I render myself to Thee and put me in Thy mercy!' he prayed as Andrew Harcla strode towards him and put the blade of his sword to Lancaster's throat.

'Stand up! There'll be time for your prayers

to your heavenly lord later when you've begged forgiveness of your sovereign lord!' he told him as he waved men forward to take the earl into captivity. 'Strip him of his armour!' said Sir Andrew.

Lancaster stood quietly as they took everything from him until he was dressed only in his shirt and braies. Then, without cloak or hood to protect him against the northerly wind, which was bringing a fresh flurry of snowfall from the overburdened sky, they dragged him from the chapel and back to the river where he was taken onto one of the boats that had brought Warde's foot soldiers.

William handed Hengist's reins to Dicken and told him to pack up their belongings and then find Ned and bring the horses to the city where he should ask after his whereabouts at the castle gate.

'I must see Lancaster secure,' he told him.

William crossed himself as the body of the Earl of Hereford was brought aboard. The two friars who were to be responsible for it stepped from the bank making the flat-bottomed boat sway on the choppy water. Bound and shivering Lancaster sat in the midst of his guards. Clifford, also stripped of his armour and with a makeshift bandage about his head, was pushed down beside him and then the boat was untied and the sail set to take them the seventeen miles downriver to the city harbour.

As they tied up at York wharf, in the midst of the trading ships, William saw Warde's armed men waiting to escort the prisoners up to the castle. He followed as they marched up the short incline, through the gate set in the high stone wall of the round gatehouse and into the crescent shaped bailey. Adjacent to the kitchen was a strongly constructed prison into which Clifford and Lancaster were taken without ceremony. William watched as the helpless prisoners were chained to the walls and he searched his conscience for some shred of pity. But all that he could think was that as soon as this was finished he could go home to Mab, and whenever he thought of her the longing to hold her and his daughters closely in his arms again eclipsed everything.

Word had come that the king was at Pontefract and wanted the earl brought before him there. It would be even more humiliating, thought William as they rode south, for Lancaster to be tried in the great hall of his own castle.

It was a Sunday, but Andrew Harcla had responded immediately to the king's summons and, holy day or not, they had ridden out at first light in the hope of arriving before nightfall.

At last, as the afternoon darkened from the south, Pontefract came into sight and they urged the tired horses on. As they approached the town, crowds began to gather at the roadside to jeer at Lancaster as he passed. At the approach to the castle even more were gathered to watch, including those who had been Lancaster's own vassals.

'King Arthur!' they cried, making fun of the pseudonym he had used in his communications with the Scots. Then one man reached for some of the slush that was still gathered at the roadside from an earlier snowstorm and, after pressing the mixture of mud and ice into a ball between his hands, he threw it. Laughing, others followed his example and Lancaster was pelted until his thin tunic was plastered to his body and his cheek bled from a laceration just below his right eye.

The royal standard was only just visible, flying from the turret, as they clattered over the drawbridge and into the outer of the two courtyards. William watched as the Earl of Lancaster was taken to his prison cell in the newly constructed tower which overlooked the abbey. Then he helped Dicken and Ned to stable the horses, unpack what they needed, and find a corner out of the drafts to catch up on some much needed sleep.

★   ★   ★

'William!' called Sir Andrew early the next morning. 'Come and attend me and you will be admitted to the hall to see Lancaster found guilty.'

William followed his lord across the courtyard and up the steps to the ante chamber. Guards in the king's surcoats were at the door, but they stepped smartly aside and allowed them in. The best chairs in the castle had been arranged along the dais for the king and his advisers. William recognised Hugh Despenser in his usual position at the king's elbow and he watched as Sir Andrew took his place alongside those who would pass judgement.

An account of the evidence against the Earl of Lancaster was read out and Robert Malmesthorpe pronounced that he had been found guilty of treason and would be condemned to death by hanging, drawing and quartering.

'What? Shall I die without answer?' demanded Lancaster and a chill ran through William as he recalled a similar trial, when Piers Gaveston had stood before them in this same hall as the condemned man.

'The evidence of your guilt is without doubt,' Malmesthorpe told him. 'It would be useless for you to speak in your own defence.'

'And I am to die a traitor's death?'

'I will show some leniency, cousin, in respect of your royal blood,' said the king with a glance at his chamberlain. 'I will show you the same mercy that you afforded to my brother, Piers. You will not be hanged, drawn and quartered, but you will be beheaded. Take him!' he instructed with a wave of his hand and William watched as the Earl of Lancaster looked around in dismay as armed men grasped him.

As he joined the crowd in the courtyard William saw a thin grey pony that looked half-starved itself. Someone pushed a dirty battered hat onto Lancaster's head and amid much laughter and jeering he was picked up and put astride the saddleless horse.

'Lord have mercy on me!' the earl cried, clutching at the pony's sparse mane as they led him out of the castle. Outside the walls he was once again pelted with mud by the townsfolk. William followed as they took him up the hill where he was pulled from the animal's back and forced to his knees to make confession to a priest.

'Turn him the other way — to the north!'

shouted someone when his head was on the block. 'If he be so fond of Scotland let him die facing it!'

Voices of assent rippled through the crowd as the earl was hauled to his feet and repositioned. Then a man took up the axe with which he was to be executed. William watched as the shivering earl crossed himself and said a silent prayer, his eyes closed and only his lips moving as he awaited his death overlooking his own castle, watched by those who had pledged him their loyalty, but were now only eager to see him die.

Despite the long wait to be rid of his enemy the bile rose in William's throat and as the axe was raised he looked away, hearing only the dull thud and the gasp of shock then admiration from the gathered crowd, some of whom gave a half-hearted cheer. William opened his own eyes to see the white face of Dicken who was staring at the scene. Damn, he thought, he should have taken more care that the boy did not witness such an event. Still, he conceded, as his hand rested on the boy's quivering shoulder, he had better get used to it. This was a cruel and violent world and there was no part in it for those whose constitution blanched at the death of a traitor. Though, as Dicken retched over his boots, he had to acknowledge that he couldn't have stomached watching it himself.

A small group of monks came forward to claim the body and William was glad to see they were given permission to take it; not for the Earl of Lancaster the final indignity of having his body abandoned at the roadside for the crows as he had done with Piers Gaveston.

Partly from a grudging respect at his good death and partly to reassure himself that Lancaster really was dead William took Dicken to the abbey. The earl's remains were laid in a coffin to the right of the altar. In place of his head the monks had put a roughly hewn stone and Lancaster's bloodied head, with the eyes still closed in his silent prayer, was laid between his thighs.

As William knelt to say a prayer of his own, he wished only that he could shield Dicken's ears from the shrieks and howls of the half-hanged men whose bowels were being drawn from their bodies and burned on stench laden fires.

'What will we do now?' whispered Dicken as the stone lid grated into place over the remains of the earl.

'Now, we will go home,' replied William.

Before they were allowed to leave every man had to swear his loyalty to the king and the following morning William, Ned and

Dicken stood in a long queue that trailed from the great hall, down the steps and across the expanse of the courtyard. It was still cold even though the high walls were protecting them from the worst of the March wind and as they shuffled up the steps, one at a time, William wished that they could at least reach the ante-chamber where there would be some shelter.

As he glanced up to see how close they were to the top, armed men of the king's household appeared and began to shout at everyone to stand aside. William recognised Robert Holland being escorted from the hall. His usually assured face was bewildered and he kept his eyes downcast as he was hurried past them down the steps and across to the tower where those fortunate enough to escape the sentence of death were being held. William saw that Sir Andrew Harcla was directing the soldiers and he remembered his own words to him that Holland was not to be trusted. It looked as if he was to be a prisoner despite his attempt to swap sides so late in the day, thought William, with a feeling of satisfaction.

At last they reached the hall and knelt before the king and took the oath of loyalty. William was rising to his feet to be hurried out, so that the next knight could kneel in his place when he saw the king hold up his hand.

'I know you,' said Edward.

'Sire, I am Sir William Bradshaigh. I came to you at Langley with proof of Lancaster's treason,' he reminded him.

'Bradshaigh. You said you were an outlaw,' replied the king.

'I was, sire.'

'You were mistaken. On enquiry I found that I had already granted you a pardon at the request of your wife, who presumed you were dead.'

'Dead?' repeated William in bewilderment. Did Mab really believe that he was dead?

He bowed before backing out from the royal presence and then he ran down the steps as fast as he could.

'Saddle the horses!' he called over his shoulder to Dicken. 'We have to get back to Haigh!'

★　★　★

'It's refreshing to see a happy face this day,' remarked a dark haired knight sourly as he watched William tighten the girth of Hengist's saddle.

'I ride home to claim my lands and my wife, after many years,' William told him with a grin. 'But you do not look so pleased my

339

friend. I take it you were on Lancaster's side.'

'I was. I am no more,' he added, as he checked the bridle of his own black stallion. 'I rode with Robert Holland and pledged myself to the king before Boroughbridge. But it is my task to take the news of the earl's death to Lancaster and I'm not sure the townsfolk there will be as pleased as some I've seen this day.'

'And may take out their displeasure on the messenger perhaps?' asked William as he paused to look at the man.

'I have men enough for protection,' he replied. 'I'll just be glad when it is done and I can ride home.'

'You have a wife?'

'I have a beautiful wife who waits anxiously for my safe return,' he replied.

'God speed then,' said William. 'For my wife is beautiful too and I will not waste another minute that could be carrying me closer to her arms — and her bed!'

The dark haired man laughed.

'Then God speed you as well,' he replied, though as William whistled to Calab to come he saw the man look puzzled at the sight of the elderly dog.

13

The Supplicant

When she woke, Mabel knew that it was a special day, but in her sleepiness it was a moment before she remembered that it was her birthday. As she yawned and stretched across the cold parts of the solitary bed, her thoughts strayed not to Edmund, but to William. She thought about her twenty-first birthday, the day they had come home to Haigh. It was the day she had begun the tradition of handing out alms to the poorest people from the surrounding district.

As she lay and listened to the early morning birdsong from the trees, she recalled that William had never forbidden her to give out alms. In a time when even Robert Holland's servants had begun to eat the trencher bread themselves rather than share it with the starving villagers at the gate, William had never once told her that others must go hungry on this day because they had so little themselves.

The first year that she had been married to

Edmund he had grudgingly agreed to her upholding the tradition, though he had kept a strict watch on what was given away, unlike William who had always left it to her to decide how much or how little she thought they could spare. And she had always given more than she should, she remembered, though he had never complained or looked at her reproachfully.

She sighed. She still missed him. There was a part of her that would never feel whole without him. No matter how much she had grown to love Edmund it would never be the same as the love she had felt, the love she still felt, for William Bradshaw.

She smiled at his insistence on being known as Bradshaigh to reflect his ownership of the lands that she had brought to the marriage. She thought about how much he had loved Bella and Amelia and even though she knew he had craved a son he had never been bitter or uttered a word of disappointment as first one daughter and then another had been born. And she thought about the way he would have scooped her into his arms if he had been here on this, her birthday morning, and insisted that he would give her the best gift she could ever want before she even managed to stumble from their bed.

Trying to push the memories to the dark

part of her mind where she usually kept them hidden, she was glad that Edmund was not there to see her smile or hear her sigh. Although he was unerringly kind, she knew that he disliked to be compared with William — and she had learnt from the way he pursed his lips, and the jealous look that flickered across his face whenever she mentioned him, that it was better not to speak of her first husband in front of her second.

But it could have been worse, much worse. She shivered as she recalled Sir Peter Lymesey. She would always have cause to be grateful to Edmund Neville for providing her with an alternative to becoming Lady Lymesey.

Edith tapped on the door and came creeping in with warm water for her to wash.

'I'm awake,' she said, pushing aside the bed hangings.

'I've made the little cakes you like so much for your breakfast,' smiled Edith. 'And people are already beginning to gather outside!'

Now that Edith mentioned it, Mabel could hear the murmur of voices.

'Help me to dress in the blue gown,' she said. 'As soon as I have eaten I will go out. I'll not keep them waiting, hungry, whilst my stomach is full.'

Bella and Amelia both hugged her and

wished her well on her birthday. Mabel clutched them tightly to her. Bella was fifteen now, almost a woman, and Edmund had already begun to make enquiries about a husband for her. Mabel knew that it would not be long before both her daughters would have to go away to homes and husbands of their own and, as she looked at them and saw William's fair hair and hazel eyes reflected back at her two-fold, she felt an ache in her throat as she desperately tried not to weep.

As soon as they had eaten, they wrapped their cloaks around themselves to go outside. The fourth of April might sound as if it should be springtime, but Mabel was not surprised to see the flurry of snowflakes as she opened the hall door.

The crowd outside fell silent and Mabel reached down into the sack that was held wide open by her daughters and took out the first loaf. From her purse she took a penny and handed them both to the thin woman who was the first in line.

'Thank you, my lady. God bless you, my lady,' she said and after giving Mabel a curtsey she moved on. They came in a polite and orderly manner, these faces she had seen grow up and grow older during the many years that she had handed out alms.

Then she noticed a stranger moving

humbly along to await his turn. The sack was growing empty and she began to worry that the loaves and pennies would all be gone before he reached her. She asked Edith if there was more inside. Although she did not know him, the cloak that the man wore with the hood pulled around his face was made from good cloth. He must have fallen on hard times, thought Mabel, and she wanted to be sure that he would not be turned away empty handed.

She had sent her daughters and Edith into the kitchen to bring out more food from the stores, thanking God that Edmund was not present to prevent her, when the man at last approached her. He said nothing, but keeping the hood pulled over his face he knelt before her and held out his hands like a supplicant. At first she thought that he might be a leper. But he carried no clapper or bell and his hands, although roughened with hard work, were not diseased.

'A moment,' she told him. 'I will not send you away hungry.'

She looked down at him again and the outstretched hands seemed familiar, as if she had known them well in some other life. Mabel chided herself for such foolish fantasies.

'Will you not put back your hood and allow

me to see your face?' she asked him, gently. 'For it would please me to know who it is that receives a gift from me on my birthday.'

'Yes, I know that it is your birthday, my lady,' said his voice and Mabel felt her heartbeat race. Her hands shook as she took the warm loaf from Edith who had just come out from the door. He sounded so like William that for a moment she was almost overcome with emotion.

'Forgive my tears,' she said, as she held the bread out to the man. 'For a moment I thought you were someone I used to know.'

'And did the man you used to know give you cause to weep, my lady?' he asked, though he did not take the bread from her.

'No! No indeed!' she exclaimed. 'He was my husband and I loved him very much. But he went away to fight and did not return and I have grieved for him for many years.'

'And do you grieve for him still?'

'Every day,' she whispered, wondering why she was confiding in this cloaked stranger who knelt before her.

'Do not grieve any more, my lady,' he said and Mabel watched as he slowly reached to pull the hood back from his face. She gasped and heard Edith beside her take a sharp breath as the loaf fell at their feet. She reached for the girl's arm to steady herself.

The man before her was so like William that he could have been his brother. His features were familiar, though the face was older and more lined than her husband's and this man's fair hair was streaked with grey.

'Do you not know me?' he asked in a puzzled voice.

'You . . . you look like my late husband, William Bradshaigh,' she said. 'You could be his kin. Do you come from these parts?'

The man rose slowly to his feet. His gaze never left her face and as she studied him more carefully, with the tears wiped from her eyes, Mabel began to wonder if God had answered her prayers and if a miracle had occurred. He reached out his hands and gently took hold of hers. Even though it was an affront for an unknown man to take hold of a lady she did not protest or pull away from him, but continued to stare into the hazel eyes that she thought she would only ever see again in her dreams.

'Do you not know me, Mab?' he asked again.

'William?' His name escaped her lips as a whisper. 'William?' she repeated as she freed her hands and stretched out to touch his face with her fingers, as if they could be relied upon to recognise him more than her startled eyes. 'How can it be you?' she asked, suddenly afraid that he was an apparition who would at any moment dissolve before her. 'How can you be real?' she asked as she traced the well-known contours of his cheeks and jaw line and finally his lips.

'I am no spectre, my lady,' he reassured her, catching her hands in his again to kiss them each in turn. 'I was condemned to live as an outlaw and could not return for fear of my life. But now the Earl of Lancaster is dead and I have come home.'

He held his arms open wide as the villagers around them clapped and cheered his return. Mabel realised that she was expected to step forward and allow him to embrace her and carry her into Haigh Hall, to a welcome reminiscent of that of the prodigal son. A fatted calf should be killed and wine should flow freely as they danced and sang in celebration until he took her to their bed and gave her his customary birthday gift.

'No!' she cried suddenly pushing him away from her. 'No!' Her hands flew to her mouth as she stared at him in confusion not knowing what to do. Then she ran inside to the bedchamber, where she slammed down the bar that held fast the door and fell sobbing to the bed.

★ ★ ★

Mabel had no idea what time of the day it was when she was awakened from a dream about William returning. Someone was banging on the bedchamber door, making the latch rattle, and Edmund's voice was shouting at her to unbar it at once before he fetched the axe to break it down.

Confused, but with a notion that something startling had happened, Mabel sat up and was surprised to find that she was wearing her outdoor cloak. She unfastened it and looked at the door, not knowing why she had secured it. Was she ill, she wondered, as she pressed a hand to her throbbing temple. She did feel unwell and her mind was in such turmoil that she couldn't even decide what day it was.

'Mabel!' came Edmund's authoritative voice once again. 'Open the door!'

Leaving the cloak strewn across the bed she walked unsteadily towards the wooden bar and grasped it in both hands. At the sound of it being raised, Edmund pushed the door open. His face was contorted with anguish. Something had happened, but she couldn't remember what. Had someone died?

'Bella? Amelia?' she asked, her voice sounding hoarse and unnatural to her ears.

'They're safe. Mistress Palmer has taken them to her house for the present. Are you harmed?' he asked.

'Harmed? I don't think so. No.' She shook her head and tried to look past him, through the doorway into the hall. She thought that she could see William sitting in his chair by the fire with Calab spread at his feet, but her reason was telling her that it could not possibly be so.

'Who is that?' she asked as she tried to pass Edmund, but his arm across the doorframe blocked her way.

'Mabel, I must speak with you, in private, if you feel well enough,' he said, looking down at her with a concerned expression. She could see Edith hovering behind him but he waved her away before grasping Mabel's elbow and urging her gently towards the bed. She sat down on the edge of the mattress and watched him as he shut the chamber door and then walked across to the window and opened the shutter slightly. Mabel saw that it was daytime and she could hear excited voices talking in the distance, yet the last thing she remembered was eating honey cakes for breakfast.

'It is my birthday!' she said, as she began to remember. 'I was handing out alms at the door and a palmer came, returned from the crusade. He looked so like William that for a moment I thought it was him . . . I think I was so shocked I must have fainted away,' she said. 'But you were not there. Have you just returned?' she asked as he stood with his back to her. 'I hope you do not bring bad news.'

He sighed and turned to face her. Apart from tiredness he did not seem harmed, although there was an unfathomable hurt in his blue eyes as he gazed at her.

'Do you still love him?' he asked.

'Who?'

'William Bradshaigh.'

'I did love him,' she said slowly. She wasn't sure how to answer. She did not want to make Edmund angry, but she could not, would not, deny her love for William. 'I think I was shocked because the man reminded me of him so much. That is all. It does not mean I love you less,' she reassured him, standing and going to him and touching her hand to his cheek.

'Don't!' he said, pushing her hand away.

'Edmund? What's wrong?' she asked in bewilderment. Surely, she thought, he was not so jealous and angry because she had seen a man who reminded her of her dead husband. Even he could not be that unreasonable. 'The beggar who came. Is it he who is sitting in the hall?' she asked, wondering why the man had been brought inside, let alone given the chair before the fire. 'Who is he?'

'You do not know him?' asked Edmund and Mabel was puzzled to detect a note of hope in his voice.

She sat down on the bed again and fought to gather her thoughts and memories and, as she pressed her face into her hands, she began to recall more clearly what had happened earlier.

'It is William,' she said at last. 'He is not dead. He has come home.'

'Are you sure?'

'Yes,' she replied. 'I'm sorry,' she told him. She saw that he had been hoping she would deny she knew the man, that she would say he was an imposter who bore only a passing resemblance to William.

'Are you certain, beyond a doubt?' he asked again. 'It is a long time since you saw him.'

Mabel looked down at her fingers clasped in her lap and remembered how she had traced his face. He was older, but his eyes and his voice were the same.

'Yes,' she said. 'I am certain.'

'Then you had better go to him,' said Edmund, turning away from her again. He tried to sound unemotional but Mabel knew that he was near to tears himself.

'Edmund?' she said as she laid a hand on his back.

'Go!' he said, shrugging off her touch.

'I'm sorry,' she whispered again after a moment of silence.

Mabel went to the door and opened it hesitantly, but when she walked into the hall it was as if she had stepped back in time. William looked up and smiled and Calab struggled to his feet and came to her with his tail wagging. She reached out a hand to stroke the hound's head and it licked at her fingers.

William was still wearing the cloak with the palmer's cross, but beneath it she could see that his tunic and hose were fashioned from fine cloth and he looked healthy and well fed.

'Mab?' He held out a hand, but she was reluctant to approach him any closer; she was still afraid that he might dissemble and fade as he always had in her dreams.

Suddenly she was aware that there were other people in the hall. Not just Edith, but others who were strangers, yet not quite strangers. From a bench below the window a man with a beard had stood up as she entered and now he bowed to her.

'Ned?' she asked.

'Yes, my lady. It is me, safe and well.'

At Ned's side his wife stood looking up at

him, her hand possessively curled around the crook of his elbow as she smiled. Mistress Kemp had waited for her husband to return without losing faith or hope, thought Mabel with regret.

By the door there was a young squire who looked vaguely familiar. She puzzled at his face for a moment until he smiled at her as if he knew her.

'Lady Bradshaigh,' he said with a formal bow.

'Dicken?' She gazed at him. He was tall and, although still gangling, showed signs that his jaw was firming and his chest broadening. 'How?' she asked. Then she recalled how the boy had disappeared the day Lymesey was attacked in the forest and brought home so badly beaten. She also recalled how she had prayed hard that he would be taken care of and now she knew that more than one of her prayers had been answered.

'Sir William rescued me. He is training me to be a knight,' grinned the boy.

'I prayed that you were safe,' she told him.

'And did you pray for me also?' asked William. Mabel walked slowly towards her husband.

'You have been in my prayers every day,' she told him.

'Even when you thought I was dead?'

'Especially when I thought you were dead.'

He was still holding out his hand and she put her palm to his palm and felt his familiar fingers close around hers. He stood up and gently put an arm around her shoulders, drawing her to him.

He smelt the same and she stood for a long time, cradled in the safety of his embrace until she slowly realised what she had done. She shrugged off his arms and took a step back as she glanced with sudden horror towards the bed chamber door.

'But I did think that you were dead. I married again,' she told him in a quiet voice. 'Oh, God forgive me! God forgive me,' she repeated. 'What have I done?'

She watched William's expression crumble into disbelief. He stared at her and said nothing. Then he looked towards the doorway and Mabel saw Edmund Neville standing there with similar look of agony on his face.

She looked speechlessly from one to the other and did not know what to do or say. She wanted to go to them both, to be comforted by them both and because she could not choose she remained unmoving, and they all stared at one another without speaking for what seemed an eternity.

'I truly believed your husband was dead,' said Edmund, at last. 'Those men, those outlaws swore that they had seen him die. I would not have married you otherwise.'

'Which men?' demanded William staring at Edmund as if the devil himself had been conjured before him.

'Stephen Scallard and William Tegg swore, before they went to the gallows for the murder of Henry Bury, that they had seen you killed at Preston,' whispered Mabel, putting out a restraining hand towards William. 'They must have said it to protect you and keep you from being hunted down. But I believed that what they said was true — and when I was free to marry again I became Edmund's wife.'

'Why?' he asked incredulously. 'Why did you do it, Mab?' He shook his head in disbelief and looked at her as if she had become a stranger to him. 'This man was my enemy. He was the one who sought out Adam Banastre and Henry Lea and had them killed, and he would have had me killed as well if he had found me.'

'William!' Mabel fell to her knees in front of him and grabbed for his hand and brought it to her lips. 'William, forgive me, please. I believed that you were dead — and I needed his protection.'

'Protection?' he repeated as he pulled his hand from her grasp. 'From what?'

'From Peter Lymesey,' she told him. 'Please do not be angry with me, William. I only accepted him because he offered to keep me safe from Lymesey.'

'This was the same Sir Peter Lymesey who beat the boy and who had the lands whilst they were forfeit to the king?' he asked.

'Yes. Do you know him?'

'I've heard about him,' said William, with a cautious glance at Edmund Neville. 'And met him on one occasion.'

'Then you were the one who attacked the man and caused him so much harm he almost died!' burst out Edmund, starting across the hall towards William as if he would seize him and call in his guards. Mabel saw William's hand fly to his tunic and she thought he was going to pull out a knife and strike at Edmund.

'No!' she cried in alarm, but William took out a letter and shook it at the sheriff.

'I have a pardon from the king for all past crimes — real or imagined,' he warned him. 'Do not think that you can be rid of me so easily! The letter also confirms that these lands are mine. You have no rights here over my land or my wife. You had better leave before I set the dog on you!'

At his words Calab sat up and awaited a command, a growl rumbling at the back of his throat. Mabel saw Edmund eye the dog with suspicion. It had never liked him and she knew that if William ordered it to it would attack him.

'Please William!' begged Mabel. 'Do not be so hasty to turn Edmund out. He has been a kind husband to me and a caring step-father to our daughters. He has provided for us and kept us safe.' She still knelt before William and clutched at his hand again as she begged his understanding.

'But Neville was the sheriff of Lancashire,' he said, looking down at her. 'And as the sheriff it was for him to decide who my lands were demised to for the year and a day. It was he who chose Peter Lymesey.'

Bewildered, Mabel looked up at Edmund who was standing with his arms folded and his eyes averted from her.

'That cannot be true?' she said to him, refusing to believe that he would have deliberately sent such a man as Lymesey to take control of her manor and to treat her so appallingly.

'Oh it's true, believe me Mab,' said William. 'And why do you think he would do such a thing? Why do you think he first persuaded you that I was dead and then showed you such an evil man before offering himself as an alternative?'

Mabel stared at Edmund Neville; at the man she had trusted; the man she had come to love.

'No,' she said, shaking her head. 'No. He is not a bad man. Say it isn't true,' she said to Edmund. 'Tell me that you did not trick me.'

'I think perhaps I should leave,' said Edmund.

'No!' Mabel struggled to her feet and held out her hands to him. 'Edmund, please don't go! There must be a way to sort this out!' She turned to implore William to ask him to stay, to let him explain his innocence, but William's face was dark and angry.

'You are not welcome in my house, Neville,' he told him and Mabel could only watch as Edmund nodded sadly and walked to the door where he called for his horse.

Mabel tried to follow him but William caught her and held her back.

'Where will you go?' she called after him.

'I will spend the night at Robert Holland's house. Tomorrow I will go home to Middleton.'

'Will I see you again?'

He shook his head, incapable of words, and left without looking back at her. She wanted to go after him, to hug him and kiss him and comfort him and assure him that everything would somehow be all right, that it could all be sorted out. But she didn't know how it could be made all right — and she could only watch as he walked away from her.

She felt William's arms come around her again and she turned and sobbed against him as he held her tightly and kissed and stroked her hair.

'It is you, isn't it?' she said at last as she held his face between her palms and gazed into his hazel eyes. Then she pressed her lips to his.

★ ★ ★

'Forgive me Father, for I have sinned,' she confessed. She had wanted to walk to the church at Wigan to make her confession, but William had forbidden it, saying that she was not strong enough and that he would send Dicken to fetch Father Gilbert.

Now she focussed her mind on what yet remained to be done before she could feel cleansed. 'Father, I am guilty of the sin of adultery,' she told him as she bent her head in penitence. 'I must make amends before man and God.'

'Mabel, my child,' sighed the priest. 'I feel complicit in your sin. I counselled you to accept that your husband was dead and urged you to take another. If I had not, then the

360

burden of sin that rests upon your shoulders would not be so heavy for you to bear. Accept my absolution and go in peace.'

'No, Father. I must make amends — before man and God,' insisted Mabel. 'Only by doing what is right and what is expected can my soul be cleansed from this grievous sin.'

'But you know what the penance is?'

'Father, I do. And I will gladly perform it to renew myself before God and to prove to my husband that I am truly sorry.'

* * *

Mabel de Haigh paused on the edge of the market place. Her bare feet were bloodied and torn and the snow-laden wind made her shiver as she limped forward, bareheaded and dressed only in her linen chemise. In her hand she shielded a lighted taper, almost burnt down now. The villagers who lined her path willed her on and gave her strength. Although the penance for adultery was designed to be a humiliation, these people neither mocked nor jeered her as she passed, but the men averted their eyes from her unclothed body and the women whispered words of encouragement and sympathy.

At last she reached the stone cross and knelt before it to pray to God for the salvation of her soul. She was an adulteress. She freely admitted her sin to God, priest and man. But she prayed that God would forgive her as easily as Father Gilbert, her confessor, and the people of Haigh who stood protectively around her.

'That is enough,' said Father Gilbert as she felt a warm cloak being placed around her shoulders and the hood raised to cover her hair which hung loose and unbraided. 'Come away now.'

She held up her hand in a silent plea for a few more moments of prayer. Then she crossed herself, put out the taper and stumbled to her feet as arms grasped hers and supported her. It was over now and she could go home, shriven, to have her feet bathed and bandaged and to recover from her long penitential walk.

As the priest helped her up from the market cross she saw Harry Palmer standing with his arm around his wife's shoulders. The battle scar across his face gave him an added charm she thought. Her daughters Bella and Amelia came to her, their eyes bright with tears, but she smiled at them to reassure them that although the penance had bruised her physically it had cleansed her soul and she was now content. Then William pushed the priest aside and lifted her from her ravaged feet.

'I am proud of you Mab,' he told her and pressed his lips to her temple. 'You have no need of forgiveness. What you did was forced on you. I love you and I always have — just as you have always loved me.'

Yes, she thought, as her tired arms clung around his neck and the familiarity of his body reassured her. She had never stopped loving him. But as he carried her to the waiting palfrey that would take her home, she glanced over his shoulder towards the northern hills and she said another, silent, prayer that Edmund Neville would also be granted absolution. For even though she would never admit it to anyone, there was a part of her that still loved him.

Author's Note

My research for this novel was greatly helped by various sources. I am grateful to the Rev. T.C. Porteus, whose small book, *New Light on the Mab's Cross Legend,* I discovered in the Lancashire Authors' Association library at Accrington. He points out that the story of Lady Mabel and Sir William Bradshaw has been told and re-told over the years and has many versions. One comes from the Bradshaigh Roll, an ornamental pedigree probably drawn up by Randle Holme of Chester about 1647. In this version, Sir William went away on Crusade and Lady Mabel married a 'Welsh Knight'. On his return, Sir William chased and killed the interloper at Newton Park. Another version of the legend comes from a manuscript 84 years older than the Bradshaigh Roll. This document is in the Harleian Collection and purports to be a Declaration by Sir William Norris of Speke Hall, dated 9th June, 1563. In it, he recounts a story told to him by Sir Roger Bradshaw of Haigh. Once again, Sir William goes off on crusade and Lady Mabel marries Sir Henry Teuther, and once again the intruder is killed by Sir William who is then pardoned by the king. However, this version does not record the penance at all, although on the Bradshaigh Roll it says the penance was performed weekly.

Porteus goes on to look at the events in the country during the years of Sir William's absence and points out that the years were from the Banastre Rebellion in 1315 until the execution of Thomas, Earl of Lancaster in 1322. It makes sense that Sir William was a rebel and became a Lancastrian Robin Hood, hiding in the forest because he was a wanted man, and it is this version of events that I have used in my re-telling of the legend.

Sir Peter Lymesey was the man who held the lands at Haigh for a year and a day, but Porteus suggests that it was more likely that it was the county sheriff, Edmund Neville, who became Lady Mabel's bigamous husband as some accounts refer to the man she married as 'Osmond'.

I am also grateful to Kathryn Warner for her excellent blog:
www.edwardthesecond.blogspot.co.uk
which provided invaluable background information for this and future novels.

The cross to which Lady Mabel de Haigh walked barefoot as a penance for her adultery can be found outside Mab's Cross Primary

School in Wigan. And in Wigan Parish Church the effigies of Lady Mabel and Sir William lie side by side — Mabel with her hands clasped in prayer, and Sir William reaching for his sword.

More information about the background history of the novel, along with photographs, can be found at my website: www.elizabethashworth.com